BLUE

Farmhouse

CHRISTMAS

BLUE

Farmhouse

CHRISTMAS

TERI HARMAN

Mirror Press

Interior Design by Cora Johnson
Edited by Joanne Lui, Lisa Shepherd, and Lorie Humpherys
Cover design by Rachael Anderson
Cover Image Credit: Shutterstock #524227753

Published by Mirror Press, LLC
ISBN: 978-1-952611-09-4

MORE BOOKS BY TERI HARMAN

Blue Farmhouse Flowers
Blood Moon
Black Moon
Storm Moon
A Thousand Sleepless Nights
The Paradox of Love

Dedication:

To my brothers, Kenneth, John, and Paul, and all the good
times we've had hunting Christmas trees.

Christmas Eve

Hill Valley, Utah
December 24, 2004, and December 24, 1974

Clara Hill shoved her feet into her snow boots. She fumbled with her coat sleeves, smiling as she caught sight of the falling snow through the back-door window. "Mom?" she yelled. "I can't find my glove." Clara dropped to her knees and looked under the wooden bench in the mudroom, elbowing boots aside. She huffed in frustration. "Mom! Where is it? MOM!"

Grace Hill shuffled into the mudroom doorway, hands around a steaming mug. She wore comfy jogger pants and an oversized sweatshirt. Her espresso-bean brown hair was piled into a messy bun on top of her head. Her eyes were hazel green, her skin smooth and white. Clara loved that she had all the same physical features as her mom, and hoped she would look as effortlessly gorgeous when she grew up. Grace raised her eyebrows. "What are you doing? *Besides* making a huge mess." She gestured her mug to the pile of outerwear and boots on the floor.

Clara shoved aside her grandpa's rain boots. "I'm trying to find my other glove. I only have one. See?" She waved her ungloved hand at her mom.

"You're going outside? Now?" Grace sighed. "Clara, it's almost dark."

"But it's *snowing*. I promised to meet Liam at the well if it started snowing."

1

"You do know you're twelve, not eighteen, right?"

Clara stopped rummaging and glared up at her mom from all fours. "Mom, come on! I'll be fine."

"What about our movie?" Grace went to the shelves and shifted a few things. "If we wait too long to start it, Grandpa will fall asleep before the opening credits. A Christmas Eve movie is tradition. Dad's picked a good one this year." She made a triumphant sound and handed Clara her missing glove.

"You mean like last year?" Clara stood and took the glove.

"*Chariots of Fire* is a classic. It wasn't that bad."

Clara rolled her eyes. "*Sooo* boring. Like the most boring movie ever made."

Grace conceded with a shrug. "You can't mess with tradition. You'll like *The River Wild*. Not boring at all, I promise."

"Are Dad and Grandpa still fighting about the trees?"

Grace frowned and took a quick look over her shoulder. "No, they're done for the moment. That's one Christmas tradition I wish we could get rid of. I swear, they haven't agreed on anything *ever*." She shook her head but smiled indulgently. "It's the downtime between harvest and early spring. They kind of go nuts without a lot of work to do."

"Why can't they just figure it out?"

"It's . . . hard when two very stubborn people have two very different ideas. They'll get there. Eventually." Grace took a sip of her tea.

Clara shook her head. "Okay. So . . . I won't stay out long. Twenty minutes?" Clara put her hand on the doorknob. "Please?!"

"Did you ever find out where Liam lives or his mom's phone number?"

Clara huffed. "No, but I will. Promise."

"I really should meet his mom if you guys are going to hang out so much."

"I'll find out. Can I go now?"

Grace sighed, tapping her red-and-green fingernails on her mug. "Fine. But seriously, twenty minutes *only*."

"Okay!" Clara was already out the door.

She sprinted down the porch steps and plowed into the fresh mounds of powdered snow. Her smile grew as the icy spray hit her face. She cut across the backyard, past the barn, and took off through the neat rows of pine trees. The Christmas tree farm stood silent and asleep, evergreen branches catching the fresh flakes. In the sky above, a blush of pink faded from the round-bellied clouds.

Exhilarated, Clara ran faster. She didn't want to waste any time getting to the well. When the sound of Liam's soft singing reached her, she picked up speed one more time. She took a sharp right turn, knowing exactly which row to cut down to find the old well. She skidded to a stop against the stone well, breathing hard and grinning.

Liam lay in the snow with his hands behind his head on the other side of the clearing. He wore old jeans, even older work boots, a thin gray coat, and a black beanie pulled low on his head. His shaggy brown-blond hair had a little natural wave in it and was usually smashed under some kind of hat. His eyes were a light brown and deeply set. Tall for his age, skinny but lean, he was only two years older than Clara, but she thought he looked like one of the cool teenagers she often saw coming out of the diner in town.

"I ran all the way," she said.

Liam laughed. "I can tell. Your face is all red. Plus, you always run all the way."

Clara lovingly ran her gloved hands over the surface of the well's stones, brushing away a thick layer of snow. The well had been built about four feet above ground level, the rough gray stones neatly mortared together. The wooden remains of a bucket rigging clung to the edges, rotting slowly. Clara leaned over the edge to look down into the black hole of the deep casing.

"I wish for a Harley-Davidson motorcycle when I grow up," she yelled into the blackness, her voice echoing. A familiar little chill moved down her neck; she shivered.

"Hey! That's *my* wish," Liam called out.

Clara shot Liam a mischievous grin. "Fine. I'll change it." She thrust her face a few inches lower. "I wish for a motorcycle that is *way* cooler than Liam's." She lifted her head to grin at him.

"Cheater," he said, smiling. "No way that happens."

"That's so happening." Clara flopped down beside him, laughing when snow puffed up into his face. He grunted and wiped it away, smiling again. Readjusting, he settled close, his elbow touching hers. She didn't move. "Big flakes this time," he said, eyes on the sky.

Clara watched the snow fall toward her face, mesmerized by its languid drift. "Real big," she confirmed. The granite-colored sky above felt endless, mystical. Clara opened her mouth and let the snow land on her tongue.

After a few quiet moments, Liam asked, "Whatcha thinking about, Clara?" His favorite question whenever they fell into silence.

Clara felt a little tug of embarrassment but wanted to answer him honestly. "I think this is my favorite thing ever. My favorite place. My favorite time of year. My favorite weather." *And my favorite person.* She kept that one to herself—so, mostly honest.

Liam nodded. "Agreed." He started to hum. Something soft and lilting.

Clara thought the notes fit the storm perfectly. "What song is that?" She looked sideways at him.

He blushed and shook his head. "Just something I'm trying to write."

"You're writing a song?"

"Yeah. I've been messing around with my dad's old guitar."

"That's awesome."

"Thanks." He shrugged. "It's nothing special."

"Can I hear it when it's done?"

Liam frowned. "It ain't any good."

Clara elbowed him in the ribs. "Then I really want to hear it so I can make fun of you." She threw him a wicked grin. "Liam and his sucky song."

Liam tossed snow at her face. Clara sputtered and laughed, throwing a handful back. Instantly, they were shoveling heaps of snow at each other and rolling with laughter. Clara crawled away to hide behind the short wall of the well. She tried to catch her breath, inhaling the smell of the old stone. "Truce!" she yelled, while forming a snowball between her hands.

"Nice try!" Liam snuck up behind her, wrapping his arms around her middle and lifting her into the air. He spun her around in circles. "Dizzy yet?" he yelled.

"Yes!" she screamed back, laughing so hard she could barely breathe. The green trees and the white sky swirled past her vision, a merry-go-round. Liam stopped spinning, and they collapsed to the ground, his arm trapped under her body. Clara watched the world turn and turn until it slowed to a stop.

Liam took a big breath and laughed. "I might puke."

Clara laughed back. "Gross." She felt her heart rate return to normal. She sat up to look at Liam lying in the snow. His

5

clothes were covered in white. "Tomorrow is Christmas," she said.

"Thank you, Captain Obvious." Liam brushed the snow off his face.

She rolled her eyes. "Well . . . aren't you excited?"

Liam's smile fell away, and his hands fidgeted with his beanie.

The clearing suddenly felt too quiet. "Your mom is still sad?" Clara asked gently.

Liam nodded. "It's our first Christmas without Dad."

"Are *you* sad?"

Liam sighed. "It's so weird without him. And my mom, she just . . ." His face creased with worry.

Clara nodded, trying to imagine her life without her dad. It made her chest hurt. "I never knew people died in rodeos."

Liam sat up to face her. He nodded. "Yeah, it's actually crazy dangerous."

"Are you going to keep doing it?" Clara's stomach tightened. *Please say no.*

Liam slowly shook his head. "No. It scares my mom too much. She's been through enough. Plus, she already sold the horses."

Clara nodded, releasing a quiet sigh of relief. "I'm sorry. I know you like it."

Liam frowned, lifting his gaze to look out at the trees. "I did. I used to love it. Because Dad loved it. It's what we did together. But now it just feels like . . . it betrayed me." He puffed out a breath. "That doesn't make sense."

"Yeah, it does." Clara wasn't sure it really made sense to her, but she wanted to offer him comfort. She waited for him to look back at her, and then offered a quiet smile. "You did music with him, too, and you still have that."

Liam smiled back. "Yeah. For sure."

6

A jolt of reality hit her. "Crap. I gotta get back. I promised my mom I'd stay only twenty minutes. We've got to watch our lame Christmas Eve movie." She jumped to her feet. "Wish you could come."

"Thanks. But I need to get back and hang out with my mom." Liam stood. "Do you think you can come out tomorrow?"

"Sure. Once we do presents and breakfast and everything. Sometime in the afternoon, I should be able to come out."

"Cool." Liam reached into the pocket of his coat. "Merry Christmas, Clara." He held out a small red box, a shy blush coloring his face.

Clara's cheeks flushed hot, and her heart did something strange. "You got me a gift?" she whispered, wishing she'd gotten him one.

Liam shrugged. "No big deal. I saw it in the store, and it reminded me of you. Here." He pushed it out toward her, laying it on her glove. He gave her a goofy grin, tugged his hat down low, and then ran off in the direction he always went. Clara blinked after him, her breath coming in short bursts. She looked down at the small box.

He got me a present.

She ripped off her gloves and hurried to lift the lid. She brought the open box close to her face to see in the dark. A flash of silver. Clara gasped.

Inside the box lay a simple silver necklace with a tiny snowflake charm. Clara blinked again, surprised to find tears in her eyes. Excited, amazed tears. Tenderly, she put the lid back in place, gripped the box tightly, and ran all the way back to her house.

Liam Cooper's teeth got cold as he ran—he couldn't stop

smiling. He wished he'd stayed to see Clara's face when she opened the necklace, but he'd been too nervous. He knew she'd like it, though. He hadn't known anyone who loved snow as much as he did until he met Clara. He'd spent most of his meager savings on the necklace and didn't regret it. That wad of cash in the toe of his old sock had been just enough for Clara's necklace and a new lighter for his mom. As soon as spring hit and the farms and orchards needed workers, he'd fill up the sock again.

The snow and the old well had brought Clara into his life. Back on Thanksgiving night, feeling trashed about his dad's death, he'd come to the clearing alone, and leaned his head deep into the well. "I want to feel better," he yelled. The words echoed into the depths, their desperate ping sounding back at him. "I want to stop hating everything." His throat was left raw, as if the words had scraped their way out of him.

As he had shuffled home, he felt stupid for trusting his desires to an old hole in the ground. But the next morning, he'd woken to a thick veil of snow, the first of the season. His favorite. He'd thrown on his coat and hat, and walked to the Hills' tree farm, somehow ending up at the well. And there sat Clara, in a pink coat and white hat, gazing up at the sky with big eyes as if it were the first time she'd ever seen snow. When she'd lowered her chin and leveled those kaleidoscope-hazel eyes on him, Liam felt a strong confirmation that the well had answered him. Somehow.

"Hi," she'd said brightly. "It's first snow, and I'm Clara."

Liam had smiled and sat down beside her. "I'm Liam."

"Do you like the snow?" she asked.

"It's my favorite."

"Mine, too."

And then they were friends, as easy as that. It became their habit to meet at the well every day. Hang out, talk, read—it didn't matter what as long as it was together.

Maybe one day, he'd tell her about that wish he'd thrown down the well on Thanksgiving.

The lighted windows of his family's small cottage blinked through the outer rim of pine trees. Liam slowed, and pulled his face into a sober expression. It didn't feel right to greet his mom so happily. He felt a quick pang of guilt that he'd had so much fun with Clara. His dad was dead, and his mom heartbroken. This should be the worst Christmas of his life.

And it would be, without Clara.

Liam went to the back door, stomped off his boots, and headed inside. His mom sat at the kitchen table surrounded by papers. He knew she was struggling to make enough money—even after she'd sold their small cherry orchard to the Hills and all the horses to his dad's rodeo friends—but did she have to worry about it on Christmas Eve?

"Hey, Mom," he said as he hung his coat on its hook behind the door.

"Oh, Liam. Where were you?" Sally Cooper didn't look up.

"With Clara, at the well."

"That's nice." She shifted some papers.

Liam frowned at her bent head. *Does she even know it's Christmas Eve?* Her blonde hair needed a wash, and her slender frame looked thinner than it had five months ago. *July 24 to December 24. Exactly five months.* Liam frowned at the realization. His dad's old flannel shirt hung off Sally's jagged shoulders. A full ashtray sat at her elbow.

"Can I make some hot chocolate?" he asked.

"Sure, sure."

"Want some?" Liam went to the fridge for the milk.

"No, I'm fine."

Liam shut the fridge. "You didn't eat dinner, Mom."

Sally finally lifted her head, her brown eyes rimmed with fatigue and grief. "I didn't?"

Liam held back a sigh. "I'll make some toast, too."

"Okay. Thanks, buddy." Liam watched her out of the side of his vision as he poured milk into a saucepan. Sally surveyed the papers and the room. She blinked several times and then quickly gathered the bills into a pile. "Hey, I bet *White Christmas* is on TV," she said, her voice forcefully bright. "Or maybe *It's a Wonderful Life*. Should we watch something?"

She does know it's Christmas.

A little tension left Liam's chest. "Yeah, sounds good."

"Sorry we never put up a tree. Our whole house is surrounded by Christmas trees and somehow, I never . . . I just—"

"It's okay," Liam hurried to say. "We could put out some of the other decorations while we watch the movie—like Grandma's carolers—or hang some lights around the fireplace. Something like that. If you want." Liam stirred the milk as he added cocoa and sugar.

"Great idea." She pushed out of her chair. "I'll go grab the box."

Once she left the kitchen, Liam let out a long sigh. He wondered what Clara was doing right now. He didn't exactly know where she lived, but he imagined a beautiful house with Christmas lights outside and a big Christmas tree inside. Her mom and dad. A big, loud family. Christmas cookies and roasted chicken. Lots of laughter and fun. No stale cigarette smoke or pile of bills.

When too much jealousy clamped down on his heart, he shook the images away. Carefully, he filled two mugs and buttered four slices of toast. He put it all on a large plate and carried it to the living room. His mom knelt in front of an old, ragged cardboard box, her forearms propped on the sagging edge, and Dad's stocking in her hands. Liam tensed at the sight of her tears.

"Mom?" he asked quietly.

She startled, sniffed loudly, and swiped at her cheeks. "Sorry. Sorry, Liam. I'm fine."

"It's okay." He set the food on the coffee table. "It's five months today."

"Yeah," she sniffed. "I know."

Liam nodded and looked away from her. The tiny living room had olive-green carpet, butter-yellow wood paneling, and a river-rock fireplace at one end. There was space for one small couch, the plain wooden coffee table, and the box television. The TV sat in front of a large picture window. Sally had made and hung white cotton curtains.

Last Christmas Eve, they'd all squeezed onto the couch to watch *Miracle on 34th Street.* Jim Cooper had kicked out his long legs, feet propped on the table. He'd teased Liam about Santa coming. Liam had rolled his eyes. Later, he'd fallen asleep on the floor in front of the TV, the Christmas tree lights blurring in his vision as he'd drifted away.

Content, happy.

And totally unaware it would be his last Christmas with his dad.

Liam looked around the drab room. A pair of his dad's boots still sat by the front door, the toes coated in dust. Sally sighed, turning the knitted stocking over in her hand. Liam wasn't sure what to do for his mom. He wanted to help her but felt completely inadequate. He flipped on the TV and turned the channels. He skipped over *It's a Wonderful Life*—it seemed somehow inappropriate right now—and stopped on *White Christmas.*

Then he sat on the couch and picked up his hot chocolate. Maybe if he pretended everything was all right, his mom would, too. Sally went to the fireplace and hung Jim's stocking. She crossed back to the box and lifted the other two. But on her way to the fireplace, she just stopped, pivoted, and collapsed onto the couch. As if she didn't have the energy to hang the others. Maybe she didn't, since all she ever did was cry, worry, and smoke.

Liam handed her a piece of toast. She took two bites.

On TV, Danny Kaye danced with Vera-Ellen.

Liam wondered if his mother had remembered to get him a present. He felt instant shame for the thought but couldn't help it. Tomorrow was Christmas. What was he supposed to do if his mom had forgotten? It was hard enough to face the day without Dad. But no tree, no decorations, *and* no present?

Liam glanced over at his mom. She'd fallen asleep, the piece of toast in her hand. He took it and put it back on the plate. Then he hung the other stockings. He draped a strand of white lights across the narrow wooden mantel. Gently, he unwrapped the ceramic carolers his grandma had made decades ago and set them up on the coffee table. Two girls in big festive dresses, two boys in suits, a small dog, and an evergreen tree. The children held songbooks, and their mouths were painted open in song. Liam turned the little dog, a brown cocker spaniel, to face the carolers, as if he were listening to the small choir.

Liam switched off all the lights, except the strand on the fireplace, and sat on the floor behind the coffee table. He finished his hot chocolate, and then started his mom's. He ate all the toast and watched *White Christmas* by himself, snow falling outside the front window.

Christmas Day

Clara woke suddenly, a sense of panic in her chest. Liam's face hovered in her mind. She'd been dreaming about him and the wishing well. She'd watched Liam jump into the well and fall deep down until he disappeared, and then she called his name over and over and over.

He never answered.

She blinked at her snow-bright window and shivered under her heavy pink patchwork quilt, wishing she'd had a better dream on Christmas morning. She moved her bleary eyes to her small Christmas tree in the corner—every room in the Hill home had a fresh tree—the white lights going in and out of focus. This year, she'd decorated it with dozens of pink glass ornaments. Her mom said it looked like a giant piece of candy. Clara wondered what Liam's tree looked like.

Do you have a Christmas tree when your dad is dead?

She wondered what it was like at Liam's house right now.

Her mind came back to the dream, to the sense of desperation as she'd called to him.

Just a dream.

Stop thinking about it.

It's Christmas morning.

Her anticipation for the day sparked, crowding out the bad dream. Smiling, Clara pushed aside the gauzy sensations and launched out of bed. She thundered down the stairs, calling out for her parents to wake up. In the big living room, with its tall windows, plush couches, gorgeous hardwood, and grand river-rock fireplace, she found her grandpa seated in the

13

brown leather armchair by the Christmas tree. He was reading an old Louis L'Amour paperback.

Lincoln Hill looked every bit a man who had spent his whole life working the land. His shoulders were broad, and his forearms gnarled with corded muscles. His skin was deeply corrugated from years in the sun. His giant hands were so strong, he could crack a walnut in his palm. Clara had always been amazed by how much her father and grandfather looked like one another. The square jaw, the dark blond hair and beard—though Grandpa's was more silver now—and the slate-blue eyes. Today, Grandpa wore a navy-blue sweater, jeans, and his Christmas tree belt buckle. Clara dove to the floor at his feet, eyes wide at the spray of presents under the tree.

Grandpa laughed, using his book to softly swat the top of Clara's head. "Easy, kiddo. Your parents aren't up yet."

"I know." Clara reached for the closest present and checked the tag. "I'm just looking."

"Did you sleep good?" Grandpa asked.

"Yep! Did you see all the snow?" Clara pointed to the windows behind them.

He nodded. "Shoveled plenty of it, too." He rubbed his bad knee, wincing. "But sure is pretty on our trees."

"Do you think the trees like the snow?" Clara asked, checking another present.

Lincoln laughed. "Of course they do. No self-respecting Christmas tree would dislike snow. Plus, the winter water is good for the roots."

He shifted in his chair, reaching behind it. "You ready for our thing?"

Clara turned to give him her full attention. She adored this tradition between them. With a flourish, Grandpa produced a small mason jar of pine nuts. "Clara Hill," he said with solemnity, but then offered her a wink. "I present to you the first batch of pine nuts from our oldest tree—the first Hill Valley Farm Christmas tree—which was planted by your Great-Great-*Great*-Grandpa Willis in 1861. I harvested these myself—which is no small feat, mind you—and then toasted and salted 'em just right. Just for you on this Christmas morning."

Clara took the jar into her hand like it was a precious jewel. "Thank you, Grandpa." She spun off the top, scooped up a handful, and popped them into her mouth. Buttery soft and perfectly salty, as always.

Grandpa laughed. "Good grief, kid. Chew. No choking on the Christmas pine nuts allowed."

Clara chomped quickly and swallowed. "Can I help on the farm when I'm older?"

Grandpa smiled tenderly. "I would love that. And one day, when I join Grandma in heaven, how 'bout you run it for me?"

"Really?"

"That's what I'm hoping for. Well, you and your dad."

"Cool," she answered simply. "What were you and Dad fighting about yesterday?"

Lincoln frowned. "Heard that, did ya?"

Clara nodded. "Mom says you guys never agree on anything. Especially this time of year, when you don't have enough work to do."

Lincoln's frown deepened. After a sigh, he answered, "We just see things a little differently. Your dad wants to add some goofy Christmas village, bring people to the farm like a tourist attraction."

"Like with a Santa and all that?"

"Yes. But this is a serious farm, not some amusement park." He shrugged. "I don't like the idea of people tromping through my trees." He shook his head. "What do you think, kiddo?"

Clara chewed another handful of nuts, considering. She thought about her and Liam at the well. She didn't want other kids playing there. She liked the quiet privacy. "I don't want other people here, either. This is our farm."

Grandpa smiled. "That's my girl."

"But it's okay that Liam comes here, right?"

"Sure. You should bring him over to the house sometime. We still haven't met this famous friend of yours."

"We like to hang out at the well."

"Ah, the old wishing well. I liked to play there, too, when I was a kid."

Clara couldn't picture her grandpa as a child. "Did you make wishes?"

He smiled. "Always. I'm pretty sure that well is magic, because some of my wishes came true."

"Really? Which ones?"

"The important ones. I met your Grandma Debbie. I had a son. And he had *you.*"

Clara smiled big in return. "I wished for a Harley-Davidson motorcycle."

Lincoln laughed loudly, shaking his head. "That's a good wish, too. I can see you on a motorcycle." He chuckled again. "You know, I knew a Liam once, a long time ago. Best foreman I ever had. He lived in the old cottage down by the cherry trees."

"The one that burned down?" Clara had always had a fond fascination for the ruins of the cottage, even though her dad had told her it wasn't safe to explore. The river-rock fireplace—so similar to the one in this room—stood all by itself, surrounded by broken, charred lumber. The similarity attracted her, made her wonder about the small building's fate and the people who had lived there. She'd once found a half-burned cowboy boot buried in the ash and dirt. There was a strange feeling there, a tremor in the air she couldn't really explain. It reminded her of when she made a wish into the well.

"That's right." Lincoln's face changed. Clara wondered why he looked so sad. He added, "Real tragic, what happened. That poor family."

Clara opened her mouth to ask for the story, but footsteps sounded on the stairs. She jumped to her feet to haul her parents to the Christmas tree.

Liam lay in his bed staring at the wooden plank ceiling. He wasn't sure he wanted to get up. Normally, he'd have been up before dawn, scoping out the haul under the tree. But this year . . . "What's the point?" he whispered. The only thing he really wanted to do was hang out with Clara at the well. But she wouldn't be there for hours.

He stayed in bed in his small room with a John Denver poster on one wall and a Waylon Jennings poster on the other. And instead of thinking about Christmas, Liam thought about the day his dad died. He'd tried really hard not to think about it lately—he'd already relived it a thousand times, awake and dreaming—but the scene came on strong, encouraged by his melancholy.

The memory of the heat always came first. Not just a vague recollection of that hot summer day, but the actual *feeling* of dry, suffocating heat on his skin. His room was icy, but Liam's skin flushed red, and he started to sweat. He remembered the dissolving delight of cotton candy on his tongue, the feel of the paper cone in his hand. He remembered the buzz of the crowd, as hot on his skin as the July heat. And he remembered the smell of the rodeo.

Before every rodeo, Jim Cooper had taken his son out

into the empty arena, smiled, and said, "You smell that, Liam? *That's* heaven, right there. Dust, sweat, and manure."

Those words had become a quiet chant of good luck as Liam had watched Jim mount the restless bronc in the bucking chute. *Dust, sweat, and manure. You got this, Dad.* Liam's mom, seated next to him, whistled loudly, and then pulled off a chunk of blue cotton candy. "Here he goes," she said. "Sure hope that bum wrist of his holds. He'll be a nightmare if he doesn't get gold this year."

Jim Cooper always got gold at The Days of '47 Rodeo in Salt Lake City.

Sally popped the spun sugar in her mouth, and added, "He's getting too old for this." Her head snapped to Liam. "Don't tell him I said that." She winked.

"He's still the best," Liam defended proudly.

Sally smiled. "Yes, he is, and one day, you will be, too."

Liam grinned, excited about a future where he followed in his father's cowboy boot footsteps. Rodeo glory.

Dust, sweat, and manure.

The gate had burst open, and the blond bronc charged out into the dusty arena. Liam and Sally sprang to their feet. Jim had one hand on his reins, the other flung out behind him in a graceful line for balance. He swung his legs to meet the rhythm of the bucking horse. In those first two seconds, Liam marveled at his dad's control and strength. The sight sent a chill up his neck. But then something in Jim's posture changed. Liam's body knew something was wrong before his mind could process it. He dropped his cotton candy at the same moment his dad lost his grip, flipped backward out of the saddle, and crashed to the ground. Sally gasped, her hand clutching Liam's thin arm. Jim had fallen many times, but Liam *knew* this time was different.

The crowd went silent.

Liam couldn't breathe. "Get up," he whispered. "Get up, Dad."

Jim didn't move. A crowd of medics rushed out onto the dirt.

Sally's grip had tightened painfully.

Liam wrenched his arm free and ran down the stadium stairs. "Dad!" he yelled over and over. He hadn't heard Sally behind him and hadn't registered the security guard who tenderly pulled him aside.

Dust, sweat, and manure. Get up, Dad!

Why didn't you get up?

In his bed now, Liam dragged in a shaky breath and wiped at his wet cheeks. He closed his eyes, willing the scene to disappear.

A quiet knock on the door pulled his attention back. "Yeah?" he answered, hurrying to blink his eyes clear.

The door opened, and Sally stuck her head in. "Did I wake you?"

"No. I'm up."

She nodded as she walked through the door. She had two wrapped presents in her hands. Liam scrambled to sit up. "Merry Christmas, Liam." Sally smiled shyly and sat at the foot of his twin bed. She handed him the two flat gifts. He guessed immediately what they were.

"Thanks, Mom." His chest felt light with relief.

Her smile grew. "Go on! Open them."

Liam tore back the red-and-green striped paper to reveal the cover of the first record. "Led Zeppelin. I heard about these guys at school."

"Wait until you hear the guitar. It'll blow your mind." Sally ruffled his hair. "Open the other one."

He tore the paper from the front. "Yes! The new Waylon Jennings." Liam ran his hand over the title of the album, *The Ramblin' Man.* "Thanks, Mom."

Sally moved closer and put her arm around his shoulder. She kissed the top of his head. "I hope you didn't worry I forgot about Christmas completely."

"No, of course, not," Liam answered to save her feelings.

"I know it's not much and it's a . . . weird Christmas. I should have gotten a tree up. There's really no excuse, but—"

"These are great, Mom," he interrupted gently. "Really. I got you something, too." He pushed off the bed and went to his time-worn dresser. From the top drawer, he pulled out her humble present. "It's not that exciting." He held it out, feeling a little awkward.

Sally took the box and opened it. She laughed as she lifted the silver lighter into her hand. "It has an owl on it. I love owls." Liam smiled with pride. Sally added, "And I like to smoke, too, as you may have noticed." She shrugged off her bad habit. "This is perfect."

Liam laughed. "Glad you like it."

"I love it. Thanks, buddy." She opened her arms, and Liam stepped into her hug. He tried to ignore the jagged angles of her shoulder blades and ribs. She eased him back, keeping ahold of his shoulders. "We're going to be okay. I promise."

A sting of emotion burned his eyes. "I know."

Sally nodded, her own eyes growing wet. She sighed, shook her head, and smiled again. "Let's make pancakes and listen to your records."

Clara lay in the pile of torn wrapping paper, her new copy of *A Wrinkle in Time* held above her face. Her body hummed with the magic of the morning. Her dad strolled into the living room, steaming mug of coffee in one hand and snowman sugar cookie in the other. He shuffled through the paper, making a circle around her. "You going out with the trash, Clare-bear?"

"Ha ha, Dad." She stuck out her tongue at him.

He laughed. "No respect for your old man!" he teased. Randy Hill needed a haircut; his dark blond hair fell across his eyes as he bent over her. His teeth were straight and white, his smile always a little mischievous. He wore old black sweats and a Garth Brooks T-shirt. Her mom often said he looked like a hippie cowboy. "How's the book?" he asked between sips from his mug.

"Good. I like Meg."

"Good. How 'bout that Lego set?"

"Already did it." She pointed over her head without looking away from her book.

"What? You did it *already*? No way." Randy looked over at the completed Lego structure of the White House. He let out an impressed whistle. "How are you so fast at putting stuff together?"

"It was easy." She shrugged.

"That's cuz you're a smartie-pants." He kicked some paper at her and went to the couch.

Clara swiped the paper away from her face. "You're such a nerd, Dad."

He scoffed. "See?! No respect." He shook his head, smiling.

She rolled over to her belly to look at him. "Why do you want people to come tromp through the trees and have a goofy Santa?"

Randy's eyes widened. "Been talking to Grandpa, I see." He took a slow sip of his coffee and, seeing Clara still waiting for an answer, said, "The farm needs to modernize, or it won't survive. Small, family-owned farms are failing all over the country. We've got to do something to keep things going, to spark new interest, and increase revenue."

"What's revenue?"

"The money we make from the farm."

"Can't we just sell more trees?"

Randy smiled lovingly. "It's not that easy, kiddo. Trees take a *long* time to grow."

"Grandpa thinks things are fine."

"I know, but Grandpa isn't always right."

Clara frowned, thoughtful. She wanted to understand so she could help.

From the kitchen, Grandpa yelled, "I heard that, and yes, I am always right! Always!"

Clara looked back to her dad. He sighed, rubbing at his forehead. "Don't start, Dad," he called back.

Lincoln stomped into the room. "When it comes to this farm, I am always right. I've been doing this my *whole* life. This was the first farm in this town; it *created* this town. And it's survived the Depression, wars, weather, bugs, fires—you name it. I think it can survive the modern age of the internet."

"That's not what I'm saying, okay?" Randy sighed again. "If you'd actually listen to me, you might know that. You assume every word out of my mouth is wrong. Like I'm still eight years old. But I've been doing this my whole life, too, and we need to be smart. Diversify."

Lincoln's face twisted with disgust. "Diversify! Give me a break. You read too many marketing books."

"Turner Barnes is starting a cut-your-own program next year."

"Oh! Well, if Turner Barnes is doing it . . ." Grandpa scoffed, rolling his eyes. "There's a reason we have always done better than the Barnes' farm."

"Well, they just might catch up next year. It's smart to have multiple streams of revenue."

"Not a chance. He'll never catch us—our trees are healthier."

"But people want the *experience* of a tree farm, not just the trees from a lot or store."

"That's harder on the farm and our staff. No. We aren't doing that."

Randy scoffed loudly.

Clara's eyes widened. She hadn't meant to start up their fight again. She looked away from the men and noticed the scene outside the windows. She rocketed to her feet. "It's snowing again!" Grandpa and Dad didn't respond to her. Quietly and quickly, she slipped into the kitchen.

Her mom stood at the sink washing dishes and shaking her head. "Here we go again," she mumbled.

"Can I go outside?"

Grace startled and turned, her soapy hands dripping on the wood floor. "Sure. You might as well escape World War Three while you can."

Clara moved toward the mudroom off the kitchen, but then turned back. "Is there anything I can give Liam for a gift? He got me this." She hooked the chain of her snowflake necklace and lifted it out to her mom.

"Oh, my gosh. That's so sweet of him." Grace leaned closer. "It's pretty. Your first gift from a boy. That is so *cute*!"

"Stop it, Mom." Clara rolled her eyes as she tucked the necklace back under her shirt. "So is there something?"

"Umm . . . probably. What does he like?" Grace dried off her hands.

"Snow and music and guitar and motorcycles. He's kind of like a cowboy."

Grace smiled. "Do you know what kind of music?"

Clara pursed her lips. "Not really. He says he likes to listen to records. Like those really old things."

Grace laughed. "Yes, I know what a record is. Okay. I'll be right back; we have tons of old records."

Clara hurried to put on her snow pants and coat. Grace came back as Clara pulled on her beanie. "What do you think of this?" She held out an old record, the edges of the sleeve bent and worn. "It's Gordon Lightfoot. Classic folk rock, sort of country music."

Clara shrugged. "Okay. Sure."

"You used to dance to this when you were little."

"I did?"

"Yep. Remember?" Grace started to sing the chorus of *If You Could Read My Mind.*

Clara's eyes widened. "Oh, yeah. I remember." She saw her younger self spinning in vague circles around the living room. "Okay, yes. I want to give him that."

"Cool. Want me to wrap it real quick?"

"No, it's fine." Clara held out her gloved hand. She and Grace turned toward the living room as the yelling got louder.

"Good grief," Grace hissed. She smiled at Clara. "They'll be fine. You go enjoy the snow."

Clara frowned, uneasy about the intensity of the words thundering from the living room. She'd never heard them yell like that. "I didn't mean to make them fight again—I asked about the trees. Why are they so mad?"

"It's okay, honey. Totally *not* your fault. I'll go talk to them." Grace opened the back door, still smiling, but Clara noticed the edge of worry in her mom's eyes. She realized she should clear out and let the grown-ups figure out their stuff.

With the record album tucked to her chest, Clara ran through the trees, so perfectly Christmas, covered in fresh snow. Who needed a fake Santa when you had this? Clara liked the farm just as it was, no change needed.

She found Liam exactly how he'd been the day before, except he looked happier, a little less heaviness in his eyes. "Hey," Clara called out as she walked around the well to sit in the snow next to him. "I brought you something." She held the record out so he could see the cover. "Merry Christmas!"

Liam lifted to his forearms. "Gordon Lightfoot. Nice!" He sat up all the way and accepted the record. "I've never seen this one."

Clara shrugged. "I used to listen to it when I was little."

"Huh. Must be older. Cool. Thanks, Clara."

Clara smiled as her stomach fluttered. "And look," she tugged off her glove to show him her necklace, "I'm wearing it."

Liam half-smiled, bashfully lowering his eyes to the record in his hands. "Looks good."

Clara returned the necklace and glove, more flutters passing through her core. "What'd you get for Christmas?"

"More records. The new Waylon Jennings and Led Zeppelin. Pretty awesome."

Clara had no idea who those people were but saw how excited Liam was about it. "Nice. Did your mom like her lighter?"

"Yep." He looked up. "She wasn't as sad as I expected. Even made pancakes."

"That's good." Clara smiled at Liam, who smiled back. At the same moment, they both looked away. Clara watched the light snow land silently around them. "How come I've never seen you at school?" she asked.

"I'm in ninth grade, at the high school. You're seventh, right? Still at the middle school?"

"Yeah, but I mean the years before that. Or around town."

"Maybe we did see each other and never realized it."

"Maybe. Kind of weird, huh?"

"Yeah. It's not like this is a big town."

Clara laughed. "Right. Guess we just always missed each other."

Liam shrugged. "I watched *Donovan's Reef* last night. Have you seen that?"

Clara shook her head. "Is it a Christmas movie?"

"Yeah, with John Wayne. It's funny, and it's in Hawaii. Have you ever been to the beach?"

"We've gone a couple times. My cousins live in San Diego; their house isn't far from a nice beach. Have you been?"

Liam shook his head. "We went all over the west with my dad for his rodeos, but never made it to the ocean. Do you like it?"

"Yeah, it's fun. I like to stand in the sand and let the waves hit my feet over and over until I'm buried up to my shins. I like jumping the waves, too. But it'd be really weird to be at the beach for Christmas. No snow? No, thanks!"

Liam laughed. He flicked some powdered snow at her.

Clara laughed, dodging.

"What did you get for Christmas?" Liam asked her.

Clara felt a little tug of guilt. She'd gotten a pile of presents, and Liam only mentioned two records. She edited it down to, "A cool Lego set and a new book. I already did the Legos."

"Nice. What book?"

"*A Winkle in Time.* Pretty good so far." Clara decided not to mention it was about a girl whose dad had disappeared.

"I think I've seen that in the library. Maybe I'll read it, too."

"That'd be cool."

"Clara!"

Clara and Liam turned toward the loud call. "That's my dad," Clara said, jumping to her feet. "What the heck? Why is he yelling?"

The call came again, louder and more urgent.

"Guess I better go," she said, annoyed and disappointed. "Maybe I can come back."

"Okay. I'll hang out for a bit."

On impulse, Clara threw her arms around Liam's neck. She hugged him quickly, barely giving him time to react, before she turned to run. "Bye!" she yelled over her shoulder, the flutter in her stomach now a rushing roar of excitement.

"Bye, Clara!" Liam yelled back.

Clara smiled, thinking about the way Liam's hands had come to her back. Her dad continued to call her name, the edge in his voice starting to worry her. She burst through the trees and nearly collided with his legs.

"There you are!" he said. "Come on, we're leaving."

"What? Why?"

"Because I said so." Randy stomped over to his gray Ford truck, the tailgate down.

Clara bristled. "Where are we going? What about Christmas dinner?"

"Change of plans," he said with a grunt as he pushed a suitcase into the bed of the truck. "We are going to stay at Liz's house for the rest of break."

Clara's pulse quickened. "No! I don't want to go! Can I stay with Grandpa?"

"Clara, no. We are going as a family to San Diego. I need a break from this farm."

"This is because you and Grandpa can't stop fighting? That's not fair."

Her dad huffed out a scoff. "Will you please just get ready to go?"

"I'm sorry I asked about the trees. I'm sorry! Please, can we stay?"

"This isn't because of what you said, baby. This is just . . ." Randy huffed. "Years of fighting. We are going. Go pack."

Clara wanted to scream at him, but instead ran past him

27

into the house. "Mom!" Clara didn't bother to take off her wet boots. She ran through the house looking for her mom. Clara jerked to a stop in the doorway of her own room; Grace was packing Clara's duffle bag. "I'm not going!" Clara announced, folding her arms.

"Clara, it's already a mess. Please be helpful."

"I don't want to go to San Diego. I want to be home, in my own house, with the snow and the Christmas trees. With Grandpa." *And with Liam.*

"Dad and Grandpa need a break." She folded a sundress. Quieter, more to herself, she added, "I knew living in the same house would be too much for them. Stubborn idiots . . ."

"Fine. You and Dad go, and I'll stay with Grandpa."

Grace sighed. "Don't you want to hang out with your cousins?"

"No. They're all so old, anyway."

"They will be so sad if you don't come."

"No, they won't, and I don't care. I want to stay here."

Grace looked across the bed, her brow furrowed. "Would you spend all day with Liam, or would you hang out with your grandpa, too?"

A burst of hope cut across her chest. "Yeah, of course. I'll hang out with Grandpa, I'll do chores. Whatever. Just please don't make me go."

Grace sighed again, rubbing at her forehead. "I don't love the idea of him spending the holidays alone." She huffed out a long breath. "Okay. Fine. You can stay."

"Yes!" Clara jumped up and down. She moved to run out of the room.

"Wait!"

"What?" Clara turned back.

"You can't go back outside right now. This storm is supposed to get worse. I want you to stay in and watch movies with Grandpa. There're leftovers from last night for dinner."

"But Liam is waiting, in case I could come back."

"Well, you *can't* go back. He'll figure that out soon enough." Grace put Clara's clothes back in the dresser. "You can see him tomorrow. Okay?"

Clara wanted to fight to go back out now, but knew she'd already asked a lot. "Okay. Fine."

"Thank you. Now, go take off those snow clothes and clean up all the wet boot prints."

Liam lay back in the snow, the cold seeping through his thin coat. He didn't want to leave. He couldn't get enough of watching the snow sway through the air above his face, and he really hoped Clara would come back soon. They hadn't had nearly enough time together.

The sun dropped low on the horizon. With a resigned sigh, he sat up. Small drifts of snow had gathered around the base of the well. Liam let his gaze move over the gray stones and then into the thick collection of trees. He wondered, not for the first time, about the men who had dug the deep shaft and placed all those stones. He wondered if some mystic force lived in the well and had heard his desperate words. And had that power really brought Clara to him, or was it just one of the strange coincidences of life?

Sometimes, he was so certain of the magic; other times, not so much. He decided to tell Clara about it next time and see what she thought. If she felt it, too, he wouldn't feel so silly.

Liam got to his feet, dusting off the snow. He lifted her gift to him into both hands. "How did I not know about this album?" His dad owned all of Lightfoot's albums, or so Liam had thought. He opened the two-sided case of *Gord's Gold*, the scent of dusty time coming off the cardboard. His eyes snagged on the recording date. "What?" he hissed as a cold tingle went down his spine. He read the date again. "1975. How is that possible?" He closed the album book to look at the faded picture of Gordon's face and the frayed edges. The album had the wear and tear of decades, and Clara had said she danced to it as a small child. But . . .

He shivered.

Lifting his gaze, Liam looked back through the pines in the direction Clara had gone. He didn't know where she lived or where she came from, other than the opposite side of the well as him.

Why didn't I ever ask?

I don't even know her last name.

His heart beat too quickly.

How does Clara have a record from 1975 when it's 1974?

He thought of her unusual clothes, the way she talked. Some of the things she said that he didn't understand. He thought of how they lived in the same town but never saw each other. Liam walked to the well and put his gloved hand on the stones. Another frigid chill moved through his body. He leaned forward to look down into the blackness.

"What did you do?" he whispered.

A Snow Storm

Clara lay at the base of the Christmas tree, propped up against two throw pillows and wrapped in an old quilt her Grandma Debbie had made. She'd angled herself to see the tree and the TV at the same time. Her mom had done this tree in all green lights and delicate silver mercury glass ornaments. The big tree, all green at night, had the most enchanting effect. Like the tree itself created the glow. It was probably Clara's most favorite tree ever; she wished they could leave it up all year.

She and Grandpa were halfway through *Donovan's Reef.* Grandpa had scrounged up the old VHS tape from his collection. She loved it. John Wayne reminded her of her dad and grandpa, and the three kids were hilarious.

Grandpa hadn't laughed much, and sat sullenly on the couch, his brow furrowed into deep lines. Clara tried not to notice. *At least, I'm not trapped in the backseat of the truck right now.* She moved her eyes to the windows, now black with night, and wondered if it was still snowing.

How long did Liam wait for me until he went home?

Sorry, Liam. I wanted to come.

The house phone rang, and Grandpa grunted as he stood to go to the kitchen to answer it. Clara reached for another chocolate from her stocking. She heard his mumbled voice answer the call. He talked for several minutes while she watched John Wayne drive a boat as the leading lady water-skied.

Clara was on her fourth chocolate when she realized Grandpa hadn't come back into the room. She sat up, reached for the remote, and paused the movie. She didn't hear his voice. "Grandpa?"

He didn't answer.

That's weird.

Clara tossed off the blanket and got to her feet. She shuffled her fuzzy socks along the wood floor into the kitchen. She froze. Grandpa sat at the kitchen table, his head in his big hands, crying.

Grandpa is crying.

What?

Watching him sob like a child stripped away her foundation. She suddenly felt five years old again, and completely uncertain of what to do. She'd never seen her grandpa cry—never even thought about the *possibility* of him crying like this. He was Grandpa Lincoln, rough and tough as John Wayne.

"Grandpa?" she managed to squeak out, her voice and body trembling.

Grandpa startled, sniffing loudly as he dropped his hands. His face collapsed into more emotion as he looked at her. He opened his arms. "Come here, Clara. I need to tell you something."

Clara didn't want to move. She hated the defeat in his face, the tremor in the air. She started to shake her head but then ran to him. "What's wrong?" she mumbled against his shoulder. "Are you sad about Dad leaving? I'm sorry I got you and Dad fighting again."

Lincoln shook his head. "No, sweetheart. That's not it. And that was *not* your fault." He turned her to sit on his thigh, exactly as she had when she was smaller. He took an unsteady breath. "That was the Highway Patrol on the phone." His voice wavered. He cleared his throat. "They are the police who help on the big roads. The storm's really bad farther south, around Cedar City. Your mom and dad . . ." His voice got tangled up in a sob.

Clara gripped his shirt, her own emotions rising cold in her throat.

Grandpa finally said, "There was a bad accident with a semi-truck and they . . . didn't make it."

Clara blinked at him. "They didn't make it to San Diego?"

Grandpa closed his eyes briefly, shook his head. "No, sweetheart, they were . . . killed in the accident." He watched her face closely through his red, watery eyes. "The paramedics tried to save them, but . . ."

Clara's chest burned. She realized she hadn't been breathing. "But . . . they . . ."

"They died," he said, his voice as soft as fresh snow.

Clara blinked again as hot tears rushed to her eyes.

Mom and Dad . . . are dead?

No.

Not my parents. They were just here. They were driving to the beach.

I don't understand.

She shook her head. Grandpa pulled her close to his side. "I'm so glad you weren't with them," he whispered.

I was supposed to be with them.

Mom and Dad are dead.

Her sobs came hard and fast.

Liam sat on his bed long after the time he normally went to sleep. He'd listened to the Gordon Lightfoot album over and over, trying so hard to understand what the date on the cover meant. He'd thought of going to look for Clara, but beyond a general direction, he didn't have any idea where to search. Besides, she'd be back to the well sometime tomorrow. He could wait.

But the waiting made him restless.

A nagging itch of instinct he didn't understand and couldn't name made sleep impossible. He kept going to the window and looking in the general direction of the well, thinking of Clara. He realized he was worried about her, but didn't know why. He swept his threadbare curtain aside and looked again, seeing only the dark winter night.

"Are you okay?" he whispered. Frustrated, he dropped the curtain and flopped back down on his bed. *Of course, she's all right. Stop it.* He reached for the record player and started the album over again, turning the volume down to avoid waking his mom. He sang along, trying to ease the anxiousness in his chest. Goose bumps rose on his arms at the line in *If You Could Read My Mind* that compared a man to a ghost from a wishing well.

The well. Something isn't right.

The record from 1975—does that mean . . . Clara is from the future?

Or is she a ghost?

Liam scoffed loudly and rolled over to face the door. "Stop being weird," he scolded himself. "But . . ."

Liam sat up.

Something is wrong. I feel it.

Is it the well? Or something else?

Liam leveled his eyes on the small window opposite his bed. "Are you okay, Clara?" he whispered. "Please be okay."

Clara lay curled on her side on the couch, watching the window-framed sky go from black to gray to sunrise pink. Grandpa sat at her side, his head slumped forward as he slept. Her body felt so heavy; it'd been hours since she moved. And it was impossible to sleep. She had no idea how Grandpa had managed it.

How can I do anything now?

How do I do this?

Part of her brain still believed it wasn't real. At any moment, the phone would ring, and a police officer would tell Grandpa that it was all a crazy mistake. But then her mind would take a wicked turn and imagine the accident, and what it would have been like to be in the truck. What her parents must have felt just before . . .

The crunch of metal, the shattering of glass, the pain.

Clara shivered.

Stop it. Stop it.

I could have been in the truck.

Her young mind wrestled with the intimidating fear of possibilities, unsure how to sort it all out.

I should have been in the truck. But I stayed.

Because of Liam.

"Liam saved my life," she whispered.

For the first time since last night, she wanted to move. She *had* to move. Silently slipping off the couch, Clara went to the mudroom and put on her snow gear. She went out the back door and down the steps. The morning sky blazed bright, apricot orange and salmon pink, the colored clouds piled high above the mountain peaks. Clara tried to take a long breath, but her chest hurt. The cold slapped her warm cheeks, not the loving greeting she normally received. She shivered and folded her arms. *Is it colder today?* She didn't feel up to running—her legs felt strange, robotic. She took her time trudging through the shin-high snow.

"My parents are dead." She tried the words out loud for the first time. Tears immediately glossed her eyes, turning icy cold on her cheeks. She smeared them away with her gloves. "My parents are dead. I have no parents. I'm an orphan."

Clara ducked under some tree branches and walked into the well clearing. Liam wasn't there.

It's too early.

Of course he's not here.

She walked to the stones and leaned over the side, looking down as she tried to catch her breath. "I wish . . . my parents weren't dead. Can you do that, wishing well?" A feral anger roared up her throat. "Bring my parents back!" she yelled, the words ripping at her throat. "Bring them back! I wish for my parents back." She stood back and kicked the well, sharp pain twanging up her leg. Collapsing to the snow, Clara let big sobs rock through her unrestrained. She put her back against the well and pulled her knees to her chest, crying so hard, it hurt down into her bones.

"Where are you, Liam?" she hiccupped between sobs. Her body started to feel heavy again, her arms and legs like sinking stones. She slipped down to her side, shivering and mumbling for her parents and for Liam. She closed her eyes and fell asleep in the snow.

The next thing she felt were two strong arms lifting her from the snow. "Liam?" she mumbled, unable to open her eyes all the way.

"It's Grandpa, sweetie." He swore under his breath. "You're frozen through. I'm taking you home to a hot bath and some food."

"But Liam . . ."

"He's not here, Clara."

Clara buried her cold face in her grandpa's chest.

Liam woke with a start. "No. Oh, no." He jumped from his bed and scrambled to get on his clothes. It was only eight in the morning, but he felt like he was late. Too late. He had to get to the well.

He tore out the back door and through the farm.

"Clara?" he called as he neared. "Clara!"

He burst into the clearing, huffing clouds of mist. He made a slow circle, stopping to squat next to an imprint in the fresh snow. It looked like someone had been lying there. Liam looked over his shoulder at the adult-sized boot prints leading away. He stood up and followed. They stopped at the tree line.

"What the—?" He walked back and started over. But the boot prints didn't go beyond the trees. They just . . . vanished. The snow between the pines in front of him lay pristine and untouched. "How?"

There were acres of trees in all directions. The Hills' blue farmhouse was about a five-minute walk or so. Besides his cottage, that was the only house for miles. But he knew for sure she wasn't a Hill; his family had always been close to theirs.

"Where does she come from?" he muttered as he stared at the last set of boot prints. Liam walked forward, slowly scanning the ground for any hint of prints. But there was nothing, not even the tiny, forked shape of bird feet. He kept walking.

He emerged from the trees behind the Hills' barn. He heard movement from inside and decided to ask Mr. Hill about Clara. It made the most sense that she came from this house, but no one had ever mentioned a Clara.

Liam went in the open doors at the front and found Lincoln seated on the ground, working on replacing a tire on his tractor. "Mr. Hill?"

There was a grunt of question. Liam moved closer so that

Mr. Hill could see him. "Oh, morning, Liam. How are you? Have a good Christmas?"

"Yes, sir. Thank you."

"How's your mom?" Lincoln pulled away from the machine and pushed his big black Stetson farther back on his head to see Liam better.

Liam had a flash of his dad, in his favorite gray hat, grinning from the back of a horse. Jim and Lincoln were about the same age and had been best friends. Liam swallowed hard. "She's okay. Thanks for asking."

Lincoln nodded thoughtfully. "Can't be easy. We sure miss Jim around here. I miss him. Good friend, good man. But you know that. Sorry."

"Thank you, sir."

Lincoln stood up. "Is there something I can help you with?"

"I'm looking for someone. A friend. I'm not sure where she lives."

Lincoln frowned. "Well, I know pretty much everybody in Hill Valley. What's her name?"

"Clara." Liam sighed. "I don't know her last name."

"Hmm. Well, I don't think I know anyone named Clara. You sure she lives in town?"

Liam nodded. "Yes. She said she grew up here."

"Hard to know for sure without her last name. I don't know all the kids' names. That's a lot of kids." He smiled. "What does she look like?"

"She's a little shorter than me, with dark brown hair and green eyes. Wears a pink coat and white knit hat with one of those pom-pom things." Liam gestured loosely to his head. "We usually meet at the old wishing well. Have you seen her walking through?"

Lincoln shook his head and clicked his tongue. "I haven't.

I guess I'm not much help after all." He lifted his chin. "Liz, you still up there?"

Liz Hill, the first child in the family and ten years old, leaned over the edge of the loft. She had bright blonde hair and the same blue eyes as her father and younger brother, Randy. There was straw in her hair and a book in her hand. "Yeah, Dad?"

"Do you know a little girl named Clara? Wears a pink coat and white hat."

Liz pursed her lips thoughtfully. "I don't think so. There's no one at school named Clara. Why?"

"Liam's looking for her."

Liz looked briefly at Liam. She shrugged. "Sorry." And then she rolled out of view.

"Thanks, sweetheart," Lincoln said to the loft. "Sorry, Liam."

"That's all right. Thanks, anyway, Mr. Hill." Liam turned to leave, angry he'd never simply asked Clara for her last name.

"Liam, wait. Mrs. Hill made way too much food yesterday. Why don't you come grab some leftovers for you and your mom?"

"Thanks. That'd be nice." Liam wasn't a big fan of the pity-laden handouts that had started after his dad's death, but he wasn't about to miss a chance for some of Debbie Hill's cooking.

Lincoln nodded, moved around the tractor, and clapped Liam on the back companionably. "You bet. Come on. Deb made roast beef and potatoes and *pie.*"

"Apple or cherry?" Liam asked, his stomach rumbling to life in complaint of no breakfast. He put a hand to his loud belly, embarrassed.

Lincoln laughed. "Both. And sounds like you could use a piece right now. Pie for breakfast?"

Liam smiled awkwardly back. "I won't say no."

"Good man."

Liam followed Lincoln to the back door of the blue house. He could smell spices and sugar before they opened it. Liam wiped his boots on the doormat as Lincoln hung his hat on a hook. "Deb?" Lincoln called out. "Liam's here."

"Oh, good!" came her response. She met them as they came into the kitchen from the mudroom. Debbie Hill was everything his mom was not. Debbie was tall, healthy, and fit. Her cheeks glowed, her blue eyes shone bright. She kept her long blonde hair in a high ponytail and adored colorful aprons. Today, she wore one made of a Christmas tree-patterned fabric, trimmed with gold ribbon, the front dusted with flour. "Merry Christmas, Liam!" She grabbed his face with both hands, patting his cheek. "You look hungry. I got tons of food."

Liam blushed and struggled to smile, as her tactile greetings always set him a little off center. "Yes, ma'am."

She smiled and went back to the counter. "There's always so much food the day after a holiday. I *always* make too much. What would you like?" She gestured to the island, nearly covered in platters.

"His stomach just growled as loud as a lion," Lincoln said as he went to the fridge. "Give him everything."

Debbie laughed. "Teenage boys' stomachs always sound like that. Sit down." She gestured to the stools at the island. No one in town had a kitchen as big and impressive as Debbie Hill's. Of course, no one knew how to use one as well as she did. She put two pieces of pie on a plate and slid it in front of him. "Did you like your Led Zeppelin record? I saw your mom a few days ago—we talked presents."

Liam picked up his fork. "Yes, ma'am. It's pretty cool music."

"They're my new favorite."

"You listen to them?"

Debbie laughed. "Yes! I'm not an old lady yet—I still like cool music."

Liam smiled and put decadent cherry pie in his mouth. "This is so good. Thank you."

"You're welcome." She turned to her husband, who was still rifling through the fridge. "Linc, what on earth are you looking for? You had your breakfast."

"I want another glass of that cider from Harold's place. Did we drink it all?"

"There's another jug in the basement."

Lincoln huffed. "All right. I guess it's worth going down the stairs for."

Debbie rolled her eyes. "Cut down a hundred trees in one day, and he won't complain one word. Go fetch something from the basement, and he whines like a toddler."

"I don't whine!" Lincoln yelled back as he left the kitchen.

Debbie turned her attention back to Liam. Her face sobered. "Hard Christmas? I can see it in your eyes."

Liam blinked. "Yes, ma'am."

She sighed, shaking her head. "You're a good support to your mom."

"Thank you. She made pancakes yesterday."

"Good!" Debbie watched him closely. "Is there anything you need, Liam?"

Liam's throat tightened. He swallowed a bite of pie. "Do you know a girl named Clara? She's twelve, wears a pink coat and white hat."

Debbie frowned. "No, I don't think so. Why?"

"She's a friend. We were supposed to meet at the old well, and she didn't come. But I don't know her last name or where she lives. I only met her on Thanksgiving."

41

"I'm sorry. Maybe she had something come up."

Liam pushed at his pie. "Maybe."

"What's wrong?"

"Nothing."

Debbie leaned her forearms onto the counter, leveling a serious gaze on him. "Nice try, mister. Come on, let's hear it."

Liam furrowed his brow. He couldn't tell her what was really on his mind; she'd think he was going crazy. He said, "Clara is always there. She's never been late. I feel like something must be wrong."

Debbie nodded slowly. "Maybe something is. Sometimes, we get feelings we can't explain, but that doesn't mean they aren't real. But if you don't know where to look, I guess all you can do is wait for her."

"I should have asked for her phone or address or . . . something."

Debbie shrugged, pushing away from the counter. "I'll make you a big basket of food. You go wait for her at that old well. It's a nice day."

Liam's chest tightened. "Thank you."

"And I'll ask around town." She grabbed a basket from a shelf. "We're here for you, Liam. Always. Remember that."

"Yes, ma'am." Liam's throat tightened again. He was too shy and too worried about being a tough fourteen-year-old to let her see the tears rimming his eyes. He dropped his head and focused on his second piece of pie instead.

Clara lounged in the bath, staring at her toes, the water no longer warm. She let her arms float at her sides. Her unmoving body reminded her of the dead fish she saw at the lake last summer. All silver and floating, lifeless. Rotting. The *lap lap* of the water pushing them against the reeds.

Dead. Everything dies.

She knew she should get out and go eat breakfast, but she didn't move. She wiggled her toes and watched the ripples move toward her chest. She felt them push at her snowflake necklace.

Why weren't you there, Liam?
Because it was too early.
We never meet before nine.
And he doesn't know.
He doesn't know.
But he would understand.

Clara knew he'd grasp exactly how she felt without her saying very much, and maybe he could tell her what to do next. What to think, what to feel. Part of her didn't want to tell him. He was already so sad; she didn't want to add her hefty grief to his. They couldn't both be broken at the same time. It seemed so wrong.

Grandpa called her name for the third time.

I'm not a dead fish.
Get up.

With a sigh, Clara got out of the tub. She dressed in her favorite jammies—the ones with fuzzy, rose-pink pants—and went downstairs.

"Oh, good. Your eggs are getting cold." Grandpa pulled out her chair, a plate of eggs, bacon, and toast in front of it.

She frowned.

"I know you don't feel like eating, but we have to keep going. I learned that when Grandma Debbie died." He nodded to the chair, and Clara sat. Grandpa kissed the top of her head. "Good girl. Eat up."

Clara picked up a piece of bacon and ate it. It felt strange that it was delicious.

I'm not dead. Bacon is still delicious.

43

Mom and Dad will never eat bacon again.

She ate another slice, trying to shut down her thoughts. Grandpa went to the stove and cleaned up the skillets. After a few minutes, Clara asked, "Grandpa, what happens now?"

He turned to her. "Well, sweetheart, we have a funeral. Like when Grandma died. Do you remember that?"

"A little. I remember the flowers in the church and how windy it was at the cemetery." Clara had been only six years old, but had known her Grandma Debbie well. Clara's family had lived in their own house nearby before Grandma died, spending most of their time at the farm. It'd been an easy thing to move into the blue house after Grandma Debbie's funeral. Clara had always wanted to live here, anyway.

She looked around the large kitchen, with its cream-colored cabinets, huge granite island, and big silver stove. This had been Grandma Debbie's kitchen. Her collection of antique plates still hung on the wall behind the long farm-house table. Clara had a few faded memories of sitting at the island while Grandma cooked. When her mom took over the cooking, Clara still liked to sit at the island, watching, talking, and tasting.

Now they are both gone. Grandma. Mom.
Dad.
Liam's dad. The fish at the lake.
All gone.

Lincoln sat at the table across from her. "It takes a few days to get ready for a funeral. I think we'll do Wednesday. Give Liz time to get here."

Clara nodded, looking down at her plate. *And one day, Grandpa will die.* She shivered. "Where are they? Right now. Do the police have Mom and Dad?"

Grandpa sighed again, rubbing a hand over his beard. "The police took them to a hospital in Cedar City. They have a special place for people who have died."

44

Clara nodded. *The morgue.* She'd watched enough TV to know that. Her imagination tried to take over again, sending up pictures of cold rooms in dark basements. Sterile, metal tables. Sour-faced doctors. Her stomach turned; she put down her fork.

"The police and doctors are taking good care of them," Grandpa soothed. "I know this is hard to understand."

"I'm not little anymore, Grandpa. I get it."

He nodded. "Of course. Sorry, sweetheart." He put his forearms on the table and leaned toward her. "There's something else I need to talk to you about." He hesitated, and Clara's anxiety perked up.

"What?" she whispered.

"Your parents want you to live with Aunt Liz in San Diego."

Clara's jaw dropped open, and her stomach constricted. "What? How do you know that?"

"Grown-ups write up special papers for emergencies like this. A will has instructions for what to do with money, houses, and any children. Your parents left instructions for you to live with Liz."

"But . . . I don't want to. I want to stay here! This is our home. I don't *ever* want to live anywhere but this blue house." Clara's breath burned in her lungs, coming in fast, tiny gulps.

Grandpa grimaced. "I know, sweetheart. But I'm old and not the best person to take care of you. Your mom and dad did a lot to help *me.* That's why you guys moved in. My blood pressure and arthritis . . ." He shook his head. "Liz and Gavin have lots of space in that fancy house and lots of money for all the things kids need. You'll be with your cousins. They can give you so much more there than I can here."

Clara's throat constricted, her jaw so tense it hurt. "I love it here. It doesn't snow in San Diego. And you have money. I

45

know you do. I don't need a fancy house or space. Just this house, this place." The tears came quietly this time, sliding down her trembling cheeks. "*Please*, Grandpa. Don't I get a say? I can take care of myself, and I'll help with everything. Give me as many chores as you want. I want to be with you and Liam and the trees and the snow."

Grandpa started to cry with her, which made it so much worse. He dragged the back of his hand across his wet cheek and then reached out and took her little hand in his big one. "I know, I know. I wish I could change it. But I can't. We have to follow what your parents wanted."

"Why did they want that? I don't understand!"

"I'm sure they were being careful and not expecting this to ever happen. But this is common. Adults want their kids to be raised by their aunts and uncles, people of similar age, with kids. Not older grandparents."

"But Liz and Gavin are old. Their kids are way older than me." Clara's panic flooded her blood. She couldn't even imagine living with Liz and Gavin and their weird, technology-obsessed teenagers. How would she survive without Grandpa and the blue house? "I'm not going. I can't. Please, Grandpa!"

"Clara, I know it's not what you want. It's not what I want, either. But . . ." He took a shaky breath, dropping his eyes from hers. "After the funeral, you'll go home with Liz."

With a full stomach and a basket of Debbie Hill's food, Liam went back to the well and waited. For hours. He waited until it got dark and then, reluctantly, went home. He returned the next day and the next.

Every day for three months, during every spare moment, he waited at the wishing well for Clara.

Then every Saturday for a year.
He waited.
She never came.

Coming Home

Fifteen Years Later
December 4, 2019, and December 4, 1989

Clara eased her 2019 Harley-Davidson Street Bob, sleek matte black with turquoise pinstriping, to a stop in front of the blue farmhouse. The engine rumbled as she idled, hands locked on the handlebars. Through the tinted visor of her helmet, Clara took in the shape of her childhood home. Her stomach tightened.

The colonial-style house looked exactly the same, with its long, rectangular shape, broad front porch, two stone fireplaces like bookends on either side of the house, and three dormer windows. In fact, it looked better. Part of her had expected to find it in shambles and falling apart, the same way her grandpa's body had broken down. But the house was pristine.

The turquoise blue paint looked fresh, the white trim and shutters gleaming. Clara looked down at her bike.

It's the same blue. I didn't even realize . . .

Gently, she touched the pinstriping, following it with the pad of her finger. *The blue farmhouse. Once my favorite place on earth.* She took a long breath before lifting her head to continue her inspection. The stained-glass windows in the double front doors depicting pine trees in front of a blue-and-gray sky sparkled in the afternoon sun. The paned windows flanking the doors were clean and bright. The *Hill Valley Christmas Tree Farm* sign suspended from the porch, the one that had been hand-carved by her great-great-great-grandpa, Willis Hill, hung perfectly level.

Clara pressed a hand to her aching chest. "I'm sorry, Grandpa," she whispered, a glaze of tears blurring her vision. "I'm sorry I wasn't here to help, like I promised that Christmas. Before . . ."

Before everything went wrong.

During that last Christmas in Hill Valley, she'd been certain she wanted nothing more than to run this farm one day, to carry on the family legacy. To stay and never leave. But those were childhood fantasies. Real life had stepped in and violently changed her path. She had a career and very different lifestyle now, far away from this small town and this farm.

Clara looked at her watch. In a couple hours, she'd sign the papers to release this place from her family for good. Her breath snagged on a wave of guilt. "Can I do that? I can't do that," she whispered. "How can I let it go?"

But how can I keep it?

I don't know anything about it. I never got to learn how to actually care for a Christmas tree farm.

And I can't stay here. This is not my life.

She dropped her hand to the ignition and shut down the Harley. The sudden quiet hummed all around her. She levered down the kickstand and dismounted. Pulling off her helmet, she noticed how Grandma Debbie's English rose bushes—which ran the whole length of the porch and down the sides of the house—still looked stout and healthy, even pruned back and dormant for winter. Grandpa had been boisterously proud of his trees, but Grandma had been deeply proud of her rose garden. Clara could easily recall the creams and pinks and yellows. The perfume on the summer air, the vases on the table full of stems cut by her mom after Grandma died. *Just like Debbie always did,* Grace would say. *She'd want us to enjoy them.* Clara remembered leaning over the table to plunge her nose into the silky, fragrant blooms.

"There's so much life here," Clara whispered. "All still so strong and alive. You kept it going, Grandpa. All these years, all alone. And now . . ." She swallowed hard against the clog of emotion in her throat.

Now, I'm going to sell it off.

Like a piece of tacky, old jewelry.

Clara placed her helmet on the seat of the bike and walked to the porch steps. She pressed her gloved hand to the rounded newel post. A thick curl of grief moved through her stomach, bringing with it the sting of that Christmas night so long ago. The night she lost her parents, her home, her best friend, her grandpa, her snow, her trees—everything, as far as her twelve-year-old mind could understand.

The last time I was here, my parents were alive . . . and then they died.

Those first months living in San Diego with Aunt Liz had been a constant pendulum swing of raging pain and indifferent numbness. Sometimes, she had missed her parents, Grandpa, and the blue house so much she couldn't eat. Other times, she pretended like none of it had ever existed.

Liz's anger toward her father—blaming Lincoln for Randy and Grace's death— hadn't helped the situation. For those first few years, Clara had asked to visit Grandpa and the farm. She'd worried about Liam and felt a desperate need to explain to him why she'd never gone back to the well. But Liz had always refused, saying she couldn't bear it. Gradually, Clara's connection to her home faded away. The only string that tied her to this place over the last fifteen years had been Grandpa Lincoln's jar of pine nuts. He'd sent it to her every

Christmas without fail. Always with a short, staccato note of love.

Love you. Miss you. Enjoy the pine nuts. Grandpa Lincoln.

Clara looked at the field of Christmas trees.

But not this Christmas.

For the first time in my life, Grandpa won't send me pine nuts.

And soon, someone else will own our first tree—all our trees.

"Miss you, too, Grandpa," she whispered, her fingers flexing on the post. She hadn't known his stomach cancer was fatal. When Liz told her that Lincoln had gone into the hospital, Clara had called him. He'd dismissed his pain. "I'm fine, Clara. Just old. Don't worry about me. I'll be fine in no time. Go build those amazing bikes."

She'd accepted his words. In her mind, nothing could touch Lincoln Hill, with his John Wayne bravado and steel-strong hands. She'd dismissed the itching in the back of her mind that told her to go see him. She'd ignored the whisper that said it was finally time to go back to Utah. But her dread of being here, like this, had been stronger than that voice. She'd stayed away for so long it'd become a habit. An obstacle she didn't quite know how to climb over.

Clara had avoided Hill Valley for years—until the funeral this morning.

And standing here, with the trees and the blue house, hurt as deeply as she'd always feared. The memories harsh, slashing cuts over her heart.

Liz's hushed words at the funeral came back to her. "Clara, I saw the will this morning. He left the farm to you. The house and the trees." She'd rolled her eyes. "All of it. I told the lawyer you'd come sign the papers that allow us to sell it. I'm sure Turner Barnes has his checkbook ready."

"Sell it? Are you sure?" Clara had responded instinctively, her fists tightening at her sides. *And who says checkbook anymore? No, not Turner Barnes.*

Liz had sighed impatiently. "Of course I'm sure. We can finally get rid of the place. Tonight at six, Bill Pratt's office on Main Street. Let's get it over with so we can get back to California before it snows."

Clara had nodded vaguely, unsure why she felt a sudden, overwhelming desire to keep the Christmas tree farm.

Clara pulled her mind back to the present. Her hand dropped from the newel post. "What would I do with forty-five hundred Christmas trees?" A whisper near her heart answered, *come home.* She frowned. "I don't do home. My home is my bike and my van and any shop that needs a mechanic."

Another quiet retort: *Stop running and come home.*

"Not a chance," she mumbled back.

A wave of exhaustion forced Clara to sit on the stairs. She propped her elbows on her knees and put her face in her hands. The grief and confusion swirled through her, pungent and raw.

Just sell the place to Barnes and move on.
No more Hill Valley. Ever.
Grandpa is gone—it's time.
Is it?

After a few minutes of letting the sting simmer, she lifted her head to look out through the trees. Her gaze went in the direction of the old wishing well. Her hand came involuntarily to the tiny snowflake charm around her neck.

I guess it's not just the pine nuts that keep me connected to Hill Valley.
Liam's necklace.
Liam.

What is he doing now?

Many times over the years, she'd taken it off and tossed it in the bottom of a drawer. It was badly tarnished and scratched. But it always left her feeling exposed, unprotected, and somehow, disloyal. None of which made any sense. Liam was just a boy she'd known for about a month before her parents died. Yet, the relief she felt whenever she put the necklace on was undeniable. And so, it stayed on, and most of the time, she didn't think much of it. But right now, it made her think of snowflakes on her cheeks and childhood wishes and Liam smiling over at her.

Clara got to her feet and started walking toward the old wishing well.

The dirt under her boots was hard and dry, the air cool and fresh with the familiar scent of Christmas trees. Hill Valley still awaited its first snow of the season. Clara glanced up at the azure sky, no clouds in sight.

It's so late this year.

Good. It can't snow until I leave.

Harleys and snow don't mix.

She thought of her parents driving in that gray truck, the road slick and icy. "And I *hate* the snow," she added in a bitter whisper.

Liam resisted the urge to throw his wrench across the garage. His body hurt from sitting on the cement, hunched over the stubborn engine of his 1947 Harley-Davidson EL Knucklehead Bobber. "You're *not* worth it," he grunted as he tossed the wrench into his toolbox. He rubbed his greasy hands together, trying to force some warmth back into his fingers. "No wonder you sat in Earl's garage for so long." Liam swore and pushed up to his feet. He groaned as he straightened his back for the first time in an hour.

With another scowl at the old bike, he walked to the open garage door and took a few deep breaths of the crisp December air. The brilliantly clear sky did nothing for his mood. He checked his watch. He had about an hour before he was supposed to meet Lyla for dinner. He turned to go back in the house for a shower, but stopped.

The wishing well flashed into his mind.

I haven't been there in . . . a long time.

He checked his watch again. A walk sounded nice after being huddled on the garage floor. He'd still have time to shower and get to town. Liam zipped up his camel-yellow Carhartt work coat, dug his hands into the pockets, and set out across the yard into the orchard.

His head filled with memories of Clara.

I haven't thought about her . . . in a long time.

He laughed at the bizarre turn of thoughts. One minute, he was angry at a vintage motorcycle, the next mushy with nostalgia over a girl he had known for a short time many years ago. "I guess it's because we both wished for Harleys," he told himself as he walked. "Wonder if she ever got hers. Hope it's better than mine." He shook his head, lips curving into a smile.

Liam strolled slowly through the healthy, six-foot-tall Scot pines, enjoying the crunch of fallen pine needles under his work boots. The trees always brought him comfort, an easy peace. Their constancy in his life were a gentle reassurance. Their partnership a point of pride. As foreman of Hill Valley Christmas Tree Farm, these trees depended on him, and he on them.

Emerging from the rows, Liam stepped into the clearing. A surprising rush of emotion hit him as he looked at the old stone well. Nothing had changed. He could still be fourteen years old, waiting for Clara to come bursting through the trees, cheeks flushed, eyes bright. His smile grew as the image of her face became brighter in his mind. He went to the well and ran his dirty hand over the rough stone.

An odd melancholy swelled in his chest as he looked down into the black hole. "I wish I knew what happened to you, Clara," he whispered. For years after that Christmas, he'd thought about her, especially on the first snow. He hated that he didn't know what had happened. The uncertainty, the guessing—it was torture. The question came roaring back to him now, those feelings as fresh as they'd been fifteen years ago.

Why didn't you ever come back?

What happened?

I missed you—a lot.

He marinated in the gloom of his wish to know about Clara until he remembered another woman was waiting for him. He pulled his hand away from the stone and realized he'd rather stay here than go to dinner with Lyla.

Liam frowned deeply.

Now, that's just ridiculous. Stop it.

Lyla Dunne was pretty, sweet, and charming. He'd enjoyed her company on their previous three dates, but . . .

A chill moved up his spine. He shook his head.

You're being weird. Lyla is great.

It's just . . .

"This place," he finished out loud. Or maybe it was much more about the hurt of his failed marriage. The paranoid distrust that now seemed a constant companion. "Lyla is not Kendra."

Liam buried his hands in his pockets again and started to walk to the trees. A sound made him stop. He turned to find a woman standing just inside the trees on the opposite side of the well. His heart stuttered.

"Oh, I'm sorry," she said, lifting a gloved hand in an apologetic gesture. She wore a slim-cut leather jacket in Harley's signature black, orange, and white. The logo was stitched on the left side, over her heart. She had on light-wash jeans under black leather chaps and solid brown boots. Her dark hair, rich as good garden soil, hung in a long braid over her shoulder.

Liam took a few steps forward. "No worries . . ." His words got lost as he noticed her eyes. Sage-green, marbled with brown. "Clara?" He instantly regretted saying it out loud. Of course, this wasn't her. His memories of this place were confusing him. He started to shake his head, opening his mouth to fumble out an apology.

"Liam?" she said, slightly breathless. Clara stepped out of the trees, stopping a few feet in front of him.

"Clara?" he repeated, taking another step forward. His heart rate spiked. Their eyes scoured over each other. Clara's hand came to her throat. Liam recognized the snowflake charm under her fingertips. A rush of heat spread through his chest. His eyes came back to hers. A hesitant smile lifted her full pink lips. He wanted to reach out for her, the impulse so powerful, it took his breath away. But he held back. Even if this woman was Clara, they hadn't seen each other in fifteen years.

"I can't believe it," she whispered. She took a half-step forward, her brow furrowed as she continued to study his face. Liam wondered what she saw, what she felt as she looked at him. Was the past plowing over her heart, too?

"Liam?" she asked once more.

"Yeah, it's me," he said with a small laugh.

Clara laughed back, and then launched herself at him,

wrapping her arms around his neck. He stumbled back from the force of her body meeting his. Liam planted his feet and immediately brought his arms around her, pulling her small, thin body close. He pressed his cheek to her hair and closed his eyes. She smelled of leather and something citrusy.

Clara jerked away much too soon. "I'm so sorry," she sputtered as she stepped back. "Whoa. That was weird. Sorry! I didn't mean to—"

"It's totally fine," Liam hurried to comfort. He desperately wanted her back in his arms. "I'm glad to see you, too."

The corner of her mouth lifted in a half-smile. There was a moment of awkward silence. Clara fiddled with her necklace, still avoiding his eyes. He warmed at the flush of embarrassment high on her cheeks. He pointed to the necklace. "I can't believe you still have that."

She laughed. "I can't, either, really." She gave a small shrug as she dropped her fidgeting hand. "And I can't believe you're *here*."

"I can't believe *you're* here. What happened to you? One day, you just stopped coming to the well."

A shadow moved over her face, an emotion that made Liam think of his dad.

Clara half-turned toward the Hill family side. "My parents died in a car crash that last night," she answered quietly. "Christmas night. After my dad called me back—do you remember?—he and my mom left for San Diego. I stayed with my grandpa. They hit a bad storm near Cedar City. The roads were . . . a bad accident with a semi . . ." She lifted one shoulder casually, but it couldn't hide the pain in her expression.

A rush of empathy filled him. "I'm so sorry, Clara." It felt good to say her name. "I wish I'd known. I wish . . ." Both their gazes went to the well. "I'm sorry," Liam repeated.

She nodded. "I tried to find you . . ." She folded her arms tightly against her body, moving slowly to the well. "I came here the next morning, but it was really early. I wanted to say goodbye before I left. I . . . wanted to tell you, but I also didn't. You were already sad about your dad."

Liam winced slightly, his worry about missing her that morning now confirmed. *How did I feel it? How did I know something was wrong?* "I came that morning, too, but obviously too late," he said. "I'm so sorry, Clara. I know exactly how you felt. I wish I could have been there for you. Where did you go?"

"San Diego, to live with my aunt." She sighed. "I wanted to stay but . . . my parents' will put me in Liz's care. I was so angry, and I hated that I didn't have a way to contact you."

"Do you live there still—San Diego?"

"Not really. I move around a lot." She shook her head, quickly dismissing the question and her answer. "And you? How are *you*, Liam?"

"Good," he answered, feeling a little shy. He had the urge to tell her everything that had happened in the last fifteen years, including his disaster of a marriage and his mother's cancer. "I'm good. Still here, as you can tell."

She smiled. "Do you still play the guitar? I never got to hear that song you were writing."

Liam laughed, stepping a little closer. "I play almost every night. Some hobbies never die." He didn't say anything about that song. He'd finished it, and it was about her. For her.

Clara's Song.

I can probably still play it by heart.

Clara smiled. "How's your mom?"

"She's . . . okay. Lung cancer. Remember how much she liked to smoke?"

Clara's expression fell. "Oh, yeah. I'm so sorry. How bad is it?"

"It's pretty advanced. She's getting treatments a few times a week, but the outlook isn't great." Liam hadn't realized how much that scared him until this moment with Clara. He'd been able to suppress the building grief, but now it exploded in a sharp burst behind his eyes. He turned his head away.

Clara stepped closer and hesitantly put her hand on his arm. Surprised by the pulse of comfort that came with her light touch, he looked down to meet her gaze. She was still a good foot shorter than him. Her eyes were misty. He knew she understood perfectly. He put his hand over hers—so small compared to his. Her skin so warm.

"That's so hard," she whispered.

"Yeah, thanks."

Wanting to lighten the mood, and unable to stop admiring how incredible she looked in her Harley gear, he asked, "Bike leathers, huh?"

Her face lit up. "Hard to ride without them. I'm a motorcycle mechanic, actually. I specialize in restoring old bikes."

"Seriously? That's incredible. I have a '47 Knucklehead Bobber. I was just working on it."

"That's a great bike! Is it running?"

"No. It's kind of a disaster. Been sitting for decades."

"That's common. The Knuck engine is one of Harley's best. It probably needs some new electrical work, a deep clean of every part. I could take a look sometime, if you'd like help."

"I'd love that. I'm not getting very far with it, but I'm dying to get it riding again." Liam realized he still had his hand on hers. She noticed at the same moment, her face flushing slightly as she gently pulled away. He cleared his throat, folded his arms. "So . . . uh . . . what bike do you have?"

"Brand new, actually. It's a Street Bob. Basically, the great-granddaughter of your bike. Custom built—by me, obviously. It's fast and powerful and way too much fun."

"Well, your wish came true, then."

She narrowed her eyes and then laughed. "That my Harley would be cooler than yours? I forgot about that." She looked at the well. "Once you get yours back to its former glory, I think it'll be a tie. Hard to compete with a killer vintage bike."

Liam laughed and nodded. "Well, I don't think it'll get there without some help. I'm kind of failing the old thing."

"I doubt that." Her smile caused tendrils of warmth to move through his chest.

"I still can't believe you're here. What brought you back, Clara?"

She blinked quickly, the joy slipping from her eyes. "My grandpa's funeral."

Liam's stomach clenched. "Oh, man. I'm so sorry. You and I got too much grief going on in our lives."

She gave a sincere nod. "It could fill up that old well."

Liam wished he were still holding her hand. "I hadn't heard that anyone died. Who's your grandpa?"

"Lincoln Hill. He owns these trees—Liam, what's wrong?"

A cold tingle started at the base of his neck. "Lincoln Hill? Of Hill Valley Christmas Tree Farm?"

Clara nodded, her brow furrowed. "I thought everyone knew . . ."

"But . . . no. No. I work for Lincoln. I'm his foreman, and I just saw him this afternoon. And he doesn't have any grandchildren."

Clara took a step back, her expression closing down. "What are you talking about?"

Liam's heart started pounding. He thought of the Gordon Lightfoot record tucked away in his extensive record collection. His old theory came thundering back to him.

No, no, that can't be possible.

But Lincoln . . .

"Clara . . ."

"What?" she asked, her face tight with confusion.

"What year is it?"

Clara's eyes popped wide. She chuckled nervously and took another step back from the wild look on Liam's face. "Liam . . . what are you talking about?"

He held up a hand. "Just . . . indulge me, please. What is the date today?"

She hesitated. *Is he crazy?* The gulf of fifteen years suddenly slammed a door shut in her mind. Moments ago, it had felt natural to be so open and comfortable with Liam, to touch him and talk with him. But this man was a total stranger. They'd been best friends for all of a month a decade-and-a-half ago. She didn't know anything about him.

And now he thinks my grandpa is alive and doesn't know the date.

"Liam . . . I don't . . ." She half-turned, ready to leave. Something in his expression stopped her, and her curiosity demanded some answers. Slowly, she said, "It's December 4, 2019."

He flinched, eyes narrowing. He looked from her to the well and back, and then shook his head. He scoffed. "It's true," he whispered. "How is that possible?"

"What's true?" Clara asked, leveling a cautious gaze on him. "Wait—what year do *you* think it is?"

Liam looked at her intently for a moment before answering. "It's 1989. Still December 4, but . . . in 1989." He shifted his gaze to the well. "I think that old well is more powerful than any of us ever guessed."

*Okay, so this guy is drunk or delusional or . . . something.
What do I say to that? He thinks it's 1989?*
Come on!

"The *well* is powerful? Do you mean because of the motorcycle thing?" she asked, searching for a thread of reason. "I don't think it really—"

"No, not that. I mean . . . maybe that, too. But there's more . . ." He trailed off, his eyes on the well. He took off his baseball hat and ran a hand back through his hair.

Clara again resisted the urge to run away, and instead took a bold step toward him. "Please tell me what you're talking about. That's just a pile of old stones—an empty hole in the ground." She pointed to the well.

Liam turned back to her, a deep crease of concentration cutting across his forehead. "Do you remember the day we met?"

Clara blinked at the unexpected question. "Uh . . . yeah, of course. Day after Thanksgiving. First snow."

"The night before, on Thanksgiving night, I was here. I had to escape my house. My mom, so deep in her grief fog, had completely forgotten it was Thanksgiving. We didn't do anything—it was just another depressing night. It made me so angry, the whole situation. So, I came here." He paused to take a breath. "I made a wish—a plea, really—to the well. I wanted to feel better, to find a way out of such a dark hole." Liam stepped closer. Clara's pulse quickened at the force in his eyes. "You showed up the next morning, and everything got better."

A flash of cold moved down her body. She looked at the well, and then at Liam. "You think the well brought us together? That it . . . *answered* your wish?"

Liam frowned. "I know it sounds weird and impossible . . . but yeah, I do. And I think it did something extraordinary to make it happen. I think it has . . . *bridged* time." He grimaced, running his hand through his hair again, then tugged his hat back on.

Clara frowned at him, her mind grappling for a solid hold. "You think . . ." A roll of dizziness clouded the edges of her vision. She spread her feet a little farther apart to find her balance. "What exactly do you think?"

"I think we live in different times." He winced, watching her closely. "You in 2019, me in 1989, and the well, *somehow*, allows us to be together here."

She made a noise that was part laugh, part whimper.

Okay. Now I really should run.

Bridged time?

Leave, now!

But Clara could only stand and stare at Liam.

Liam stepped closer, rushing on with his explanation. "I know, I know. Stay with me. The Gordon Lightfoot record . . . remember that?"

"Yes." In her memories, Clara saw clearly the excitement on Liam's young face. She felt the sensation of hugging him for the first time. The thrill of it. Not so unlike what she'd felt a few minutes ago when she'd hugged him for the second time.

"You told me it was old—it looked old—but then I saw the date inside. The album was recorded in 1975."

"Right . . ."

"To me, it was 1974. That Christmas, it was 1974. Same year my dad died." He said the words slowly, his gaze penetrating, almost pleading. "That record was the first clue. Then I started thinking about how we never saw each other in town or at school. Your clothes, how you talked. It all felt a little . . . off. But that date on the record—that really got me wondering. When you never came back to the well, I had no way to know for sure."

The information clogged her mind. "You're saying . . ."

He's not saying what I think he's saying.

Is he?

Clara looked at him more closely. The cut of his jeans was old-fashioned, but that didn't really prove anything. His coat was similar to many work coats she'd seen. His light brown hair was shaggy, curling out underneath his navy-blue Utah Jazz baseball cap, the logo and colors definitely in the '80s style. His expression was eager but sincere.

He still wears hats and has messy hair.

Am I dreaming?

Did I fall asleep back on the porch steps?

She swallowed hard. "You're saying that . . . we live in different times," she finished, her voice weak. A tremor moved up her spine. "And the . . . well brought us together."

Liam nodded seriously. "That's what I'm saying, as weird as it sounds."

Clara scoffed. *Okay, that's enough of this.* "I think I better get back to the house. It's been a . . . hard day. I can't . . ." She turned. Liam moved quickly to her, a gentle hand on her arm. She looked up to meet his eyes, the color of coffee with cream.

"Clara, wait." He took a shaky breath. "Your grandpa, Lincoln Hill . . . I know him so well. He's a big, old cowboy type, always wears a black Stetson, and knows everything about growing Christmas trees. He and Debbie have two kids, Randy and Liz. Liz just got engaged to a guy from California, Gavin. And Randy recently started dating a local girl named Grace." He scoffed quietly, half-smiling. "You look just like her," he whispered.

Clara could hardly breathe. Her heart and head sprinted away from the confusion and the swell of grief Liam's words churned up.

He knows my parents and Grandpa.

To him, they are alive.

But I've lost them all.

Clara jerked her arm from his grip. "Stop it," she breathed.

Liam looked stricken, but she didn't care.

She turned and bolted off into the trees.

Bridged Time

L iam hesitated for only a breath before tearing after Clara.
Wait! We can't leave it like that. I'm sorry.
"Clara! Wait, please."

But several feet into the trees, he realized she wasn't there. Not just that she'd gotten ahead of him, but that she wasn't there at all. He skidded to a stop and tried to catch his breath. He scanned the row, the trees turning to shadow in the failing light. "It's just like before, when I tried to find her that morning," he said quietly. "She ran back into 2019, and I'm stuck in 1989."

He jerked off his hat, welcoming the frigid air on his head. He lifted his face to the violet sunset sky. "What did I do?" Liam felt he was right about the well, but wondered if maybe he'd pushed too hard too fast in sharing his theory with Clara.

"First time I see her in fifteen years, and I act like a crazy person," he whispered. "How can this be the truth?" He found no satisfaction in the confirmation of his theory. If Clara lived in another time, he had no way to reach her or to see her again. He'd already waited too long to see her. He couldn't do that again.

His mind snagged on a forgotten reality.
Oh, crap. How late am I?
He brought his watch close to his face and swore. He only

had fifteen minutes before he'd be late for his date with Lyla. He looked back in the direction of the Hills' blue house. "She's Clara Hill, Lincoln's *granddaughter*. And she went to his funeral today." He shook his head, amazed and broken-hearted. "And then I threw all that at her. Talked about her family, alive and well." He swore again as he started to jog toward his house. "I am an *idiot*!"

Liam picked up his speed. He couldn't fix things with Clara right now, but he could hurry to avoid screwing things up with the woman who lived in his time.

What just happened?

The question repeated in her head as Clara sprinted through the rows of pines. She didn't hear Liam behind her, but checked over her shoulder a few times. Her confusion twisted into a tighter knot when she realized she was disappointed he wasn't coming after her.

Now, that's just stupid.

I don't want that head case following me.

A magical wishing well that can break the barriers of time.

Seriously?

The blue house appeared at the end of the row, and she pushed harder to get to it. Huffing for breath, she looped around the house and collapsed on the front porch steps, laying back with her head against the top stair edge, her feet spread wide at the bottom. Her heart pumped against her ribs. The conversation at the well replayed in her mind, growing more confounding in recollection. "Both 2019 and 1989," she mumbled. "Uh . . . I don't think so, Mr. Casually Sexy Liam." She pulled a hand across her forehead and scowled up at the sky.

If it's true . . .

He knows my family. They're all alive . . .

An involuntary hysterical laugh burst out. She slapped a hand to her mouth until she was sure the impulse had died away. *Get a grip, Clara.* When she dropped her hand, she said, "Maybe he has a brain injury. Maybe *I* have a brain injury."

"Are you all right?"

Clara sat bolt upright at the unfamiliar voice. A gorgeous, older woman and an equally impressive Old English Sheepdog stood to the right of the porch steps. Both looked at Clara with apprehension and a touch of amusement. Clara felt that manic laugh bubbling back up and swallowed it down. She hurried to her feet. "Sorry. Uh . . . sorry. I'm fine. Totally fine. Promise." She gave a burst of nervous laughter and then shook her head.

Yeah, real fine.

"Uh-huh. I can see that." The woman raised her thin eyebrows. She had a sort of farmer elegance going for her. Long white hair in pigtail braids, creamy skin deeply wrinkled around her gray eyes, but hardly anywhere else. She wore ripped-knee jeans, tall, red Hunter rainboots, and a floral-print bomber jacket.

"Sorry. I'm fine. I'm Clara Hill, Lincoln's granddaughter." She meekly clasped her hands behind her back, doing her best to put on the expression of a mentally sound person.

The woman smiled, an impressive look that lit up her whole face and showed off white teeth. "I figured. Hey, Clara. It's Winnie Sparrow. Remember me?"

Clara blinked at Winnie. Childhood memories of stacks of books came rushing back. "Winnie? Oh my gosh! You look amazing!"

"Ha! I look *old.* Remember, I'm just a few years younger than your grandpa." Her eyes immediately clouded; her smile slipped away. "Still can't believe he's gone."

"Me, either. How did I miss you at the funeral?"

Winnie shook her head. "Not really my kind of thing. Me and this beast went for a long walk instead." She nodded to the big dog.

"That is such a gorgeous dog."

Winnie let the leash out a bit, and the dog came forward for some attention. "This is Ollie. She was Lincoln's dog."

Clara blinked in surprise. "Really?" She squatted down to better engage the giant teddy bear, ruffling her soft hair. "I didn't know he had a dog," she whispered. "I didn't know anything."

"He talked about you all the time," Winnie offered. "He loved to brag that his granddaughter could fix and ride a motorcycle better than any man."

Clara's lips lifted again, but sadly. Tears burned the back of her eyes. She could only nod.

Winnie came closer. "Killer bike, by the way."

Clara took a breath and managed to find her voice. "Thanks. It really is. Do you ride?"

Winnie laughed, shaking her head. "I dated a guy once who had one. That was basically the only thing he had going for him. It didn't last long, and then that kind of put me off motorcycles for a while. Though it does look fun. Is it fast?"

"Sometimes I can't drive fast enough." Clara pressed her teeth together. She hadn't meant to blurt that out.

Winnie nodded, compassion in her gaze. "I bet that thing nearly flies. And there's something about the wind in your face. Right?"

"Yes, exactly." Clara straightened up, but kept her hand on the dog's head. "Do you still own the bookstore?"

"Of course I do. Someone has to keep reading alive."

Clara laughed. "Do you still do the mug thing? I always loved all the mugs in your shop."

"I've got about five hundred or so now. Not exactly sure. Kind of lost track around three hundred."

Clara smiled, remembering trips to the bookstore with her mom. Winnie's loud laughs echoing in the store, the bowl of chocolates she kept behind the counter. "Every book I read from the time I was born until I was twelve came from your store."

Winnie grinned. "And that, right there, is why I keep it open. The memories that go with the books."

"I will have to stop by soon."

"Yes, you will. I'll round up some recommendations."

"That'd be great. Thanks."

Winnie nodded and then startled. "Speaking of which, I gotta get back. Here ya go." She held out the leash to Clara.

Clara took a step back. "What's happening?"

"She's yours, kid. She comes with the trees and the house. Lincoln's wishes."

Clara pressed her teeth together again, feeling incredibly guilty. She didn't want to say that, soon, she'd sign away her inheritance and go back to her nomadic lifestyle. She read in Winnie's face and tone that she expected Clara to stay and pick up where Lincoln left off.

But that's impossible. Grandpa, I can't.

Not a farm. Not a house.

And certainly not a huge dog.

Winnie took another step forward. "I know this is rough. I know it's been a hard day. Ollie is great companionship. I think you'll enjoy having her around."

Clara blinked down at the dog. "But . . . I've never had a dog. I don't even know the first thing. And I live in a *van* . . . not a lot of space. I travel a lot."

"Her food and water bowls are in the mudroom."

"What? I don't—"

"Lincoln was very clear about this. She's yours now." Winnie smiled empathetically as she placed the leash in Clara's hand. "Ollie is as easy as they come. Just feed her when you eat, keep her water filled, and good luck keeping her from sleeping on your bed. I'm not kidding when I say Lincoln seriously spoiled her."

"But . . ." Clara sputtered. "I have to go to town to meet Liz and the lawyer—like right now. Ollie won't exactly fit on my bike."

"She's totally fine to stay in the house. Lincoln installed a dog door in back."

"Okay . . ." Clara looked down at the dog, who panted up at her with an eager expression. Her stomach tightened.

Oh my gosh! What is happening?

Not a dog. Not a living, breathing thing.

"You got this," Winnie added as she turned to walk away. "Stop by the shop after the lawyer thing. I'll have those books waiting." She waved over her shoulder and headed toward the barn.

Clara blinked after the woman, panic itching under her skin. How was she supposed to process all this stuff in one day? She watched Winnie get into a vintage truck. It had a bulbous frame—characteristic of the forties and fifties—a short bed, white-wall tires, and a gorgeous melon-orange paint job. A square black-and-white vinyl sign on the passenger door read, *Pages on Main Bookstore.*

Clara looked down at Ollie. "Winnie has great taste in cars." The dog huffed lightly and wagged her tail. Clara frowned. "So . . . I guess we better go inside?" She checked her watch. "Ugh. I'm gonna be late. Yep, inside. Hurry up." The dog led the way to the back door, pulling an overwhelmed Clara behind her.

Clara hesitated on the back porch. Ollie's leash slipped

from her hand as the dog went in through her dog door. Clara heard the rustling of her childhood snow pants, the whisper of the fresh powder over her boots. She slowly opened the door. The mudroom was clean and well-organized, her grandpa's boots all lined up under the long wooden bench. The same bench that had been there fifteen years ago. The air smelled like pine, of course. A smell that, to her, was not just Christmas, but childhood. That smell was *before.*

The dog noisily lapped at her water bowl.

Clara shut the door behind her.

Heart thundering, she stepped into the kitchen and instantly felt she'd stepped back into that Christmas night. She saw her grandpa sitting at the big wooden table, face in his hands, crying. She felt her small body sitting on his lap. The deep sounds in his chest. She recalled perfectly how she had thought it strange that her mouth still tasted like the chocolates from her stocking while she was crying over her parents. As if it were impossible to taste something sweet while her whole world turned to ash.

And the crash of grief—she felt that as sharply now as she had that night. Perhaps more now with all the years of loss compounding into *this* moment.

Mom. Dad. Grandpa.

My life here, where it should have been.

My home. Taken away.

Clara's knees wavered. She dropped to the floor and let the storm of tears rage out of her. Ollie lay down beside her, quiet, solid warmth.

"Liam? You okay? *Liam?*"

Liam startled and turned to face Lyla. He blinked a few times, disoriented. Her arched brows knitted down in concern. A rush of noise came back to him. He looked around the crowded but cozy Italian restaurant, taking in the room of couples leaning toward each other over small tables, bowls of pasta, and votive candles, their expressions content and attentive.

While I worry about a woman who ran away from me.

"Uh . . . sorry, Lyla. Sorry. What did you say?" Liam forced his attention back onto his date and away from what had happened at the well.

How long was I staring off into space like a jerk?

She smiled indulgently and shook her head. "You keep staring out that window, face all serious and far away. Everything all right?"

Lyla Dunne, beautiful and effervescent, should have been more than enough to keep his attention. Her porcelain skin, eyes the color of glacier ice, and warm laugh pulled on the attention of every man she came across. Especially tonight in that red dress. But Liam's mind wanted only to stray to Clara.

He reached across the small table, between their empty plates, and took Lyla's hand. "I'm sorry. Tired, I guess."

She squeezed his hand. "Are you worried about your mom? She has another treatment tomorrow, right?"

"Yeah, in the morning. Are you working?"

"Yep. I'll make sure I'm there to help."

"You're her favorite nurse. Probably everyone's favorite nurse."

Lyla smiled sweetly as she tucked her short, white-blonde hair behind her ear. "We can call it a night if you're tired."

"No, of course not. I'm fine. I promised you a sampling of all my favorite places in Hill Valley. We've covered dinner." Liam gestured to the candlelit room. "Enzo's is the best place in town to eat a quiet dinner. So unless you want any more pasta . . . ?"

Lyla laughed lightly. "I couldn't eat any more pasta if my life depended on it."

Liam smiled. "Then let's head over to the bookstore. My most favorite place in town." He released her hand to pull out some cash. He paid the bill, and then helped Lyla into her long, black wool coat. Everything she wore whispered of high quality and high price tag. He'd spent his whole life surviving on so little, he and his mom scraping by, that his senses had become fine-tuned to comparisons. Even now, despite making a decent salary working for Lincoln, Liam felt uncomfortable around people accustomed to money. His thrifty habits never seemed to die away.

Lyla lived and worked in Salt Lake City. They'd met at the cancer clinic where Sally had been receiving treatments. Lyla's parents lived in a large house in Holladay, an affluent suburb of Salt Lake. Liam was certain she'd never wanted for anything. Did she notice that his slacks were at least five years old, his suit jacket a little worn at the elbows, and his evergreen scarf a hand-me-down from his dad? Did she care that he drove a ten-year-old truck and did all the repairs on it himself? Did it bother her that he wore flannel shirts and boots to work and not a suit and tie?

Liam shook off his feelings of inadequacy and led Lyla outside. As they walked down Main Street toward the bookshop, she hooked her arm in his. "This street is so charming with all the Christmas decorations. All we are missing is the snow," she said.

Liam looked up at the clear night sky. His mind filled with the image of Clara standing at the well, her anxious fingers playing with his snowflake charm. He forced it away. "It'll come soon, I'm sure. Hill Valley always gets a white Christmas."

Lyla answered with her warm laugh. "Well, it can stay

away as long as possible. I hate the snow. I really should move to a warmer place." She shivered to emphasize her point.

Liam turned his head to hide his disappointment. The snow had always fascinated him, and he eagerly awaited its return each year. Winter was a time for rest, hibernation, and preparation for rebirth. All winter long, the earth soaked up the water, taking it deep into the ground. A good snow season meant a good growth season for the pine and fruit trees come spring. A healthy farm needed the snow in winter.

He thought of Clara's love for the snow. Did she still feel that way, or had the years in San Diego changed her? *You're drifting again!* He took a breath and turned back to Lyla. "But you can't have Christmas without snow, right?" He gestured to an elaborately decorated tree behind the window of Big Bobbin Quilt Shop.

She shrugged casually. "I'd be totally fine with palm trees."

What did Clara say that Christmas?

They'd been talking about Donovan's Reef.

She liked the beach but couldn't imagine Christmas without the snow.

Liam decided to change the subject. "Pages on Main is just a little bit farther up the street. I love this bookstore. I've been coming here my whole life, pretty much every week. I know they have bigger shops in Salt Lake, but I doubt any have Pages on Main's awesome charm. There's a really cool section of music biographies, a fun kids' area with a giant stuffed octopus, and used paperbacks for fifty cents. The owner, Winnie—hilarious, quirky woman—collects coffee mugs. There are hundreds of them mixed in with the books." They stopped at Pages on Main's door, and he opened it for Lyla. "It always smells like books and coffee in here. It's really great."

"I've never been to a bookstore on a date," she said as she moved past him.

Is that a good thing or a bad thing? He couldn't tell from her tone, but she smiled as they moved into the shop. *Would Clara be excited to come here on a date?* He wondered if Pages on Main still existed in 2019.

Liam raised a hand to Winnie, who sat on a stool at the cash register. The wall behind her was divided into small wooden squares, each with a mug. Mostly animal themed: cows, cats, dogs, chickens, and one with jellyfish. A few small paperbacks were wedged into the slots, companions for the mugs. Silver Christmas garland framed the wall, and Winnie had taken a couple of strands of red and green lights and haphazardly draped, tucked, and wound them among the mugs. A sign taped to the register read: *The mugs are not for sale. Buy as many books as you want.*

"Hey, Winnie," he said. "How are you?" Winnie had an easy-going charm that everyone gravitated to. She knew everyone's name and favorite book genre. Her recommendations were miraculously spot-on, every time.

"Well, hello, Liam. Nice to see you. Did you finish *Fried Green Tomatoes?*"

"Of course. Incredible storytelling, great humor. Such a powerful story of friendship. I loved it. Idgie reminded me of you."

Winnie grinned. "And *that* is why you're my favorite customer. Most men wouldn't even read that, and then you do *and* you totally get it!" Her friendly eyes moved to Lyla. "This man is amazing!"

Liam blushed and said, "This is Lyla. It's her first time in Hill Valley. I'm showing her all the best spots."

Winnie smiled, her eyes lighting up. "That's wonderful. Welcome, Lyla. This is probably *the* best place in town, but I'm not biased."

Lyla laughed. "Thank you. It's a cute store."

Liam frowned at Lyla's use of the word "cute."

Cute? That's not the right word at all.

This is a bookstore, not a baby store.

And this is Winnie's bookstore.

Winnie looked back at Liam, something knowing in her expression. "You two let me know if you need anything. Look around, enjoy. Most couples prefer the music section for a good make-out session. Most privacy there."

Lyla's brows rose as she looked at Liam with a *did she really say that* look.

Liam scoff-laughed, trying not to blush too hard. Though he was used to Winnie's blunt sense of humor (and loved it), Lyla was not. "Gee, thanks, Winnie. Very helpful."

"Anytime!" Winnie winked and turned to help another customer.

Liam took Lyla's hand, and guided her deeper into the store. When they were far from the desk, Lyla whispered, "She's kind of weird, isn't she?"

Liam held back a flinch. He didn't like the way Lyla had said that. Why couldn't she just laugh about it? He whispered back, "Winnie loves to say stuff that throws people off. But she's amazing. I really admire her."

Lyla shrugged and shook her head.

Liam frowned, forcing himself to shake it off. "So . . . what's your favorite kind of book to read?" he asked. "Fiction? Nonfiction? Smutty romance, grisly true crime?"

Lyla lifted a Christmas picture book from a themed display table. "I don't really read that much. A novel here and there, I guess. When a friend recommends something."

Liam forced his face not to react.

She doesn't like snow AND she doesn't read.

Kendra didn't read, either.

Nope. Stop. Don't compare Lyla to Kendra.

77

Not everyone is a nerd like you.

"Okay. Cool," he said, keeping his tone light. "There's a popular fiction shelf over there. Let's start with those."

Clara loved to read. I remember that.

We spent a few days just lying by the well reading, two happy nerds.

There's something intimate and comfortable about lying next to someone while you both read your own books.

I want that.

Liam rolled his eyes at his disastrous thought patterns. He had to stop pulling on the past. Lyla was right here in front of him. Kendra was long gone, and the odds of seeing Clara again were incredibly slim.

He put his hands on Lyla's shoulders and his mouth close to her ear. "Pick the first cover that jumps out at you. Read the back. If it sounds good, hang on to it. If not, put it back. The one that sounds the best is the one to buy. My treat."

Lyla laughed, leaning back against him. "That sounds fun."

Clara steered her Harley onto Hill Valley's Main Street. It didn't look much different than her memories. A narrow two-lane road lined with brick shop fronts and huge maple trees. The streetlamps were on, casting warm circles of light onto the twilight street. Many of the shops were the same: Weller's Antiques, Big Bobbin Quilt Shop, Hill Valley Family Medical Clinic, and, of course, Pages on Main Bookshop. Memories sparked in her mind, dashes of color and scents and people. She couldn't wait to see all those mugs still scattered among the books in Pages.

Main Street had been decked out for Christmas. Wooden, lighted candy canes almost as tall as her lined the road, and red and silver garland had been wrapped around the lampposts. Every one of those big maples overflowed with white lights. A massive *Merry Christmas* banner in vintage script hung over the street like an arch, welcoming everyone who drove underneath it.

Clara frowned, more memories of her family's ties to Christmas filling her head. She'd worked hard over the years to avoid all this. Every tree and decoration was a sharp reminder of what had happened that Christmas night.

Sighing, she forced her attention away from the sore spots in her heart. She noted a new coffee shop and bakery, and wished she had time to stop before the meeting; she could use some caffeine courage. As Clara rode past, she deeply inhaled the smell of coffee and spices.

I'll stop after, before Pages.

It'll be post-dealing with Liz and a lawyer therapy.

Clara continued to the far north end of the street, pulling into a spot outside Pratt Law Offices. Her stomach roiled and her jaw ached from pressing her teeth together. She silenced her rumbling bike engine and stared at the unremarkable door into the office.

"What am I going to do?" she whispered inside her helmet.

The door pushed open, and Liz appeared. She summoned Clara with an impatient wave. "Come on. You're late." Liz had the same slate-blue eyes as Clara's dad and a similarly shaped nose, but she lacked any of Randy's cowboy chill. Liz was all business. She lived by schedules, clean counters, and neatly ironed oxford shirts. She was wearing one now, in pale pink, with black slacks and black flats. Her artificial brunette hair was pulled back into a simple, low ponytail. Clara always thought that Liz belonged somewhere like Vermont or New Hampshire, lording over a school board or community charity, and not as a housewife in carefree San Diego. And certainly not Hill Valley, Utah, even though she'd been born and raised here.

Clara rushed past her aunt with a quiet apology. Her Uncle Gavin and Bill Pratt sat at a long conference table, papers spread out between them. Gavin looked up with his jolly smile on his round face. He was not nearly as sophisticated (or high strung) as his wife. Gavin carried around about twenty extra pounds, smiled constantly, and spent a lot of his free time watching the DIY Network, though he didn't even own a hammer. But give him a computer software problem, and he would fix it in record time. "Hi, Clara," he greeted cheerfully. "Come in. Sit down." He gestured to the older man in a handsome gray suit. "This is Bill Pratt, your grandpa's lawyer."

Bill stood, removed his glasses, and held out a hand. "Hello, Miss Hill. I'm sorry for your loss."

Clara shook his hand, unnerved by his stiffness. "Thank you, Mr. Pratt. Sorry I'm late. I was dealing with some stuff at the house." Liz flashed her an inquiring expression, but Clara pretended not to notice while she put her helmet under the chair and sat.

Mr. Pratt took his seat, replaced his round glasses, and pulled a paper in front of him. "As you already know, Miss Hill, Lincoln left the farm business, land, and house to you, which comprises basically all his assets. He did, however, leave a small amount of money to Mr. and Mrs. Roberts here." Pratt looked up, meeting Clara's gaze. "Mrs. Roberts tells me you'd like to sell everything, that you have no interest in this inheritance as is. You would, of course, keep the money from the sale. Do you desire to sell Hill Valley Christmas Tree Farm?"

Clara gripped her hands together under the edge of the table. She wanted to take off her jacket—her back had begun to sweat. Her stomach heaved.

I wish they'd open a window.

There's no air in here.

Clara licked her dry lips. "I . . . I'm not sure, actually."

"What?" Liz instantly reacted. "Clara, please don't be ridiculous. Just sign the papers." She shoved a pen across the table.

Clara automatically reached for the pen, tucking it tightly into her palm. She was used to giving Liz whatever she asked for. Clara had always felt guilty for intruding on Liz and Gavin's family. Though they often told her she was as much their child as her cousins, Peter, Alex, and Mia, Clara had always felt like an outsider or a guest, and behaved as such, never challenging or inconveniencing. Her only real rebellion had been going to motorcycle mechanic school in Florida instead of a traditional college as Liz and Gavin had pushed for. Liz had talked at length about math and engineering degrees, lecturing almost daily for all of Clara's senior year of high school. *"If you're so good at putting things together, why waste that on motorcycles? Be an architect, a scientist, a surgeon."* Even after Clara was in Florida, her aunt's weekly calls always included a rough segue into more traditional career paths.

What would Liz do now if Clara didn't want to sell the farm?

Though Clara had never moved back into the Roberts' house after school, and she was now twenty-seven years old, she knew Liz and Gavin still felt obligated to help her. Liz had never really relinquished her role as stand-in mother, which usually Clara tolerated, but this . . . This had to be her decision, not Liz's. Just like mechanic school.

"Miss Hill?" Pratt prompted after a long silence.

"Sorry. Uh . . . I want to keep it," Clara said quietly.

Oh, no. Here we go!

Liz scoffed. "And do what? Stay here, become a farmer?

You don't know *anything* about running that place, and you haven't lived in the same spot for more than six months since you were twenty."

Clara sat up straighter before answering. "I can't be the Hill who ends our family legacy, Liz. It means too much. That place started the town, for heaven's sake. That's not something we should hand off the first chance we get." She finally met her aunt's shocked eyes. "It feels wrong."

"Really?" Liz said, blinking quickly. "Even after . . ." She pursed her lips, the words too sour to say.

"Maybe even because of that. I loved that place. Leaving was unbelievably hard. Grandpa wanted me to keep it going, and I think Mom and Dad would want that, too."

"But they fought over those trees. That's why Randy drove into that storm."

"I know that! I was there! They were fighting because of something I said." Clara paused to take a calming breath. "And standing in that house again was incredibly hard, but it also reminded me how much Dad loved it. He had as much passion for the farm as Grandpa. That's *why* they were always fighting. And my mom loved that house so much. How can I let someone else live there with Grandma Debbie's stove and roses?" She leaned forward, unable to stop now. "Yes, Dad drove off angry, but I don't think that's reason enough to give up the farm that's been in our family for generations. What happened was bad luck, bad timing. It's not the farm's fault." Clara took another quick breath, her hands cold in her lap. "And it's not Grandpa's fault. Liz, please, can't you see that?"

Liz blinked even more, pulling back slightly. Gavin cut in gently, "Are you sure, Clara? That's a lot to take on."

She turned to her uncle. "I know it's a lot, but it feels way worse to turn away from it." Her apprehension churned; she felt nauseated.

What am I doing?

"What about your career? You fought so hard for all of that, and it takes you all over the country. How can you run a farm here in Utah?" asked Gavin.

Clara had a gift for restoring older bikes. Shops called her in to help on difficult projects. Currently, she was working for Clive's Custom Choppers in Santa Fe, restoring an ancient BMW R32 from 1923, one of the first bikes made by the company. A wealthy collector had acquired the iconic machine and brought it to Clive for full restoration. Clive had emailed Clara after hearing about her work for a friend's shop in L.A. The project would take about a month, and then she'd be on to the next.

"I'm not planning to give up anything." A scrappy sort of plan formed in her head. "I'm going to take some time off to figure out the farm. I can own it, oversee it, without giving up my life. Semi-absentee—isn't that what they call it? I'll figure it out." She shrugged. "I just know I *can't* sell it. Hill Valley Christmas Tree Farm is our family legacy. That meant everything to Grandpa, and Dad. And it used to mean everything to me."

Liz winced at that, turning her face away. "Turner Barnes would buy the farm in a heartbeat. He's been gunning to be number one around here forever. I say we let him."

Clara's jaw dropped. "Grandpa would die all over again if he knew we'd sold the trees to Turner. He never liked him, and I doubt that changed recently." She looked to Mr. Pratt.

"They certainly weren't friends," the lawyer confirmed. "Though Barnes is a dedicated farmer. He could handle it and has already expressed interest."

Clara's eyes widened. "He asked you about the farm?"

Pratt adjusted his glasses. "Yes, after the funeral today. A bit uncouth, to be sure, but he does have the capital and the ability to take it on."

"Are you kidding me?" She turned to Liz. "We can't sell to that man. He asked you at the funeral? That's just terrible and in bad taste. No way." Clara looked at Liz, but she wouldn't look back.

Clara frowned and turned to her more congenial uncle. He gave her a proud smile and said, "This is very noble, Clara, and I understand why you want to keep everything. I think if you want to try, you should. If it doesn't work out, you're not stuck. You can sell at any time."

Liz made a quiet scoffing noise.

Clara nodded, ignoring her aunt. "Right. Exactly. Thank you." A tiny feeling of triumph came to life in her chest.

I'll figure it out. It'll be good.

"I don't think this is a good idea, Clara," Liz said, some of the fight gone from her voice. "Just because something has always belonged to us doesn't mean it has to belong to you. That farm is a *huge* burden. I know—I grew up there. My mother hated how insanely dedicated Lincoln was to those trees, to our *legacy*." Her eyes grew watery. "That is not something you need to inherit. It already took your parents. Don't let it take your freedom."

Clara reached for Liz's hand, emotions rising in her throat. "I understand. Really, I do. I'm not giving up my freedom; I just want to keep it going. I have to try."

"Running that farm is a twenty-four-seven, three-hundred-and-sixty-five kind of job. Who is going to do all that work? Who is qualified and willing to do it without owning it? How will you pay them, if you do find someone crazy enough?"

Clara swallowed hard. "I'm not sure. But that's what I need to find out."

"The farm has a dedicated, experienced foreman," Pratt said. "It should be simple to be a semi-absentee owner, Miss Hill."

"Good! Yes. See?" Clara smiled a little, relieved by the news.

Liz's face fell in resignation. "Going to motorcycle school was less crazy than this," she murmured spitefully. She withdrew her hand, and Clara flinched at the sting of hurt.

Mr. Pratt cleared his throat. "All right, Miss Hill. If you're decided, please sign here. This transfers the deed to you." Pratt presented her an official-looking document. Clara adjusted the pen in her hand, the barrel slippery from her sweaty palm. She pulled the paper close and pressed the pen tip down. She took a slow breath.

"This is a mistake," Liz said, venom in her words.

Gavin reached out a hand to touch her arm. "It's her decision, Liz." He smiled at Clara. "Up to you, Clara."

Clara nodded.

I hope this is the right thing to do.

Clara signed her name.

Mr. Pratt handed her the deed to Hill Valley Christmas Tree Farm and the blue farmhouse.

Coffee and Books and a Farm

Clara stood outside the law office with Gavin. Liz had immediately walked away and gotten in the car. Not a single word or glance in Clara's direction. Clara shook her head. "She'll never speak to me again."

Gavin sighed. "It's not you, really. She feels Lincoln's death more deeply than she wants to admit. She never really fixed things between them, and now it's too late. You taking on the farm will always be a reminder of that."

Clara winced. "Oh, man. I hadn't even thought of that. I'm sorry."

"Don't be sorry. You did the right thing. I'm proud of you, Clara." He gave her that jolly smile.

"Thank you, Gavin. That means a lot." Clara looked toward their silver BMW parked up the street. Liz sat ramrod straight, eyes forward. "She won't appreciate you supporting me."

Gavin laughed. "I'm used to it. Don't worry about me. You got a farm to run." He nodded. "Just remember: She really does love you."

"I know." Clara put her hands in her pockets and looked at the ground.

"If you need anything, call me right away. We're leaving first thing tomorrow. Sorry we can't be around to help you get settled."

Clara nodded. "I'll be fine. Have a good flight. It was nice to see you guys, despite the circumstances."

"Agreed. Have a good night, Clara. Enjoy that nice blue house."

"I will. Bye, Uncle Gavin."

Gavin gave a little wave and walked to the car. Clara watched them drive away; Liz never turned around.

Unsure what to feel or think, Clara drove her bike back up Main Street toward the coffee shop. It was too late in the day for caffeine, but she didn't care. She could practically hear all forty-five-hundred trees, seventy-five acres, the four-bedroom house, and that big dog mocking her for expecting to be able to take care of them. "I've never even committed to a long-term lease on an apartment," she whispered. "I'm in way over my head. Even if it was the right thing to do."

Clara heard her mother's voice in her head. *Good things never come easy. Learn to like hard work.*

She parked her bike and hurried inside the coffee shop, stumbling to a stop just inside the door. "Whoa," she marveled, surprised by the interior. The walls were painted a warm cottage-green, bright yet refined. To her left, a section of the wall had been filled with disks of raw wood of various sizes. Hung against the wood was a chalkboard menu done in a flourished script. Above it, a sleek, backlit metal sign had the café's name: *Café Shanti.* The front counter curved off from this wall, a white register tablet waiting on an easel. Multiple small chandeliers hung above round tables with padded chairs. A bouquet of gold Christmas ornaments hung from each light fixture, filling the air with sparkle. A tall Christmas tree in the center of the tables boasted white lights and more gold ornaments. Gold tinsel garland framed the ceiling.

Clara was certain the tree had come from the land she now owned. She swallowed hard, looking back to the counter.

This café looked like something she'd find in California or a posh magazine spread, not Hill Valley.

A striking man came from the back kitchen to stand behind the counter, his skin the color of caramel and eyes intensely dark. "Good evening," he said with a dashing smile. He took her in. "Rough day?"

Clara scoff-laughed. "Understatement." She stepped to the counter.

Her gave her a sympathetic smile. "Well, in that case, I recommend a cardamom latte and the orange madeleines."

"Cardamom?"

"It's a popular spice in India. It's calming, good for digestion."

"I've heard of it. Just not in a latte."

"Trust me. It's amazing." He grinned.

Clara smiled back, unable to resist his charm. "Okay, bring it on. To go, please." She handed him her credit card. "Are you the owner? This wasn't here the last time I was in town."

"Yes, I'm the owner . . . and the chef, barista, bus boy, manager, accountant . . ." He dramatically rolled his eyes. Clara laughed. He went on. "I'm Hiran. My wife and I moved here about six years ago, opened this place right away. We love it here. So much better than Chicago, where we lived before."

"That's great. Chicago is really cool, but very big-city busy. I'm Clara."

"Oh, of course. Clara Hill." He returned her card. "Nice to meet you, Clara. The bike leathers threw me off, but I recognize you from the funeral. Lincoln was the best. He came in almost every day—black coffee and a cranberry scone. We'll really miss him."

"Thank you." Clara put her credit card back in her pocket.

All these strangers knew my grandpa better than me.

"Well . . . welcome back," Hiran added. "Sorry it's not under better circumstances."

"Me, too."

"I'll have your order out in a moment."

The café was mostly empty. A man with a laptop and headphones sat in the back corner, and two teenage girls huddled over their phones and whipped cream-topped drinks near the front door. Clara leaned against the counter to gaze out the large front window. Her mind went to the deed in her saddlebag.

I own it. A farm, a house, a dog.

All things that can't fit in my van. All things that need someone to take care of them every day.

Things that need someone to know more than how to adjust post-style cantilever brakes.

She silently swore as she brought her hands to her face and rubbed at her temples. She'd spent most of her adult life denying permanent ties. Avoiding, really. And now, she'd purposefully taken on this massive anchor. She shook her head, the itch of regret tickling under her scalp.

I hope I can do this.

Wouldn't want to prove Liz right.

The front door opened, and a couple about her age came in. She half-glanced at them as she moved to step aside. Her attention pulled to the woman's face. There was something familiar in the sharply pointed nose and rectangular face. The woman's gaze snagged on Clara's, and she stopped walking. Her eyes narrowed. "Clara? Clara Hill?"

Clara cocked her head. *I should know her . . . oh my gosh!* "Regan?"

Regan rushed forward to swamp Clara in a dramatic hug. She smelled like lavender and sandalwood. In her head, Clara heard school bells and playground laughter.

"Clara Hill," Regan cried in a voice that was a little too high, just as Clara remembered it. She pulled back to survey her old classmate. "Look at all this leather. So . . . rocker. Is that *your* motorcycle? We noticed it coming in. Mason likes motorcycles. Isn't it dangerous, though? I can't believe you're here. But, of course you are. The funeral and all." She pursed her lips. "How long has it been? We were in fifth grade—no, sixth—when it happened, right? Oh my gosh! I can't believe you're here."

Clara forced a laugh, feeling a little overwhelmed by all those sentences at once. Regan's habit of talking too much had obviously not faded with adulthood. "Nice to see you, Regan. You look wonderful." And she did. As a kid, Regan's sharp angles had been awkward and strange, but now she looked refined, like a Paris runway model. She also had the too-skinny thing going, like those models. She wore white yoga tights and a long, thick-knit cardigan in soft gray.

"You, too! I always wanted your hair color. So rich and dark." She touched her own hair. Clara remembered a plain light brown color, but now Regan's shoulder length waves were a lush bronze. "So how are you?" Regan went on. "I mean, besides being here for your grandpa's funeral . . ."

Clara held back a grimace. *Not so tactful.* "I'm okay, thanks. You?"

"Great. I own the yoga studio a few blocks over. It's called Balanced Body."

"Hill Valley has a yoga studio?"

Regan laughed, a little too loudly. "I know. Crazy, huh? Our little town is somewhat cool now. Small-town trendy, you know? It really fits in the whole Joanna Gaines world. What are *you* doing with your life?"

"I'm a mechanic. I restore vintage motorcycles."

Regan's perfectly shaped brows lifted skeptically.

"Really? That's so . . . unusual. Do a lot of women do that?" The man who'd come in with Regan stepped quietly up behind her. She gasped and gestured to him. "Oh! Clara, this is my husband, Mason. Do you remember him? He was two grades ahead of us in school."

Mason held out his hand. "Hello, Clara."

Same age as Liam. Or . . . sort of.

Not at all, if Liam's crazy theory is right.

Clara shook Mason's hand, vaguely remembering his face. "Were you on the basketball team?"

He smiled with perfectly straight white teeth. He reminded her of Brad Pitt and was as sleek and fit as his wife; they could pose for a fitness magazine. They probably had. "Yeah, that's right," he said. "Now Regan has me doing yoga every day. Never been in better shape." The couple grinned at each other.

Clara felt a twinge of jealousy. These two were nothing like her kind of people, but she still envied their relationship, their permanence. Her life wasn't exactly conducive to long-term relationships. "Sounds nice," she offered. "Do you guys remember a Liam Cooper from school? He would have been your age, Mason."

Regan and Mason looked at each other; Regan pursed her lips. "Liam? Hmm. I don't think so. Mason, ring any bells?"

Mason shook his head. "No. Sorry. I think there was a Fred Cooper. Does that help?"

Clara smiled, wondering if Mason's looks outpaced his brains. "No. But thanks."

"Why do you ask?" Regan said.

"I ran into him earlier. Just trying to remember him from school."

"Doesn't sound at all familiar. Sorry." Regan shrugged it off. "How about you, Clara? Anyone special in your life?"

"Uh . . . no. I travel a lot for my work, so . . ."

The longest I've ever dated a guy was four months.

Kolby Jones, during mechanic school.

He wanted to move in together. End of that.

Regan nodded. "An independent woman. How cool."

Clara did not like the way Regan said that.

Okay, I'm done with this judgey conversation.

"Well, it was nice to see you both. I'll let you go order." Clara pointed loosely to the counter and was relieved to see Hiran coming toward them.

"And here comes *your* order," Regan announced. "What did you get? Everything here is so good. But you do have to be careful—very rich."

Clara and Hiran shared a brief look. "A latte and madeleines. I like rich."

"How indulgent! I guess on a day like today, you deserve some comfort food."

Would it be wrong to punch her in her pristine face?

Clara accepted the hot coffee and small bag from Hiran. "Thanks so much, Hiran." She stepped away. "Nice to see you, Regan, Mason."

Regan took Mason's arm. "Yes, so nice to see you, Clara. And please come by the studio for some classes while you're here. I'm sure you could use the time to breathe, center, and burn a few calories. We have a great guest-pass option."

Seriously? No, thanks! Clara forced a smile. "Have a good night."

"You, too! Bye!" Regan gave a little wave, and they moved off.

Clara hustled out of the café.

Breathe and center? Burn a few calories?

Rude!

And don't insult my comfort food. I'm sure you don't even know what a socket wrench is.

Clara half-grinned at the image of Regan trying to fix a difficult timing gear without getting grease on her no-doubt expensive, white yoga tights.

Who wears white tights?

When did she get so snotty?

When did I get so sensitive?

Clara opened the small white paper bag. The petite cakes resting in the bottom were butter yellow, one edge dipped in smooth chocolate. Heavenly citrus and cocoa scents lifted to her face.

"Oh, I like this place," she breathed.

She took a bite of a delicious, firm madeleine. "Oh my gosh! These things are *amazing.*" She sampled her latte, closing her eyes when the earthy sweetness of the cardamom hit her tongue. "Wow and *wow.*" She started to walk toward Pages on Main, her anxieties lost for a moment behind the deliciousness of Hiran's food.

Taking the last bites of the madeleines, she took in the lines of Christmas lights hung like garland between the lampposts and large wooden, lighted candy canes along the road. Somewhere far away, Christmas songs played, the familiar notes drifting on the cold air. All that was missing was the snow. Clara's fingers found her necklace.

The first snow.

Liam and the snow.

Stop it.

Her mind turned to the gigantic problem she'd just burdened herself with. *How am I going to do this?* She took a slow sip of her beverage. *Liam can help.* She flinched slightly at the unbidden thought and dropped her hand from the snowflake charm. She was certain the last thing she needed was help from Liam the Delusional.

He helped run the farm.

Helps—present tense to him? Good grief.

Either way, he knows what to do.

She scowled at that treacherous detail.

"I'm not going back to that well," she mumbled into the rim of her cup.

She turned her mind to easier problems. If she now had to take care of a dog, she couldn't stay in her van at the RV park on the edge of town. She'd have to go get the van and stay at the house. She frowned deeply, an ache rising in her chest.

The last time I slept at the blue house was the night before Mom and Dad's funeral.

But now it's mine. Really, legally mine.

The image of twin glossy silver caskets filled her mind. The overly decorated *fake* Christmas tree in the corner of the chapel. She'd been so offended by that fake tree. Which was easier to focus on than her parents in boxes.

She blinked the memories away, swallowing the lump in her throat.

It's just a house.

And it'll be a nice change from the van.

Clara's phone buzzed in her pocket. She tossed the empty madeleine bag into a nearby garbage can and reached for her phone. A text from her closest friend, Kiki.

Kiki: *Are you surviving? I'm imagining all kinds of dramatic, emotional scenes. Call me so I know what's going on.*

A small smile lifted Clara's lips. Kiki had been the only other woman in mechanic training. No one could do an oil change faster than Kiki, or make Clara laugh as easily. And even though the two women lived almost a whole country apart, they remained close. Clara clicked on Kiki's contact and pressed the phone to her ear.

Kiki answered almost immediately. "*Girl!* Has it been totally awful?" Kiki's voice was always a bit too loud.

Clara laughed. "It was until I found this amazing coffee shop."

She gasped. "Always important—find the best local coffee. But do they even have that in Utah?" Kiki laughed. No one could laugh with as much carefree energy as Kiki.

"Of course! Though it was almost ruined by a run-in with a yoga tights-wearing mean girl."

"Eww. No, thank you. Someone you know?"

"Just a girl from school. No big deal."

"Avoid her. Anyway . . . how are *you*? Really and truly?"

Clara sighed, running her finger along the rim of her cup. "I sort of inherited the farm and the blue house. Oh, and a giant dog."

"WHAT? Your grandpa left it *all* to you? That's . . . *heavy*."

"Yep, and I had a chance to sell it, take the money and run, but I didn't. The deed is burning a hole in my saddlebag as we speak." She breathed out a long sigh. "I don't know what I was thinking."

"I totally get it. I had constant heartburn for three weeks after Carlo and I bought this little condo. But a whole Christmas tree farm! I can't even believe that's a real thing people actually do. Wait! Does that mean you're staying in Utah? I can't picture you as a farmer. Your van will be so lonely."

"Ha ha. And where did you think Christmas trees came from?" Clara teased. Kiki laughed. "Honestly, I'm not sure what I'm going to do. I want to keep the farm in the family, but I can't stay here. I don't do *staying in places*."

"Crazy idea: Maybe you could try it? It won't kill you, I promise. I didn't think I'd like living in Miami, but now I love it. It's really grown on me over the last few years, and now I can't imagine living anywhere else."

"Not here, Kiki," Clara answered quietly. "I can't stay here."

"I know, babe. I know." She let out a long, dramatic exhale. "I wish I was there with you. I'm so sorry."

"Me, too."

"Is there something else? Did Liz freak out?"

"Well, yeah, she did, but I'm used to that. I . . . I don't know. It's . . . everything. And earlier, I ran into a guy I used to know. And it was . . ." She let the thought hang in the air, unsure how to describe Liam at the well.

"What kind of guy? Like old *boyfriend* kind?"

"I was *twelve* last time I was here, Kiki."

"So? I had my first boyfriend in kindergarten." She let out a quick, playful laugh. "This was a bad run-in? Has he lost his hotness? Fat and bald, right?"

Clara thought of Liam's tall, muscled body and his arms around her. "No, he definitely didn't lose his hotness. But he was . . . different. At first, it was so great to see him, but then it got awkward." Clara scoffed. "Fifteen years is a long time."

"Awkward how?"

"I think it was just too much for one day. My head is a mess."

There was a short pause. Clara knew Kiki sensed her avoidance, and thankfully, Kiki was great at not pushing. "Okay, girl. There's no way around it—it all just sucks. You must embrace the suck."

Clara sighed.

"Wait!" Kiki burst out. "Did you say you got a giant dog somewhere in there?"

Clara laughed hard. She adored how Kiki's mind sporadically jumped topics, but somehow never missed a thing. Clara answered, "Yes. An Old English Sheepdog, named Ollie. She's hard not to love instantly, even though she's one hundred pounds."

"How did you not *immediately* send me a picture of her? I can't believe you have a dog! I've always told you that you should get one to keep you company. I love dogs."

"I know. The giant bulldog face on your bike lets *everyone* know. How is Hank?"

"He's great. Sitting right here with me. Aren't you, big boy?" Kiki made high-pitched cooing noises to her faithful dog. "Oh! I didn't tell you—I added some chrome paw prints to my fenders. It's *adorable!*"

Clara laughed again, stopping outside Pages' door, which had a big neon-pink wreath on it. Winnie's amazing vintage truck was parked outside. She put the phone on speaker and said, "I'm sending you a picture of this really cool truck. The bookshop owner's truck." She snapped the pic and then texted it to Kiki.

"Oh! Wow. I like this person. Sweet paint job—I don't think I've ever seen that orange. Like a ripe cantaloupe."

"Exactly. Winnie seems really awesome. I'm at the bookstore now. She said she'd pull some books for me."

"Books are the perfect escape when you're stressed. You need that right now."

"Very true!"

She and Kiki talked for a few more minutes before Kiki had to take Hank for a walk. "Call me tomorrow," her friend said, concern in her voice. "And when you're ready to talk about what happened with that guy, I'm ready to listen."

"I will. Thanks, Kiki."

"And find out more about that orange truck. I wanna know what engine she put in it."

Clara laughed. "Of course. Love you."

"Love you, too!"

The call had done Clara as much good as the food. She still had no idea what she was doing, but at least she felt less like freaking out. She opened the door and stepped into the bookshop.

Lyla decided on a Danielle Steel novel, and Liam grabbed an old paperback of *My Name is Asher Lev* by Chaim Potok. At the register, Winnie said, "Liam! Such a good choice. This one will blow your mind. I can't wait to hear what you think."

"Thanks, Winnie," Liam said. "Glad I can occasionally pick a good one without your help."

Winnie laughed. "I've taught you well." She picked up Lyla's choice and turned to her. "These are great, relaxing reads. Perfect for propping up your feet and sipping a hot beverage."

Lyla smiled. "That does sound nice."

Winnie took Liam's cash and then handed them the books. "Have a great night, you two. Merry Christmas."

"See you later!" Liam said as he guided Lyla out the door.

"That was fun," Lyla said as they exited Pages on Main.

"Good. Glad you enjoyed it," Liam answered. He checked his watch. *Ugh. It's only nine. I expected book browsing to take longer. Now what?* They stepped to the edge of the curb. Lyla adjusted her coat.

"The diner has great pie. Interested in dessert?" Liam offered.

"Not really. I'm still pretty full from dinner."

"Okay. We could go for a drive so you can see the farm."

Lyla stepped close. "I like the sound of a drive." She nuzzled her chin onto his shoulder. In a sultry whisper, she added, "Especially if there's somewhere nice to park."

Liam froze, surprised. More by his instant rejection of the idea than her forward offer. *You're really going to turn down this gorgeous woman?* He turned his head and pressed his lips to her forehead. "Yeah, I know a good spot."

They drove through the farm, taking the service roads. Liam pointed out different areas and gave Lyla little facts about the trees. She asked questions, which made Liam feel a little better about the evening.

Finally, he pulled the truck to a stop on the high road above the Hills' property. The old farm road ran along the hillside, offering a sweeping view of the valley. Lines of trees curved over the land for miles in all directions.

Lyla leaned toward the windshield. "It's beautiful up here. The farm is very cool."

Liam smiled as he put the truck in park, the old Chevy's beastly engine rumbling down to an idle. A smooth black sky boasted shimmering stars, and the wide valley below twinkled with yellow lights from the houses. To the right, tucked between the trees, he could just see the pitch of the Hills' blue farmhouse.

Is Clara there now? I mean, in her time.

Ugh. Don't start wandering again.

Focus on Lyla.

He kept his left hand on the wheel, and out of habit, propped his right arm on the back of the bench seat. Lyla took it as an invitation to slide next to him. He pressed his teeth together, eyes still on the view.

"It's so different than the Salt Lake skyline," Lyla whispered.

Liam hummed his agreement. "I'd take this view over a cityscape any day."

"Really? Don't you ever want something more . . . exciting?"

He thought of the places he'd been while following his dad's professional rodeo career. The dizzying lights of Vegas, the suffocating crush of people in Denver, the frustrating backup of cars in downtown Salt Lake. It'd never held any appeal to him, and coming home had always been a relief. He shook his head. "Nope. I like the space and the quiet here in Hill Valley. Plus, things on the farm are always changing. It's exciting and interesting every day." He felt Lyla's confused disappointment in the way she narrowed her eyes and shifted her hands.

We have nothing in common.

'Course, Kendra and I had lots in common so . . . who the heck knows?

Lyla reached out and turned the radio knob. Soft rock music filled the truck cab. She rested her head on his shoulder and put her hand on his thigh. Liam couldn't deny that the warm contact felt good, the attention flattering. It'd been a year since things ended with Kendra, and he hadn't dated anyone until Lyla. But he also couldn't deny the significant way Clara kept slipping back into his thoughts.

"What are you thinking about, Lyla?" he said softly, remembering the way he'd always asked Clara that question when they fell into long silences.

She laughed lightly. "I was thinking I like that this truck has a bench. Very convenient." She shifted closer.

Liam laughed. "It is a nice feature." He brought his right arm to her waist, hugging her close. In one fluid movement, her lips met his. The energy of the kiss felt a bit frantic, forced, but Liam tried to give it space to settle into a groove. The opening notes of Gordon Lightfoot's *If You Could Read My Mind* sounded from the radio, and Liam jerked away. Clara's face flashed in his mind with a physically painful jolt of light. He blinked quickly, unsettled.

Lyla's hands fell to his chest. "What's wrong?" she asked, a bit breathless.

He searched her face, unsure what to say. "I, uh . . ." His pager vibrated, and he flinched again. "Sorry . . ." He reached for it at his belt, grateful for the distraction. But his stomach tightened when he saw the number. "It's my mom," he breathed. "She never beeps me."

Lyla scooted away to her side of the truck. "We better go, then." She smoothed back her hair, keeping her eyes averted.

"Yeah." He took a steadying breath. "Yeah, okay." He adjusted in his seat, tugging the gear lever into drive. "Sorry," he mumbled. Lyla shook her head, a small, stiff smile on her lips. Though he was now anxious about his mom, Liam couldn't deny the sense of relief hanging in the air between them. He frowned.

Well, I think that ends that.

He cranked the wheel of the old truck and headed down into the valley. He drove quickly, roaring into the driveway in just under five minutes. Lyla followed him into the cottage. "Mom?" he called out when he found the couch empty. A slap of worry had him rushing into the kitchen. He found Sally sitting on the linoleum floor by the fridge, the cordless phone resting in her lap. Liam had purchased it earlier in the year and admonished his mom to keep it close. She'd gotten in the habit of carrying it in her robe pocket, and he was so grateful for that now.

"I'm so sorry, Liam." She shook her head. "I didn't want to disturb your date—"

"What happened?" He knelt beside her. Sally had always been too thin, but now she looked wasted to skin and bones. Pale, weak, and a decade older than her real age. She wore a tattered, red terry-cloth bathrobe over brown flannel pajamas.

"I'm fine, fine. It's so stupid." She gestured down to her ankle with an exasperated grunt, which turned into an ugly cough. After a moment, she managed to say, "I twisted it. My slipper caught on the edge of the rug and . . . I don't even know how it happened. So dumb."

Liam looked down at the obviously swollen ankle. Lyla came around him to inspect the injury.

"Oh, Lyla," Sally cried. "I'm so sorry, honey. Please don't fuss. I just couldn't get back to the couch." Sally put her face in her hands. "I ruined your night! I'm sorry!"

Lyla smiled sweetly. "Stop that. Don't worry about it. This looks pretty bad. Dr. Oliphant will probably want to do an X-ray tomorrow, just to be safe." She glanced at Liam. "Let's get her to the couch. It needs ice and elevation."

Liam easily lifted his frail mother into his arms and carried her to the couch. Sally gushed out more apologies. "Mom, it's okay," he gently stopped her. "This is exactly why I have the pager and you have that fancy phone. I'd come running for a paper cut."

Sally smiled and weakly slapped his chest. "Don't be ridiculous. I can't believe I may have broken my ankle tripping over the stupid kitchen rug."

Liam smiled back and lowered her onto the couch. "Don't worry about that yet. Might be just a sprain. We'll know for sure tomorrow."

Once she was settled, two pillows under her foot and a bag of ice draped over the ankle, Liam and Lyla stood in the kitchen. He was unsure what to say or do next.

"You better stay with her," Lyla said. "She can't walk on it; she'll need help getting around."

Liam nodded, running a hand back through his hair. "Yeah. I'm really sorry—"

"Stop apologizing," she said with a kind smile. "She needs you. It's good you're around. You're a good man, Liam."

He felt a pulse of guilt that things hadn't gone better tonight. "I wanted tonight to be fun."

"I know. And it was. I had a wonderful time. Nothing to feel bad about."

He sighed and looked at her. It was obvious she was ready to go home. "I'll drive you back to your car."

"Thanks."

Liam drove Lyla back to her car parked at Enzo's. Neither of them said anything until they arrived. "Thank you for your help," Liam started, reaching for a way to end the night gracefully.

"Of course. I'm glad it wasn't something worse—your mom, I mean." Lyla smiled as she lifted her purse and book into her hands.

"Lyla, I—"

She shook her head to stop him. "Liam, it's totally fine. I had a good time. But . . . maybe we aren't as compatible as we both hoped." She shrugged.

Liam let out a long breath. "Yeah, you're right. Sorry about that."

She laughed lightly. "Nothing to be sorry about. That's just how it goes. We tried. It was fun. But . . ."

"Yeah. I agree."

Lyla sighed and opened her door. "Thanks for dinner and the book. I'll see you tomorrow at the clinic, okay?"

"Okay." He nodded, the tightness in his chest releasing. "Good night, Lyla."

"Bye, Liam."

Liam waited until Lyla got in her car safely and pulled out of the parking lot. He regretted that things hadn't gone better, but he also felt an odd kind of relief.

Because . . . Clara.

I need to see her again.

Liam drove home, allowing the rush of thoughts and memories about Clara to finally flow freely, things with Lyla soon forgotten.

A Little Romance

The smell of cinnamon hit Clara square in the face as she entered Pages on Main. The explosion of color made her stop and gape. Winnie had hung neon-colored garland and tinsel all over the shop. Draped over bookshelves, pinned to the ceiling. Pink, green, yellow. Orange. Not nice orange like her truck, but garish, neon orange. For Christmas.

What is happening in here?

Winnie emerged from around one of the shelves. "Good. You came."

"I didn't know they made Christmas decorations in neon colors," Clara said, holding back a grin.

"Oh, sure. It's different and fun. Nice, don't you think? One can only take so much red and green."

"I guess so."

Winnie pursed her lips. "Are you making fun of me in your head?"

Clara burst out laughing. "No! No, I would never."

"The lies! You are absolutely making fun of me and my neon Christmas. I am deeply offended." Winnie shook her head, smiling, as she came to the check-out counter. "I see you found Hiran." She gestured to Clara's coffee cup. "God bless that man, am I right?"

"A thousand times right. So good." Clara came to the counter, marveling at how easy it was to talk to Winnie. "This cup brought me back from the brink."

"Bill Pratt has that effect on most people. Even his poor wife."

Clara laughed again. "Not Bill—though, yeah, I get what you're saying. So stiff! Is that a lawyer thing?" Clara set her cup on the counter. "But really, it's the farm, the trees. I own it now. It's mine and—not gonna lie—I'm sort of freaking out."

Winnie nodded, a sage expression on her face. "It's your destiny. That's always a bit scary."

Clara wasn't sure how to respond to that.

Destiny? I don't know . . .

More like bad timing.

Winnie reached under the counter edge and produced a tall stack of books, which she slammed down on the top. With a satisfied expression, she announced, "Recommendations, at your service."

Clara widened her eyes. "For the rest of my life . . ."

"Very funny. I remember how much you read. I assume that's still the case?"

"You assume correctly. But I live in a van, so I kind of went Kindle."

Winnie gasped dramatically, putting a hand on her heart. "How could you? There is always room for real books. Take them or else!"

"Okay! Geez. I've never been threatened with books before."

Winnie chuckled. "I like you, Clara Hill."

Clara laughed. "Well, thanks. I like you, too. Am I allowed to look at the books before I take them?"

"I suppose." Winnie pushed them toward her and then leaned her forearms on the counter.

Clara set down her coffee and shuffled through the stack. "Winnie . . . these are *all* romances."

"Yep. You got your gothic romances, some romantic

105

suspense, some smutty romance—my personal favorite. It's fabulous. Start with *Dragonwyck* by Anya Seton. An old classic, and so good! This farm girl from Connecticut ends up at this ancient manor house. Of course, there's a handsome man at said manor."

"A tempestuous novel of passion and violence," Clara read from the cover. She raised her brows at Winnie.

"What could be more perfect?" Winnie grinned. "Just go with it."

"Why all romances? This isn't my normal genre preference. Give me a good nonfiction history or some good sci-fi, but . . ."

Winnie scoffed. "Then it's high time, *and* this is exactly what you need right now." She said it so matter-of-factly, with such absolute certainty, that Clara wasn't sure how to argue with her.

"Okay." She shrugged. "I guess I'll trust you."

"You *guess*? You'll *thank* me. That's a promise."

Clara laughed as she reached for her credit card and held it out. "What do I owe you?"

"Nothing." Winnie didn't accept the card.

"No, no. Take the card, Winnie. That's way too generous."

"Nope. Lincoln's granddaughter gets her first batch on the house."

There was something in Winnie's expression when she said that—a pain or sadness. Clara dropped her hand. "Sounds like you two were close?"

Winnie paid extra attention to the cash register, avoiding Clara's eyes. "Us old people got to stick together, you know?"

"I envy that," Clara whispered. "That you were close to him. Not that you're old."

"Rude! You'll be old one day, Clara Hill." Winnie looked

up, eyes a little misty but seeming grateful for the humor. "I spent a lot of time with Lincoln over the last several years. He talked about you often."

"I always wondered if he was terribly lonely after the accident. All of us just . . . gone. I hated leaving him alone."

"He was lonely for a few years. For a while there, we all wondered if he would make it. When something like that happens to a person . . . well, I don't need to tell you."

Clara nodded, her heart aching.

Winnie went on, "He rarely came into town, never socialized. He kept his trees healthy with an almost manic obsession, but that was it. Jad, the foreman, came in here one day really worried—I sent him home with a book on meditation. But anyway . . . that night, I took it upon myself to annoy Lincoln back to life." Winnie grinned, eyes still dewy with the memories.

Clara laughed. "What do you mean?"

"I mean, I packed up some books, some groceries, and some Hiran coffee, and drove out there. When he opened the door, I pushed right past him and told him I was cooking dinner."

"Seriously?" Clara could picture it perfectly. Winnie seemed just the sort of person to do something that bold.

"Yep. He growled and groused, like a sour old rhino, but I ignored it. The next week, I did it again. And then it just became part of our routines. Dinner every Thursday night." She sighed. "It took about six months before he started laughing, but finally, one of my stupid jokes broke through."

Clara's breath caught in her chest. The tears she'd been holding back the last hour slipped through. She shook her head and swiped at her eyes. "Sorry!"

Winnie only smiled sweetly. "It's okay. Cry all you want. I've been crying quite a bit myself."

"I just . . . I'm so relieved he had someone to do that for him since I couldn't. Leaving him was so . . ."

"I know, Clara. I know."

"I wish I'd come back sooner. I should have. I . . ."

"He understood how hard it was for you." She leaned her hip into the counter. "You know that he and Liz would have these fights over the phone? He must have called her twice a week about visiting or letting you come out here. But Liz . . ." Winnie shook her head.

"Yeah, I know. A force to be reckoned with. He really did that?"

"Of course he did. He even thought of getting a lawyer to fight for custody, but he worried so much about upsetting your life again by taking you back from Liz. He also worried that would really ruin his already fragile relationship with his daughter. But he wrestled with it. Liz insisted you were happy and well-adjusted. So eventually, he gave up."

"She said that?" Clara scoffed. "She lied. I would have given anything to come back here. I wish she hadn't done that. I wish . . . they'd listened to me and she'd listened to Grandpa."

"She was hurting, too. It's hard to make choices when the hurt gets in the way." Winnie sighed, shaking her head. "I'm so sorry, kid. I'm sure she did what she thought was best."

"Oh, yeah. Don't get me wrong—Liz does her best. She was helping in the only way she knew how. And really, I can't complain too much. It's just . . ." Clara shrugged, unsure exactly what to say. "What could have been . . . you know?"

"I get it. Lincoln got it, too."

They slipped into a brief silence. Clara ran her hand over the cover of *Dragonwyck*. The handsome man on the cover had the same build and hair color as Liam. She scowled.

Winnie suddenly clapped; Clara jumped. "So I'll see you tomorrow for dinner?" Winnie asked.

"What?"

Winnie shrugged. "Might as well keep it going; tomorrow is Thursday. I'm sure you'd like to hear some stories about your grandpa, and we can work on easing your mind about the farm." She gave one authoritative nod.

Clara didn't think she could say no if she wanted to. But she didn't want to. She liked Winnie's company a lot. "Sounds great." She hefted the stack of books into her arms. "I'll see you tomorrow. Thanks again, Winnie."

"My pleasure, kid. Say hi to Ollie for me."

Clara nodded, and headed out the door.

When Liam had come back from dropping off Lyla, he smelled the cigarette smoke before he stepped in the back door. Sally kept promising to stop, but never did. He didn't say anything this time—he didn't have the energy. Liam simply helped his mom to her bed, said good night, and then emptied the full ashtray.

Now, alone, the night was too quiet, even with the murmur of Sally's TV from her bedroom. He knew it'd be no use trying to sleep tonight. Liam stood in the cottage's tiny front room, arms folded, glaring out the big window. His mind was fully alert and venturing on an epic journey down memory lane. The first stop was back at that Christmas night fifteen years ago. The last time he saw Clara. The first time she'd hugged him. The surprise of it, the way it had made his whole body feel more alive. It had felt the same earlier tonight. But now his adult body knew what all those sensations meant. The attraction, desire. She fit in his arms like no woman ever had. It felt so right. But how could he feel all that so intensely for a woman he hardly knew?

She's a stranger. Fifteen minutes at the well means nothing.

Right?

He moved his attention over to more mundane memories from that night. The hot chocolate and the ceramic carolers. The way his mom had been too exhausted by grief to hang his stocking. His anxiety over the possibility of no presents. The dust on the toes of his dad's boots. Those boots that were somewhere in the back of his closet right now.

Tonight, the Christmas trees at the edge of his property looked bare without snow. By now, they should have a good, thick layer of white. Like they had that Christmas.

So long ago and yet . . . here we are.

Well, here I am.

Clara isn't even alive right now, in this time.

She doesn't exist here. Only at the well.

Bridged time?

Liam shook his head, doubting his theory. Hating how he'd lobbed it directly into her face earlier. His mind turned back to the past, desperate to avoid the impossible time-bridge conundrum.

Liam remembered the Saturday after that Thanksgiving fifteen years ago. Just a few days into his friendship with Clara. She'd come thundering into the clearing, full speed ahead, as seemed to always be her pace. The sun was brilliant on the fresh white snow, the air crisp with the smell of winter.

"Ta-da!" she had announced, thrusting a large plastic baggie over her head as if it were a great archeological discovery. "My mom made cookies!"

Liam had not been able to recall the last time his mom had made cookies, and his young mouth had watered. They sat in the snow, backs against the cold stone of the well, and ate the entire bag. He couldn't recall what they'd talked about, but he could remember Clara's laugh. The sweetness of the chocolate chip cookies. The way the sun felt on his face.

Such a small, insignificant thing and yet . . .

At the time, it meant everything.

Liam sighed, running a hand over his face. Things had been better with Clara in his life. After she'd disappeared, he'd retreated to his loner ways. He'd asked Lincoln for a job a couple of weeks later, desperate for a distraction. During high school, he spent more time working on the farm than socializing with friends or doing homework. It'd taken him over a year to stop thinking about Clara every day. Another few years to only think of her rarely. And now, once again, she was all he could think about. It was a familiar feeling somehow.

Will I ever see her again? Or was it just a cruel glimpse?

Liam glared at the trees.

It's going to be a long night.

Clara parked her black camper van by the big white barn. Her Harley was towed behind it on a small trailer. She shoved a few things from the van and all her new books into a duffle bag and headed to the house. It looked bigger in the dark, looming and threatening. *Don't be dramatic.* She curved around to the back door, starting up the wide back porch stairs. She stopped halfway, free hand on the railing, and turned to look in the direction of the well.

"Are you there now, Liam?" she whispered before thinking. A strong impulse to go check the clearing took her breath away. *No. No way.* She shoved the desire aside and went to the door. She heard the dog's nails on the hardwood as she turned the knob. Clara stepped into the mudroom. The dog blinked at her, hesitating for a split second before padding over for some attention. Clara frowned. "Sorry I'm not him, Ollie." She rubbed the dog's head.

Clara flicked on the light switch. Memories pushed in from all sides. She closed her eyes as her mother's laughter echoed in her head. The hum of the dishwasher, the smell of pork chops and mushrooms. Her dad humming classic Garth Brooks and George Strait songs while he walked among the trees. The smell of pine on her young hands.

Ollie stood at her side, looking up with big black eyes. "I'm not going to cry again," Clara said to the dog. Her throat tightened. "I promise." She took a long breath. "Let's go to bed, huh? This day needs to end." The dog walked off toward the stairs. Clara followed, suddenly heavy with fatigue, her feet slow. Ollie went to the master bedroom door. "No, girl. Not there." She thought about peeking in on her grandpa's room, but didn't have the strength to face it tonight.

Clara moved to the doorway of her old room. "This one," she whispered before turning on the light. The twin bed stood in the center, parallel to the two windows, with the same pink patchwork quilt and lace curtains from her childhood. The oak dresser and small desk with a tiny blue lamp were also the same.

He never changed it.

Oh, Grandpa.

She brought her hand to her heart. "Can I sleep in a room frozen in time?" she whispered, feeling twelve years old again. Ollie went to the bed and sniffed at the blanket. Clara followed, running her palm over the quilt's texture. The fabric smelled freshly washed. "You washed the bedding, Grandpa?"

You knew I was coming.

You knew you were dying.

Why didn't you tell me when I called? Why didn't I listen to my instinct that you weren't telling the truth?

Dropping her bag to the floor, Clara went to the windows. She brushed aside the gauzy curtain to look out at the silent night and sleeping trees, trying to quiet the questions in her head. The impulse to go to the well returned as she looked at the indented shadow of the clearing. An urge to go to Liam. Her chest ached.

Those weeks with him were a bright spot in her childhood; he'd been her only best friend until Kiki. At school in San Diego, she'd kept her head down and focused on being a good student. She hadn't socialized, instead spending all her time working on an old Harley that Gavin had indulged her with. Taking it apart and putting it back together. Learning to ride. Liz, of course, had hated it. Gavin had spent a good two nights on the couch after he'd brought it home for Clara. But he'd only smiled and told Clara it was worth it.

Clara smiled at the memory. "Poor Uncle Gavin."

She had thought about Liam a lot over the years, the necklace she couldn't take off a constant reminder. While she'd work on that first bike, she'd often wonder what he was doing, where he was, and if he ever thought about her. Did he ever get a motorcycle?

And now he's here. Back in my life.

Liam would certainly be a good distraction.

I could listen to his wild theories, look at his nice face, and forget about the fact that I now own this place.

Stop it! I'm not going.

Quickly, she changed into some sleep shorts and a camisole, brushed her teeth, and slipped under the heavy quilt with a long sigh. Ollie jumped onto the foot of the bed, settling her chin on her paws. Clara was too tired to protest. The dog's weight and warmth were an unexpected comfort, anyway. *Now I get what Kiki is always talking about.* Clara wiggled her toes under Ollie's belly and closed her eyes.

Liam's face filled her mind.

She placed his childhood image next to his adult one, picking out the differences. There were now deep creases etched into the skin between his brows. She wanted to stroke the worry from those folds with the pad of her index finger. His deeply set, light brown eyes were still bright, but now carried the weight of the years, the knowledge of life. Which made them all the more alluring. His childhood thinness had been replaced with grown-up, hard-earned muscles. Broad shoulders and thick arms were evident even under a heavy coat. And his hands had grease on them. A thrill moved through her stomach.

"Good grief, Ollie," she whispered, "his hands had engine grease on them. And just so you know, there's nothing sexier to a woman motorcycle mechanic than a man with engine grease under his fingernails." The dog blinked at her without lifting her head. "Yeah, I know. Shut up and go to sleep."

With a huff of frustration, Clara rolled over to face the windows. The weak moonlight turned the lace curtains to silver. As a kid, she used to open the windows all the way and watch the curtains lift and sway with the breeze. A dreamy dance of fabric that always lulled her to sleep.

Clara got out of bed. She opened the windows halfway and smiled at the immediate push of winter breeze into the room. Instantly, it smelled like pine trees. She hurried out into the hall to grab an extra quilt from the linen closet. She draped the quilt over Ollie's back and up to her pillow. Back in bed, she inhaled the fresh air. She watched the curtains waltz with the wind, thinking of Liam, until she drifted off to sleep.

Liam stood next to the wishing well, his guitar hanging from his left hand. "What am I doing here?" He lifted his face to the dark sky and the gibbous moon. For hours, he'd paced the cottage, the tune of the song he'd written for Clara all those years ago set on repeat in his head. Finally, he'd grabbed his guitar and walked here in the cold. At the time, it had seemed like a good idea, a way to put an end to his hike through his memories, but now . . . "What am I *doing*?" he hissed at the old well.

He dropped his chin to glare down at the guitar. Shifting, Liam sat on the edge of the well, wedged the instrument onto his thigh, and started the slow picking pattern. The notes came back to him effortlessly.

A white winter sky and snow falls all around you.
The air like glass, your face in the sun. Time slips through.
For a moment, there is only you and me. I say your name.
But do you hear me? Do you feel the same?

Winter sun, low in the sky. I think of your small hand in mine.
How we came together, how time disappears under the pines.
Lost to the cold. In the black night, I call your name.
Can you hear me call your name?
Because I don't hear you.

Time is not on our side. It takes all that I have and never gives.
Your touch is only an echo now, gone but impossible to outlive.
Winter grows old, the snow falls on the trees.
But you're not here to see it; everything freezes.

Winter sun, low in the sky. I think of your small hand in mine.

How we came together, how time disappears under the pines.

Lost to the cold. In the black night, I call your name.
Can you hear me call your name?
Because I don't hear you.

I refuse to let the winter end without you here with me.
I refuse to let your memory fade away. I force myself to see.

Your face close to mine, your body melting with mine.
Can you find your way back to the snow and the pines?

I think of you nearly all the time.
And how you disappeared from under the pines.
Lost to the cold. In the black night, I call your name.
Can you hear me call your name?
Because I don't hear you.
And now, I don't have you.

Liam ended the song with a slow strum and dropped his hand to his side. His body hummed with energy, his heart aching. He hadn't expected the song to bring tears to his eyes.

Why does she make me feel this way?

"Liam?"

He jerked around at the sound of Clara's smooth voice. She stood between the trees, a giant dog beside her. She wore oversized, tall, black rain boots, gray shorts, and a heavy coat that had obviously belonged to Lincoln. He saw her younger self in the haphazard outfit. A crash of relief took his breath. He'd been certain he'd never see her again. He'd hurt her earlier and didn't want to do it again, so he held back his eagerness.

"It's late, Clara," he whispered, keeping his head angled away to blink the tears from his eyes.

"I know." She tugged at the hem of her shorts, which did little to cover her tan, lean legs.

Liam swallowed hard and cleared his throat. "And it's freezing." He stood up from the edge of the well. "Why are you here?"

She shivered at his words. "I'm not really sure . . ." She frowned, narrowing her eyes at him. "I woke up and couldn't get here fast enough. Why did I come out here in the cold, dressed like an idiot?"

He started to smile, but it quickly fell away. "I don't know. I'm not really sure why I'm here, either." He walked over to her. The big gray-and-white dog met him halfway, eager for attention. He laughed. "Who's this?"

"That's Ollie. She's—" Clara blanched and then sighed. "She *was* my grandpa's dog."

Liam looked over the fluffy, friendly dog. "This is Lincoln's dog? I can't picture him with a dog, especially not this one. He's so . . . practical."

"I had the same reaction." She folded her arms, leveling a serious gaze on him. "It was nice to hear you play again. You've gotten really good. What was that song?"

Liam hesitated as he watched Ollie walk to the well, sniff the stone, and then sit. "It's your song, Clara. I wrote it that Christmas, after you didn't come back to the well. I wrote it here . . . waiting for you."

Clara's hand went to her heart. "You waited for me? You wrote me a song? That beautiful song? It's so . . . forlorn. But enchanting at the same time." She shivered. "It's amazing."

"Thank you," Liam answered quietly, his chest tight from her perfect description of the song. A thrill of pride warmed his face. "I haven't played it in years. But I guess after earlier . . ."

"It all came back," she finished. "I thought about you, too—after I was in San Diego, I mean. I felt so bad I didn't get to say goodbye. I'm sorry you waited."

Liam nodded. He wanted to reach out and take her into his arms, help her stay warm, and keep her close. "And I'm so sorry about earlier. I didn't mean to throw that all at you like that. I know I sounded insane, and it was inconsiderate and . . . *weird.*"

Clara gave a half-smile. "It was definitely weird. I was worried about the farm and Grandpa and Liz and . . . I'm sorry I ran away. It was just too much."

"I understand. I'm sorry I added to all that stress. I didn't mean to."

"I know." She sighed. "Is it still 1989?"

"Yeah, it is. I promise."

She nodded, folding her arms and taking a step closer. "Still 2019 on this side. Can this really be a thing, Liam? Is this really happening?"

"I guess so. I wish I could explain it better." He had an idea. "Here, look." He leaned his guitar against the stone wall of the well and reached into his back pocket for his wallet. "My driver's license. Look at my birth date." He held it out to her.

She took it, wary, and brought it close to her face to read in the darkness. She let out a small gasp. "Well, according to this, you're fifty-nine." She lifted her gaze. "You look really good for your age."

Liam smiled, accepting the license back. "And you're not even born yet."

Clara shuddered. "I'm in 2019 and you're in 1989. I can't wrap my head around this."

"Me, either."

Clara walked to the edge of the well and looked over the top; she shivered again. "It's just rock. Just a big hole in the ground," she whispered.

Liam joined her, looking into the obsidian depth. "I tried to follow you this morning—to apologize. But when I walked on that side of the well, there was nothing. You . . . vanished."

They both winced, gazes moving to the trees to the left.

"Does that mean we can only see each other here, in the clearing?" Clara asked, brow furrowed. "That's . . ."

"Discouraging." Liam took a step closer. Clara nodded but didn't look at him.

"Let's test it," she said, gaze still on the depths of the well. "Test it?"

She looked up at him. "A theory is nothing unless you try to prove it, right? So . . ." She started to walk toward her side of the clearing. "Follow me."

Ollie was first to obey and jumped up to trot beside Clara. "Wait, Clara—"

"Just into the trees and then turn around," she called over her shoulder.

Liam jogged to catch up. He watched her closely, saw her as she stepped through the branches of the trees, brushing them with her right arm, and then . . . "Clara!" He was alone, the night quiet around him. Quickly, he turned and moved back into the clearing. She was already there, blinking and frowning.

They looked at each other for a tense moment.

"The other side," Liam whispered. "My side." He led the way, Clara and the dog only a few feet to his left. A short distance into the trees, he stopped and turned in a circle, peering hard through the trees to the row she'd gone down. "Clara?" No answer.

This is unreal.

This is impossible!

Liam hurried back into the clearing. Clara stood gawking at the well, Ollie alert at her side. The dog let out a faint whimper. The air felt electric with their discovery and clouded by their confusion. Liam's heart raced in his chest. A sear of anxiety heated his face.

We can only see each other here, in this place.

Only here.

But I want more.

Clara's pulse tripped over itself; a wave of dizziness clouded her vision.

He was just . . . gone. He's not crazy.

This is real.

Clara shuddered.

This can't be real. It just can't!

I'm dreaming.

She wanted to look at Liam, to see his expression. Instead, she looked up at the clear, star-filled sky.

Why am I so drawn to him?

Why is this happening?

Liam took a hesitant step toward her. "Clara?" he asked in a tender whisper that sent another tremor through her.

"The snow is late this year. No first snow yet," she whispered back, her mind rebelling from the reality of their situation to drift back to who she'd been the last time she was in this place. "Do you have snow in 1989?"

"No, it's late here, too."

"Do you remember that feeling just before it snows?"

"Yes. The pause in the air, like an inhale."

"Exactly. That's beautiful. I haven't thought about that in a really long time. I haven't seen snow in a *really* long time. I always make sure to take jobs in warm places in the winter. The snow . . ." She pressed her teeth together, the swirl of confounding emotions tightening her throat. "It's so weird to think that back when we were kids, we lived in different times and didn't even know it."

"I know." Liam took another step closer.

"But you guessed it? Because of the record?"

"Yes. That was the first real clue." He furrowed his brow. "You haven't seen snow since you left?"

Clara shook her head. Finally, she turned to him. "I missed you, Liam. I didn't realize it until I saw you earlier today."

Whoa, didn't really mean to say that out loud.

Liam's expression looked pained. "I missed you, too, Clara. I—" His hand reached for her but then dropped. She was both relieved and devastated.

Think clearly. Solve the problem. Fix it.

I can't fix this. This is . . . beyond anything I know.

Liam went on, "I wish I could have been there for you after the accident."

"Me, too. I wanted that. I wanted to stay. Liz wouldn't let me."

"I'm so sorry."

"She meant well, but . . . I think I will always hate her just a little bit for that. Maybe that's one of the reasons I couldn't sell the farm."

Liam's eyes went wide. "She wanted you to sell it?"

Clara sighed. "Oh, yes. Cut and run. Never look back. But . . . I just couldn't. It's mine now. Even though I don't know a thing about it."

"I'm so glad you didn't sell this farm. It belongs to you. And I can help." Liam shook his head. "Well, sort of. I guess we can *talk* about the farm."

"Right. Because we can only see each other *here*, in the clearing," she said slowly. Ollie pushed her head into Clara's leg, and Clara buried her hand in the dog's hair. It brought a small sense of grounding, a stroke of comfort.

"Yes. Looks like it." He folded his arms and dropped his chin.

"What are we supposed to do with that?"

He looked at her, eyes dark and serious. "I don't know. What do you want to do?"

Clara scoffed. "This is new to me. I'm open to ideas."

Liam nodded thoughtfully. "I guess we make plans. Meet me here. Tomorrow night, around sunset. It's so late right now; we're tired and a bit in shock, I think." He smiled. "Maybe tomorrow, we can make more sense of all this. Want to give that a try?"

"Good, yes. Practical." Clara exhaled, waiting for the plan to bring comfort. It did not. "Oh, wait! I have dinner with Winnie. But I'll come after that. Does that—" She watched Liam's face crease with confusion. "What?" she asked.

"Do you mean Winnie Sparrow?"

"Yes . . . you know her? From Pages on Main?"

"Yes. I was just there earlier tonight."

"Me, too."

Clara's stomach twisted.

This is so bizarre.

Liam shifted. "Okay. That's weird. It's so strange that we know lots of the same people and places . . . but decades apart."

"Winnie's in her late eighties now," Clara said.

Liam shook her head. "Crazy. She still . . . Winnie?"

Clara smiled. "Oh, yes. The shop is decorated in all neon Christmas décor. It's like a visual seizure."

Liam laughed, nodding his head. "Yep. That sounds right."

"She used to have dinner with Grandpa every Thursday. I guess we're continuing the tradition. That's why she's coming over."

"That's nice. I'm glad." He stepped closer. "So yes, let's

meet after your dinner. I'll be here." He held her gaze. "I want to see you again, Clara. As much as possible."

His words affected her far more than she wanted them to. Clara had the fleeting thought that she should wish Liam luck in 1989 and say goodbye. End it now. Never return to the cunning well. *This feels too serious, too complicated.* But she couldn't bring herself to do it. She wished she knew if it was because of curiosity or something more. Finally, all she said was, "Me, too. I'll be here."

Liam leaned toward her. "I wish I could walk you back." His devastating half-smile sent a wave of warmth through her. She wanted to reach out and finger the hair flipping out under his hat.

That's why I can't say goodbye.

Because . . . this is Liam.

Without thinking, Clara put her hand on his arm; a flutter moved through her stomach. She smiled. "I still know the way with my eyes closed. Even after so long."

Liam's smile grew. "I'm sorry this is so strange. I'd change it if I could."

"I'm just relieved you're not delusional." She gave him a teasing smile.

Liam laughed, the deep sound coming from his chest. "I'm glad you walked out here dressed like an idiot." His eyes went to her bare legs, and she felt a flush of heat in her cheeks, a twist of pleasure in her stomach.

"I don't have a winter coat anymore. Had to improvise."

"You did well."

She laughed and rolled her eyes.

Liam put his hand on top of hers. "Good night, Clara."

Clara had a flash of laying in his arms, under a thick quilt, here in the clearing, looking up at the sky.

Oh, no. Stop that!

She took a step back. "Night, Liam."

Liam gave Ollie's head a tussle. "Keep her safe, Ollie."

The dog gazed up at him with what looked very much like understanding.

Clara reluctantly headed back into the pines. Back into 2019, and so much further away from Liam than she had ever realized before.

Time is Not on Our Side

Early morning sun pulled Clara from a fitful sleep. It took her a moment to realize where she was. She didn't remember falling asleep on the living room couch. With a groan, she sat up, her neck stiff. A shot of panic had her scanning the room.

"Ollie?"

The dog came trotting in from the kitchen, her chin wet from her water bowl. Clara reached for her and sighed with relief. "Good girl," she whispered. Grandpa had done right by giving her Ollie; it was much easier to have a companion while she acclimated to the blue house. So much space, so much quiet. Accustomed to her cramped van, noisy RV campgrounds, and chaotic bike garages, waking to silence felt abnormal. Though the house was achingly familiar, it was also foreign to step out of her memories into the real thing.

Clara went to the kitchen to make coffee. As she ground the beans, her shadowy meeting with Liam in the clearing came back with startling clarity. The lyrics of his song repeated in her head.

Time is not on our side. It takes all that I have and never gives.

Clara sighed.

That's so perfect.

So true and so frustrating. How is this happening?

Part of her still held tight to the theory that it'd all been a dream. That Liam and the well's magic were all a fantasy of her grief-muddled mind. But the memory of his touch was much too clear to be anything but real.

She glanced at the clock. "Dinner with Winnie and meeting Liam—those are the only things on the schedule today, Ollie. What are we going to do the rest of the time?" She filled Ollie's food bowl, and the dog happily munched away. Her gaze moved to the ceiling, considering the task of going through Lincoln's things. "It's too soon," she whispered. "Not yet."

She poured the coffee into a mug, adding a little maple syrup. Her body felt stiff. "How about a walk, Ollie?" The dog turned from her bowl, eager and ready. Clara laughed. "Okay! Let me get dressed."

After putting on some ripped jeans, an old Harley-Davidson hoodie, and sneakers, Clara opened the back door and let Ollie lead the way. Clear skies and bright sun told her that the snow certainly wouldn't be coming today. The scent of pine saturated the air, an intoxicating perfume that embodied everything she remembered about the farm. She inhaled deeply as they approached the large white barn.

The paint had been recently refreshed. She peered up at the large silver weathervane of Santa and his sleigh. It'd been her mom's idea. Her dad and grandpa had rolled their eyes and teased her when she brought it home, but then dutifully installed it. Clara smiled at the memory, sipping her coffee.

Calling to Ollie, who'd wandered into the trees, Clara went to the side door of the barn and opened it. She and the dog ducked inside. Large equipment lived in the main, open area. Clara only glanced at the looming shadow of the tractor as she headed to the back of the barn and her grandpa's office. She remembered it as a small room with one window, one desk, and neat piles of paperwork. When she opened the door, she found it hardly changed.

She crossed to the tall leather desk chair and put her hand on the back, looking over it at the desk. The scent of Lincoln's favorite mint candies still hung in the air, subtle, but enough to conjure memories of her grandpa sitting here, crunching down on a mint as he looked over paperwork. There was a MacBook laptop—that was certainly new—and a stack of manila file folders. She touched the cool surface of the laptop.

Clara's perusal snagged on the two framed pictures on the desk. The first was of Liz and her kids before Clara had become one of their family. The second was Clara and her parents, captured that Christmas morning, in front of the tree in the living room, pajamas and all.

Fifteen years ago, frozen in time.

Before everything changed.

There were no recent pictures. Clara leaned forward to touch the frame of her family's picture. "That day changed everything for you, too, didn't it, Grandpa?" she whispered. She was ashamed to admit she hadn't spent much time thinking about how the tragedy affected her grandpa. She'd been young, and then he hadn't been in her life other than casual phone calls and annual pine nuts. Now, with the lens of adulthood, she grew keenly aware of how deep Lincoln's hurt must have run. The shame, the regret, the what-ifs. The *blame.* His son, his daughter-in-law. Dead. His granddaughter taken away. Liz's anger heaped on top of everything else.

It must have been dark, replete torture. Isolated. Every day.

Oh, Grandpa. I'm so sorry!

How did you survive it?

A fresh anger came rising to the surface. "We should have been able to face this together. To help each other heal. What would that have been like? All those years, together instead of apart. My parents' will was wrong." The anger seared the back of her throat. The tick of a clock somewhere in the room grew annoyingly loud. "I should have done better. I regret . . ."

I regret so much.

Why was I so selfish?

She turned away from the pictures.

The source of the ticking was a large wall clock hung next to the door—also new. The space was quaint, full of light. Neat and clean.

But she couldn't stand it anymore.

Clara hurried out of the office, Ollie behind her. Back in the open air, she pulled in several breaths, hoping the cold air could tame the furious heat burning the back of her throat. She shook her head and looked at Ollie. "More walking, less emotions, huh, girl? Lead the way." Clara gestured to the thick expanse of evergreens, and Ollie was all too happy to trot into the rows.

Clara pressed her cold hands to her hot mug and followed the dog. A partial peace found her, the anger slowly dissipating. Being tucked in between the trees, the blazing blue sky above the deep green, worked to ease her old wounds. She let the sounds of the birds fill her head, the rhythm of her breath do the work of clearing out her emotions. She was so lost in the wandering, she didn't even realize when Ollie took her to the well clearing.

A few steps in, Clara stopped suddenly, blinking at the stone structure. She turned to the dog. "Think you're funny, don't you?" Ollie tossed her head and went to sniff at the well.

"Clara?"

Goose bumps rose on her arms as she looked up to see Liam coming out of the trees. *No way.* She watched as Ollie trotted over to Liam, happy as could be. Clara shivered. "Liam . . . hi. What are you doing here?"

Liam's face showed he was as surprised to see her as she was to see him. "My mom has a cancer treatment in an hour and . . . it's always hard. I thought I'd take a walk before we go." He shrugged lightly. "I didn't really mean to end up here."

Clara scoffed quietly. "Me, either. That keeps happening to us." He looked effortless in his jeans and black hoodie. No hat today, and she couldn't get enough of his loose waves falling over his forehead and flipping out above his ears. The style was most definitely not 2019, but she loved its messiness. He ran a hand back through it before lifting his gaze to her.

"Sorry about your mom," she said.

"Thanks. She twisted her ankle last night. I'm worried it's broken. It's really swollen this morning. She can't walk on it at all."

"Cancer *and* an injured ankle? That's not fair."

He smiled. "Agreed." He shrugged. "We'll see later today."

Clara nodded, unsure what else to say.

Liam filled the silence. "Speaking of ending up here, you . . . uh . . . get any sleep last night?" he asked. A small flush reddened his cheeks.

She smiled. "A little. You?"

"Not much. How's being at the blue house?"

Clara sighed. "It's weird. Good and bad, you know? I was just in the barn and my grandpa's office. He has two pictures on his desk—one of Liz's family and one of mine—both from *before* the accident. Nothing recent. It kind of breaks my heart. He must have been as stuck in that moment as I've been. Maybe worse. Actually, probably much worse. We all left him alone."

Liam moved a little closer, slipping his hands in his pockets. "I imagine it was really hard for him. I feel like my mom has been stuck in my dad's death all these years. It's an easy place to get stuck."

"Yeah, it is. I'm glad you and your mom have each other. Wish I'd been there for Grandpa. Wish he'd been there for me."

"It helps, having each other. It was hard when I wasn't at home. I know that sounds weird—" He stopped short, and his brow furrowed.

"What do you mean? Where were you?"

His face flushed, and he dropped his eyes. "I was married. Only for two years. We lived in town. Close, but still. Anyway, it didn't work out." His expression contorted; there was sharp pain in that sentence.

Clara blinked, surprised more at the bolt of jealousy than the actual news. She swallowed it down. *What is there to be jealous about? Stop it.* Her curiosity took over.

I wonder what happened?

From his face, his tone, it sounds bad.

Poor Liam.

"I'm sorry," she said softly.

He shrugged. "Yeah, me, too. But at least I can focus on Mom. She's having more and more trouble doing everyday things. Doesn't feel comfortable driving anymore, gets tired really quickly—stuff like that. And now she can't walk on her ankle."

"Is she doing chemo and all that?"

"Yeah, not pleasant."

Clara really wanted to ask more about his failed marriage; she was weirdly curious about the type of woman he'd loved before. And, mostly, why any woman would divorce him. But she knew it'd be intrusive. She didn't really want to tell him all about her failed relationships.

Liam shifted his weight. "You said you were at Winnie's shop—still read as much as I remember?"

"I do, yeah. Winnie, of course, had this huge stack of

books she insisted I read. I think she overestimated my reading speed, but I trust her. Her recommendations were always spot on."

Liam smiled. "She's kind of magic that way. A book witch, my mom always says."

Clara laughed. "For sure. That's perfect." She suddenly felt awkward just standing with so much space between them. She went to the well and sat on the edge, realizing it was because she wanted Liam to be closer. She fought the urge to pop back up and stay standing. Ollie laid down at her feet.

Liam ran his hands through his hair again and then joined her, sitting close. He smelled freshly showered, his nails clean of grease today. Clara's face flushed hot; she kept her chin lowered, as if looking at Ollie, to hide it.

"I just started *My Name is Asher Lev*," Liam said. "It's incredible. Have you heard of it?"

"Yes, it's amazing! I read that a couple of years ago. Found this beat-up, yellowed old paperback in a used bookstore in Montana. The language, the emotions. It's kind of unreal."

"Exactly. One of those rare books. I'm glad you've read it. It's not as well known." He folded his hands in his lap. "I also recently finished *Dune*. I'd wanted to read it for years."

"*Dune* is incredible. Frank Herbert was a genius. I read it last Christmas, after putting it off for years, too. Something about the size of it—I didn't think it could keep my attention through all those pages. But I was totally hooked from page one."

"Me, too. It's so gripping, you hardly notice the massive length."

Clara gave him a big smile. It felt so good to talk to someone about books. She'd never really dated a reader, and never really realized how wonderful that might be. From his expression, Liam seemed to be enjoying it as much as she was. "Winnie gave me *all* romances. Seriously, there are twelve of them."

Liam chuckled. "Why all romances?"

"She said it's what I need right now." A ripple of energy moved between them. *Oops. Shouldn't have mentioned that.* "Weird, right?" she added awkwardly.

"You'll have to let me know if they're any good. I've never actually read a real romance novel."

"Me, either."

Liam looked down at his hands. "What were you doing in Montana?"

Not the most subtle change of subject, but Clara was relieved. "Bike job in Bozeman. A 1947 Indian Chief. Great bike, needed a full restore. The transmission rebuild was really fun. Then the paint guy finished it in this deep maroon with glittery gold trim. It's gorgeous."

"Sounds like it." He leaned slightly toward her. "Your job is so cool."

"Thanks. Yours, too." Clara wanted to touch him, to move close enough that her leg would press against his. *Stop it.* "So . . . should we talk about the whole time thing or just pretend it doesn't exist?"

Liam laughed quietly. "I only have a few more minutes, so let's pretend."

"I like it." She smiled, and he held her gaze for a moment. Clara broke away first, looking down into her empty coffee mug. "Tell me about my grandpa. What's he like as a middle-aged man? I only knew him as an old guy."

Liam grinned. "He's intense but also laid back. He's stern but also makes us all laugh. He buys the crew beers every Friday during the harvest season. He's so devoted to his family—that one, you know. I wouldn't want to work for anyone else."

"That sounds just like him. I can't believe I inherited the farm. It's not real yet."

"I'm sure that will take a while to set in." Liam turned more toward her, his knee touching hers.

"I'm terrified I'll screw it up somehow."

"Not a chance. Do you have a good foreman?"

"Winnie says so. I haven't met him yet."

"Then you'll be fine. He'll manage everything." His gaze moved over her face. "Does that mean you're staying in Hill Valley?"

Clara wanted to wince at the eager hope in his voice. She'd seen this hope before, the need for her to stay, to be permanent when she couldn't. When she didn't know how. "I'm not sure yet. Still trying to figure things out."

"Of course." He hid his disappointment well. "I'm glad to hear you kept the farm in the family. Lincoln is so proud of this place."

"Turner Barnes is *not* happy, I'm sure."

Liam scoffed. "That guy is still around?"

"Yep. Asked my grandpa's lawyer at the funeral if the farm was for sale. *At the funeral!*"

Liam sucked air in between his teeth. "That's just wrong. I think Turner is the only man Lincoln doesn't get along with. The only man he genuinely doesn't like. He's so great with everyone else."

"And that's why I could never turn the trees over to him. Liz was all ready to wash her hands of it and let Turner take over. But I . . . I couldn't do it."

Liam nodded, his expression thoughtful. He looked about to say something else, but then flinched and checked his watch. "Oh, wow. I got to go. We have to drive all the way up to Salt Lake for these appointments."

"Oh, right," Clara said, a wave of disappointment moving

through her. They stood at the same time. Clara looked up at him, only a foot away.

Should I hug him?

I want to.

But...

Liam put his hands in his pockets, and Clara shook off the urge. "Hope all goes well with your mom's appointment."

"Thanks. We still on for tonight?"

"Of course. I'll see you then."

Liam nodded and smiled. He took his hands out of his pockets and then put them back. "See you then," he said before moving off into his trees.

Clara stood for a moment, watching the space he left empty.

You're making it hard to leave this place, Liam.

But I have to leave eventually.

If we get close, leaving will hurt you. And me.

I can already feel it.

Suddenly exhausted, the lack of sleep catching up, Clara turned for her own trees.

Liam sat in the hall of the clinic, his right leg bouncing nonstop and eyes fixed on the gray door to the X-ray room. Sally's doctor had ordered the pictures as soon as he saw her ankle. How had his mother become so fragile that a little trip over a kitchen rug could cause so much damage? She was already in enough pain; she didn't need this, too. The sound of someone approaching pulled his attention away from the door.

Lyla stopped next to him, slim and professional in her blue scrubs. "Still in there, huh?"

"Does it normally take this long?"

"Dr. Oliphant ordered several views, so yes. This is normal. Everything is ready for her chemo when they're done. I'll meet you back in the treatment room."

Liam's chair started to squeak from his leg's constant shaking. He pressed the heel of his hand on his knee to stop the nervous movement. "Thanks, Lyla."

She smiled supportively. "I started that book last night. It's pretty good. I'm already wondering who did it."

It took him a second to realize she was talking about the Danielle Steel mystery novel she'd picked out on their date. Their dinner and bookshop browse felt ages ago, the details pushed aside by Clara and his mom. But it had only been last night. He forced himself to smile. "I'm glad you like it." He couldn't help but think about his talk with Clara this morning. She'd read *Asher Lev* and *Dune;* they could really talk books.

"Dinner was nice, too," Lyla added.

Liam nodded. "Sorry, again, that things got cut short."

"Don't worry about it." Disappointment clouded her eyes for a moment before she smiled again. Neither of them directly mentioned what had happened, or what *hadn't* happened. "See you in a minute," she said quietly.

Liam nodded. Lyla hurried off down the hall. He watched her, a fleeting sense of regret tightening his chest. If he couldn't make it work with Lyla—an amazing person who lived in his own time—what chance did he and Clara have? He wasn't good at relationships, as his failed marriage so obviously proved. What could he possibly offer Clara?

What are we doing? How will this ever work?

Maybe it's not a good idea to keep meeting at the well.

He startled when the X-ray door opened. The technician rolled Sally out in a wheelchair. Liam hated the way the chair emphasized her frail figure, so obviously displaying her sickness.

"How'd it go?" he asked, pushing up to standing.

"I don't know how they expect anyone to put their ankle in those positions, even if it wasn't swollen and tender," Sally answered with a shake of her head.

"She did great," the male technician interjected. He was tall and thin, and wore glasses a little too large for his narrow face. "I'll take you to the treatment room now. The doctor will look at the X-rays and come talk to you."

Sally frowned. "Knowing my luck, it'll be broken."

"We don't know that yet, Mom," Liam said as he stood.

She sighed, tugging at her thick black sweater. "This guy already knows but won't say anything." She jerked her head toward the technician.

"Mrs. Cooper, you know I would if I could. Hospital policy."

"I know, I know. All these policies. It's *my body*, for heaven's sake."

Liam held back a sigh. She was in one of her dark moods, and who could blame her? "Hey, I was thinking I should make a pie to take to the Hills' party tomorrow night. What do you think?"

She glared up at him, no fool to the fact he was trying to change the subject. "Are you insane? Debbie Hill makes the best pies in town—possibly the whole state of Utah. So, I think that's a ridiculous idea."

He smiled. "I don't want to go empty-handed. Feels rude. What did we take last year? I can't remember."

"We can take some flowers."

"Good idea. We'll stop and get some on the way home." The idea of going to the Hills' house for the annual Christmas dinner sent a shiver through Liam.

They are Clara's family.

Who are all dead in her time.

All gone from her life.

And I will spend tomorrow night with them, as I have many times before.

The technician guided them into the treatment room, a large, open area with lots of windows, fresh flowers, shelves of books and magazines, and several comfortable chairs. Each chair was home to an IV tower and a cancer patient. The group already settled in for treatment looked up and smiled wanly as Sally came to join their ranks. Liam watched his mom's shoulders sink and face harden. Despite the sunshine and comfy chairs, no one liked this room.

Liam and the X-ray tech helped transfer Sally out of the wheelchair; she winced when her ankle got jostled. With a bland smile, the tech left them. Sally rubbed at her forehead.

"Headache?" Liam asked.

For a moment, she didn't answer. Then, "Do you think grief did this to me?"

Liam frowned, lowered into the companion chair, and rested his elbows on his knees. "Smoking did this."

"But I smoked too much *because* of the grief. Your father's death is killing me." She dropped her hand and closed her eyes. "Slowly. Jim got to go quick, doing what he loved, but me . . ."

A flare of his own grief made Liam press his teeth together too hard. He didn't want to listen to this or think about the time when she would leave him, too.

Everyone I love dies or leaves.

Dad, Clara, Kendra, and soon, Mom.

Clara is back, but will she stay?

Will I lose her a second time?

The thought brought an unexpected sting to the back of his eyes. He pushed it aside to focus on his mom, right here, right now. "Do you remember Clara?" he asked.

Sally opened her eyes. "Little Clara, from that first Christmas without Jim?"

It surprised him she could remember anything from that time. "Yeah, that's right. She's back in Hill Valley."

"Really? You saw her?"

"I did. Last night and this morning."

"How nice! You guys were such good friends for that little bit. You were happy when she was around. Why did she leave all those years ago?"

"Her parents were killed in a car accident."

Sally's face clouded. "Seriously? Both of them? How awful."

"Yeah. She went to live with an aunt in San Diego."

"Poor girl. Too bad she didn't stay—you two could have helped each other heal."

"Our thoughts exactly."

"So hard." Then with a tired but mischievous smile, she asked, "Is she single?"

Liam scoffed. "Really? *That's* what you ask?"

"I sensed that things didn't work out with Lyla—sorry about that, by the way. I hope it wasn't my fault. This stupid ankle interrupting things."

"No. No, of course not. It just . . . didn't work." He shrugged. "We didn't have that much in common."

"That happens. Attraction isn't worth much if you can't have a good conversation. At least you didn't marry her before you figured it out."

Liam's jaw dropped open. "Ouch! Thanks for that."

Sally gave him a wan smile. "Kendra had us all fooled. I would have never guessed she'd cheat like that."

Liam looked at the cream tiled floor. The sting of betrayal burned the back of his throat, even now, a year later. "Yeah. Well . . ."

"But what about Clara? Any potential there?"

"Yes, she's single. But . . . she's only visiting." *From the future.* Liam shifted uncomfortably.

I'm going to lose her again.

There's no way to make this work when we live in different times and can't even leave the clearing.

Heavy sadness sat down on his shoulders.

His mother watched him closely. "You like her. A lot."

"Mom, it won't work."

I should stop seeing Clara.

End it now.

I need to stop fooling myself.

Sally scoffed. "How do you know that so soon after she's back? She might stay if she had a reason. It would really help your dear, old, dying mother to know you had someone great to spend your life with after I'm gone."

"Seriously? You're playing the cancer card on my love life?" He bumped his knee against hers, relieved to see some of the dark mood clearing from her expression.

"Use what you got, I always say."

He laughed. "That's low. Clara is . . . amazing. I mean, I don't really know her anymore, but I won't deny there's something about her. There's something there."

"There ya go! Are you seeing her again?"

"Tonight." *Hopefully. If she comes. If something doesn't go wrong.* A new tremor of fear sprang to life.

What if the well severs the connection?

What if it stops working—for whatever reason?

What if we don't even get a chance to say goodbye this time?

End it on our terms.

"Liam? Are you nervous about seeing her?" Sally touched his arm to get his attention.

He offered a smile, attempting to hide his stormy thoughts. "No. Just hoping she actually shows up."

Sally smiled back. "Of course she will! I mean, look at my handsome stud of a son. Just like his father. Irresistible!" She leaned forward to slap his shoulder.

Liam rolled his eyes.

"Wear the blue flannel. It goes well with your eyes, shows off your shoulders."

Liam laughed again, but he stopped short when he noticed the doctor approaching. Dr. Oliphant was a no-nonsense man, short but powerfully built. He had a kind smile, one he used to soften the blow of the news he often delivered as an oncologist. He was wearing that smile now.

Sally scowled up at him. "It's broken, isn't it?"

"I'm afraid so. Two stress fractures as well as the bad sprain."

Sally looked at Liam. "Told ya."

Liam dropped his gaze to her wrapped foot. "That seems a bit extreme for such a simple accident. Is the chemo affecting her bones?" He looked up at the doctor.

"It could be. A loss of bone mass from chemo can make fractures more common."

"I feel a 'but wait—there's more' coming," Sally said, voice thick with sarcasm.

Dr. Oliphant nodded. "It could also mean the cancer itself has spread to your bones. I want to run a few tests."

Liam looked at his mom. She wouldn't meet his eyes, only sighed and shook her head. "Fine. Run your tests."

Dr. Oliphant nodded. "I'll write up the orders. We'll start after your treatment. It'll probably take a few hours. Is that all right?"

"That's fine," Liam answered. "Whatever needs to be done."

"Remember: We don't worry until we have a reason to. Okay?" Dr. Oliphant said.

"Easy for you to say," Sally mumbled.

Liam and Dr. Oliphant shared a concerned look. The doctor said, "I'll be back in a bit," and then left them alone.

Liam's stomach twisted. He reached for his mom's hand; she held on, her grip weak and fingers so frail. "I'm sorry, Mom."

She tried to smile, but it morphed to a bitter scowl. "I'd give anything for a cigarette right now."

Liam tried to smile for her. "No smoking allowed. Sorry. There're enough oxygen tanks in here to blow up half of Salt Lake. "

Sally sighed, the humor lost on her. She reached into her pocket to pull out her old owl lighter. She carried it everywhere, and it often appeared when she was stressed. Her own version of a worry stone, she rubbed her thumb over the owl, half the body now gone from the constant friction. Emotion clogged Liam's throat; he cleared it. "What else can I get you? Anything?"

"A ginger ale sounds nice. Helps with the nausea."

"You got it. I'll be right back."

Liam forced himself not to run from the room and from the pain on his mother's face.

Sitting at the kitchen table, Ollie asleep on the rug under the sink, Clara finished up some emails. Clive had told her to take her time; the restoration job could wait until she was ready. Grateful for his understanding, she shut the laptop, one less thing on her mind. Not that it cleared up much space; her head felt as frenzied as a shaken snow globe that refused to settle. She'd drank too much coffee and only eaten a little here and there. She was ragged and considered heading upstairs to take a nap.

Clara tapped her phone to look at the time: four-fifteen. Winnie hadn't actually said what time she'd arrive for dinner. To Clara, dinnertime was usually between seven and eight. Sometimes as late as nine. She guessed that wouldn't be the case with Winnie and also hoped not—she didn't want to be delayed in getting to the well. An anxious energy in her stomach had kept her thinking about meeting Liam all day.

I should call Winnie and cancel.

Is that rude? Ungrateful?

Clara's phone buzzed with a text from Kiki.

Kiki: *That dog is AMAZING!! She's so sweet-looking. I want to snuggle her so bad.*

Clara laughed, shaking her head. The response was exactly what she'd expected after sending Kiki a picture of Ollie in the pine trees. She typed her response.

Clara: *Ollie is a champion snuggler.*

Kiki: *Of course she is! I'm so happy for you. What you doing tonight?*

Clara: *My grandpa's friend—possibly girlfriend—is coming over to make dinner.*

Kiki: *His girlfriend? Seriously?*

Clara: *Not sure, but from what she said yesterday, they seemed really close. Like, more than friends. I might be reading into it.*

Kiki: *That could be interesting. Or bad. What do you think?*

Clara: *She's great—different, fun. Her name is Winnie. I think it'll be good. I'm just exhausted and not feeling very social.*

Kiki: *Understandable after yesterday. Funeral and Liz and a farm and all that. Reschedule??*

Clara: *Maybe. I was just considering it.*

Kiki: *Did you see that guy again?*

Clara's thumbs paused over the keyboard, wishing she could tell Kiki everything and get her opinion. But somehow, typing *he lives in 1989 and we can only see each other at this old wishing well* didn't really seem like a good idea. She decided to go with the normal facts.

Clara: *I did. For a minute this morning. I'm supposed to meet him after dinner tonight.*

Kiki: *WHAT?! Now, that sounds interesting. Tell me more.*

Clara: *There's not much to tell. I really shouldn't go. It's not like I'm staying in Hill Valley. We shouldn't start anything.*

Kiki: *Christmas fling?*

Clara: *It's not really a fling situation. It's too . . . I don't know. Also, I learned he's divorced. Recently, I think.*

Kiki: *The plot thickens. Do you know why?*

Clara: *Nope. But the way he talked about it, his face—I think it was her fault. I think he's really hurt.*

Kiki: *Gotta be an affair. You should ask him tonight.*

Clara: *I can't.*

Kiki: *Yes, you can. Just get it out in the open.*

Clara: *Right, and then I'll have to tell him I've never had a long-term relationship. That'll be a fun conversation.*

Kiki: *Hahaha. Might as well get that stuff out in the open in the beginning.*

Clara: *I should just end it now. Save us both the trouble. Maybe that conversation would do the job for me.*

Kiki: *My poor, sad Clara. If there's something there with this guy, you should explore it. Take a chance. It might be what you need. What he needs. You protect yourself too much.*

Clara closed her eyes. Kiki was way too right. She thought of Winnie's romance novels. *It's what you need right now.* Clara shook her head and typed her response.

Clara: *I know. But it's hard.*

Kiki: *I know, babe. Hey, you have a dog now. That's big! A man could be the next step.*

Clara laughed, then typed: *Oh yes, it's just that easy to go from dog to a committed relationship.*

Kiki: *You'd be surprised at the similarities.*

Clara laughed again, louder. She was about to type her response when the back door opened. She startled, nearly dropping her phone.

"I'm letting myself in!" came Winnie's voice from the back door. Ollie jerked awake and went loping into the mudroom.

Clara hurriedly typed: *Winnie just walked in. Gotta go. Love you!*

Pushing her chair back, Clara left the phone on the table and turned to Winnie as she moved into the kitchen. She carried two bulging paper grocery sacks, one in each arm.

"Hey, Winnie," Clara said. "Let me take those bags."

"I got it," Winnie huffed as she shifted them onto the island. She wore a jean jacket over a Bon Jovi T-shirt and jeans. Her white hair was still in pigtail braids.

Clara looked into the bags. "Did you invite ten more people I don't know about?"

Winnie laughed. "Very funny. I thought you could use some extra food. Stock the fridge so you actually eat. I know you young, modern women don't believe in eating."

Clara smiled and shook her head. "Thanks. I haven't been to the store yet. But not because I don't believe in eating. I am an avid food worshiper."

"Glad to hear it! Because I will make too much food

tonight, and it will be decadent and include butter. I hope you like a good old-fashioned steak, roasted potatoes, and arugula salad?"

"Sounds divine. What can I do to help?"

Winnie started lifting food out of the bags. "If you cut potatoes, I'll tend to the meat."

"Got it!" Clara put a few things in the fridge and then set to work on the potatoes.

Winnie had the steaks out on a cutting board when she said, "I know we talked about this a little earlier, but why exactly didn't you ever come visit your grandpa?"

Clara's hand froze, knife over a potato. A sharp slice of guilt cut her heart. Winnie's voice was tender, not accusatory, but the question still stung.

"Sorry—that was blunt." Winnie smashed her knife down on a clove of garlic "I'm not trying to make you feel bad, promise. I just want to understand. Maybe it's because I read too many books and get all that inner dialogue insight. I'm curious about your inner dialogue."

"I . . . uh . . ." Clara had no idea what to say. *This was a bad idea.* She kept her eyes on the potatoes, her stomach tight. "It's not easy to talk about," was the only thing she could think to say.

"Right, right. Sorry—we don't know each other well enough yet. I just knew Lincoln so well, and he talked about you a lot. You feel familiar."

"Were you and my grandpa . . ." Clara wasn't sure how to phrase it.

"More than friends?" Winnie helped her out. "Yes. He actually asked me to marry him a few years ago. I said, 'We are so old. What's the point?' We both laughed and went on the way we always had. Which was just right."

Clara finally looked over at Winnie; the older woman's

eyes were misty, her smile loving. "I wish I'd known about you. He was so casual on the phone. Never any real details."

"Lincoln wasn't great at sharing. He had a hard time with Liz and—as an extension—you. He didn't want it that way, but . . ." She shrugged and began to mix butter and herbs. "Relationships are messy."

"I didn't want it that way, either. I *should* have visited; calling wasn't enough. I wanted to for years. Liz wouldn't let me go and then . . . then it just felt impossible. I'm not really sure why."

"I imagine it's hard to be here after what happened. You were probably avoiding the pain."

"Yes, that was a big part of it. It's not easy to be here again." Clara looked over at the table, reliving the moment Grandpa gave her the news. "I didn't want it that way—never visiting. I really didn't. I feel awful I didn't come sooner. I'll always regret it. I thought . . . there was still time." Clara let out a shaky breath.

Winnie nodded slowly. "Time is tricky that way: feels abundant, but it's always scarce. You're here now. That's important."

"Is it, though? I feel too late."

"Lincoln had one dream: that you would run this place. That it would stay in the family and bring you home." Winnie put a cast-iron skillet on the large gas stove. "It's not too late for that."

A flush of guilt heated Clara's face. *But I'm not staying.* She didn't have the strength to confess that to Winnie right now. She busied herself with tossing the potatoes in olive oil.

Ollie came over to the stove, the smell of the meat drawing her forward. Winnie tousled her head. "Don't worry, girl. I'm making one for you, too." She opened a bag of arugula. "Tell me about your job. It sounds fascinating."

Clara released a little tension from her shoulders as the conversation steered away from the past. She told Winnie about the motorcycles she'd restored and the places she'd been. They finished cooking the meal and sat together at the table. Winnie told hilarious stories of some of the odd people who'd come into her shop over the years and more about Lincoln. Clara savored every bite of the homemade dinner, realizing it'd been a long time since someone cooked for her. She also cherished every detail about her grandpa.

"How did he come to have Ollie?" Clara asked as they sat back in their chairs, plates empty. "I feel like there's a story there."

Winnie grinned. "I'm afraid that was my doing."

Clara laughed. "Really?"

"A friend of mine in Idaho breeds Old English Sheepdogs. She had a litter just at the right time for Lincoln's seventy-fifth birthday. You should have seen his face!" Winnie laughed, slapping the table. "It was worth it just for that expression when I put that puff-ball puppy in his hands."

"I can just imagine," Clara said, smiling. "I asked for a dog a few times when I was little, and my dad and grandpa both said no way. Too much trouble, they said."

"Well, she was a lot of trouble as a puppy. He'd call me at three in the morning and chew me out as he had to take her outside. But I'd just tell him, 'You'll thank me one day.'"

"And did he?"

"Of course! Once Ollie slept through the night and didn't pee on any carpets." Winnie winked. "But then he just loved her to death, and she him. It was good for him—to have someone in the house with him. To have that unconditional love. He needed that."

Clara nodded, looking over at Ollie sprawled out in the walkway between the mudroom and the kitchen, her own plate empty. "She is good for that. I know I like having her around."

Winnie nodded. "Humans are pack animals. We don't like to be alone, even though we try to be."

Clara thought of how hard she'd tried to be alone the last several years. How distant she kept herself from Liz, Gavin, and her cousins. Every boyfriend at arm's length, every friendship casual. Kiki was her only close friend, but there was distance there, too, living so far apart, hardly seeing each other. Clara thought she was enjoying that freedom. But was it really freedom?

Was I really enjoying it or just pretending?

A thick melancholy clamped down on her throat as she tried to work that question out in her head.

Winnie slapped the table again. "Well, my girl, I think that's all for me." She pushed back from the table. "I tend to be pretty useless after eight these days. Time to lay in bed and watch *Golden Girls* or *Murder, She Wrote.* Not that you know what those shows are."

Clara shook off her introspection and smiled. "Sophia Petrillo is one of the best sitcom characters of all time, and I've seen every episode of *Murder, She Wrote.* Some twice." Clara laughed at Winnie's raised eyebrows. "Netflix and Hulu— good times."

"I knew you had good taste, Clara Hill." Winnie laughed.

Clara checked the clock: seven-thirty. "Thank you, Winnie. Everything was so delicious."

"I figured you could use a homecooked meal, and I'm happy to get to know you in person. Not just Lincoln's nostalgic ramblings of a little girl."

Clara smiled. "Next Thursday?"

"Count on it." Winnie kissed the top of Ollie's head, then smiled at Clara. "Next time, you'll have to tell me what you think of *Dragonwyck.*"

"I'm starting it tonight."

"Good. Enjoy."

Clara followed her to the back door. "Good night."

"Night." Winnie waved over her shoulder.

Clara stood with the door pushed open, looking out into the cold, dark night. Liam's face filled her mind, bringing with it a surge of giddy excitement. She lunged back into the mudroom to grab Lincoln's winter coat.

"Come on, Ollie. Let's get to the well."

Wishing Well Conversations

L iam felt hollowed out, wasted. The only thing keeping him on his feet was the potential of seeing Clara. His mom's additional tests had added nearly two hours to their time at the hospital. By the end of it all, Sally had plunged into one of the darkest moods he'd ever seen her in. The long drive home had been tense and silent, the black cloud over Sally's head thickening with each mile.

As they approached Hill Valley, Liam forced himself to say something. "Do you want anything from the diner or maybe Enzo's? I know you love the ravioli. I can run in really quick."

Sally didn't turn away from the window. "No. Not hungry." Her words were short, clipped.

Liam was hungry—starving, in fact. They should have eaten lunch hours ago, and chips from the vending machines only lasted so long. Was it wrong to stop for himself while she was like this? He chewed his lip for a moment. "Okay if I grab a burger from the diner? I'll be fast."

Sally lifted a few fingers in an indifferent gesture. Liam pressed his teeth together, trying desperately not to be mad at her sullenness. He pulled up in front of the diner and got out without another word. As he stepped in, Lincoln turned from the counter.

"Liam," he said solemnly. "Everything okay? Looks like your mom's appointment ran long. That can't be good."

Liam looked around, grateful the diner was mostly empty. "No, sir. She's not doing very well." Liam looked at his boss closely, marveling that this energetic and alive man was dead and buried in Clara's world.

Lincoln frowned, turning his hat in his hand. "I'm so sorry. If you need some time, take it. Not much going on right now, anyway."

"I'll take the rest of the day, if that's okay?"

"Of course. And if the party tomorrow is too much, don't worry about it."

"I'll have to see how she feels. I'll be there—I don't want to miss it—but don't count on my mom."

"Understood. Debbie can pack her up some food."

Liam smiled. How many times had Debbie packed him up some food over the years? "Thank you, Lincoln."

Lincoln nodded. "One day at a time, huh?"

"Yes, sir."

Lincoln clapped him on the shoulder. "See you tomorrow."

Liam nodded and stepped aside for Lincoln to pass. He had a fleeting memory of his dad and Lincoln standing near the horse paddock on the cottage's small acreage. Forearms leaning on the rails, hats pulled low. The summer air had smelled of hay and Debbie's fresh sweet tea. The men had been laughing about something, Liam too far away to hear the details. But he remembered smiling and admiring both men with everything he had inside him.

If only Dad had lived. If only . . .

He glanced out the diner window. His mom had her head against the window, her eyes closed.

How different things would be right now if he'd lived.

151

The Christmas tree brightened up the tiny living room, but Liam had a hard time accepting its cheer. Since that first Christmas without his dad, he'd faithfully put up a tree the day after Thanksgiving every year. Even when he lived with Kendra, he'd come over and managed the tree at the cottage. He couldn't stand another year without a Christmas tree, and so he hadn't let it happen again.

Sitting on the couch now, he stared at the white lights until they blurred out of focus. Sally was asleep in her room. He'd tried to get her to eat, but all she'd managed was a few bites of applesauce with cinnamon. Without meeting his eyes, she'd shooed him away.

He checked his watch. Only 6:20.

How soon is too soon to go to the well?

He had no idea when Clara would end her dinner with Winnie. It was better to sit by the warmth of the fire inside than in the icy shadows of the clearing.

Isn't it? It could be hours still.

Or maybe she's there now?

He snatched up the TV remote from the end table and flipped through the channels, not registering anything on the screen. Instead, in his mind, he saw Clara. Her sharp eyes, slim body. He wondered what it'd feel like to touch her hair, to kiss her. If he tried to kiss her, would she return it or flinch away?

But kissing her was a big step in a direction he wasn't sure he should travel. The ground felt so unstable around them— full of cracks and hidden pitfalls. The wishing well had set them right down in quicksand.

But I want to kiss her. To hold her. To be close.

And then she'll leave me just like always.

"Stop it," he hissed at himself. "You don't know that. Don't assume."

The last year had been one dark rain cloud after another. Things with Kendra imploding, his mom's cancer. Clara felt like the sun breaking over the mountains. That was the feeling he wanted to hold onto; that was what he wanted to trust. Not this quicksand anxiety.

One day at a time. Just like Lincoln said.

And today, I get to see Clara again.

Finally, at seven, his antsy anticipation pushed him to his feet. Liam threw on his coat and headed to the well.

Clara walked at an even pace, though part of her wanted to race, arms pumping, like she had as a kid. Even back then, she couldn't seem to get to Liam fast enough. The night air hung still and cold, the black sky clear and crowded with stars. The pines stood like sleeping bears around her, their perfume rich.

Ollie kept running ahead and then circling back to make sure Clara was keeping up. When they neared the clearing and Ollie ran ahead but didn't come back, Clara knew Liam was there. Waiting for her.

She stopped, a hand to her bubbly stomach.

I've never felt this way.

What do I do?

After a long breath, she stepped into the clearing. Liam was bent over Ollie, giving her the attention she demanded. When he lifted his head, Clara saw the exhaustion beneath his warm smile. "I hope you didn't wait too long," she said.

Liam shook his head. "Not long. How was Winnie?"

"She's . . . interesting. Blunt and funny and kind."

Liam smiled. "Yep, that's her. She still wear those two braids?"

"Yep, and rocks it. I hope I'm that cool when I'm in my

eighties." Clara stopped, the dog between them. "And your mom?"

His expression said everything. "It's pretty bad. Her ankle is broken. They did all these blood draws and MRIs to see if the cancer has spread to her bones. Put an ugly cast on the foot." He shook his head. "Of course, we won't know the results of all those tests for a week. Medicine is a sadistic waiting game."

"No, that's terrible. I'm sorry." Clara wondered if her parents' sudden death was somewhat of a mercy. To watch your mother die slowly, painfully—that was unbearable. The burden of it looked heavy on Liam's shoulders. "How's she handling it?"

He sighed. "Not well, at all. She's always been a bit depressed since Dad, but this . . . it's something darker. I feel like she's . . . giving up." Liam winced, rubbing at his forehead. "Sorry. Didn't mean to just dump all that on you first thing."

Clara stepped closer, her heart aching for him. "Let's sit. You can dump all you want."

Liam smiled and nodded. He followed Clara to the well, and they sat on the cold ground, backs to the stone, and shoulders touching. Clara thought of adjusting to put some space between them, but couldn't bring herself to do it. "Do you think her cancer has spread?" she asked. Ollie settled at her side, chin resting on Clara's thigh.

Liam rubbed his hand at the scruff on his chin. "It's highly likely. She's not really responding to the treatments. And she's still smoking despite all my best efforts and loud, lecturing rants."

"That's some stubborn commitment. I think I'd like your mom."

Liam gave a short laugh. "Yes, I'm sure you would. I wish you *could* meet her."

Clara braced, hating the reminder of their bizarre situation. "I know this question is usually futile but . . . is there anything I can do to help? I have a stack of romance novels, if she needs something to read. I can find any motorcycle part she could ever want. Carburetor from 1950? Gas tank with a skull airbrushed on it? I'm sure that's helpful."

Liam laughed, some of the sadness leaving his face, which was exactly what Clara had hoped for. She smiled back, and suddenly, her hand was in his. She wasn't sure if she'd reached for him or he'd reached for her.

They both froze and looked down.

Clara's pulse spiked; she pressed her teeth together and held her breath.

"Clara . . ." Liam whispered. His grip tightened slightly. His hand was perfectly warm despite the cold December air.

"What are we doing?" she murmured back. He lifted his head, meeting her eyes, and she never wanted him to let go.

"I don't know. I . . ." He shook his head, brow furrowed.

"We can't leave this place. We can only see each other here. What are we supposed to do with that? We can't ignore it forever."

"Can't we?" He gave her a steamy half-smile. "I know this is impossible, but I also know how I feel."

Her breath stopped again, a tremor moving through her core. "What do you feel?"

"That I want to be with you." There was such honest, pure tenderness in his tone. "I thought about this all day, struggled with it. I'm kind of terrified—for many reasons—but when it comes down to it, I can't walk away from you."

Closing her eyes, Clara let the warmth of the words fill her chest. "But Liam . . ."

"I know." He took a long breath. "I have this fear that the bridge or connection or whatever it is will suddenly stop. That for some reason, the well will shut this open door. And . . ."

"Me, too." Clara studied her hand tucked into Liam's. "Also . . . I don't know if I'm staying in Hill Valley. I have my job, my bikes. And I suck at relationships. I'm not good at them."

"I'm right there with you. I'm the one who's divorced, remember?" He squeezed her hand. "So you're not staying to help run the farm?"

The hurt on his face tore a hole in her heart. "I don't think so. I don't know anything about running it. The foreman will handle it. I have this whole life I've built. I can't just walk away from it."

Liam nodded. His free hand traced a circle on the back of hers. "You could always start your own garage—bring the bikes to you. The barn on the farm has plenty of space."

"I . . ." The idea sent her mind spinning. "I hadn't thought of that."

My own garage?

But . . . that's not my thing.

Is it?

Liam shook his head. "Sorry—ignore me. I said that for purely selfish reasons. So that you'll stay, and I know I don't have the right to suggest you change your life so we can hang out at this well." He sighed. "Let's just enjoy right now."

"I like the sound of that." Clara lowered her head to his shoulder, for the comfort, but also to conceal the struggle in her thoughts.

I could do that. Couldn't I?

Start my own garage here.

Stay in one place.

But that doesn't change the fact that Liam lives in 1989.

That only solves one problem.

After a quiet moment, she said, "Has it snowed in 1989 yet?"

"No. Nothing. It's so late. Normally, these trees are all wearing their winter coats by now."

Clara smiled at his description. "Do you love what you do—running the farm?"

"Yes, I do. These trees feel like a part of me. Lincoln and I have spent years developing the best ways to keep them thriving. Our trees look healthier because we use holistic methods, not chemicals. We recreate the forest conditions in the soil as best we can. We . . ." He stopped and laughed. "Sorry—don't get me started. I'll talk all night about trees and soil."

"Keep going. You sound just like my dad and grandpa."
Our trees.
The trees in my world are descendants of Liam's work.
Our trees.

Liam went on, "It's kind of like an orchard, or maybe, more like a flower farm. We grow these Scots pines to be cut down. To sit in someone's house and bring joy. The scent, the form, the symbolism. Each one spends a month or more as part of people's lives during this season that means so much to everyone." He lifted his hand to point to the trees. "It takes, on average, about seven years to get a tree of about six feet. Sometimes more. It's kind of crazy—very few farmers wait that long for a harvest. It requires a lot of planning to have a viable crop every year. It's just . . . complicated and rewarding and . . . very cool."

Clara smiled at his passion. "It *is* cool. I kind of forgot about all that while I've been gone. It's incredible the farm has done so well for so long. Generations of Hills, Dad, Grandpa, you, and now . . . me." She sighed, feeling the pressure of that responsibility tighten her stomach. "I wish you could be the foreman now, in my time."

"That'd be amazing," he whispered.

Neither of them said it, but Clara knew they were both thinking it: If time didn't stand as a wall between them, they could run the farm together. It was much too easy to imagine Liam in the blue house, seated at the kitchen table, smiling at her over morning coffee. Walking through the trees, calling out to each other during the chaos of harvest. Her bikes in the barn, his hand in hers. A shared bed. A shared life. A breathe-easy kind of permanence such as she'd known as a child.

Whoa. Taking it too far.

Stop it.

The vision brought a sour sting of tears to her eyes. So easy to picture, so impossible to enjoy.

It's not fair.

Liam turned his head and pressed his lips to her hair. "This isn't fair," he said, his words echoing her thoughts so exactly that goose bumps lifted on her skin. Clara closed her eyes.

For a long time, they were quiet, the night lengthening, the air growing colder. Clara relished the heat and support of Liam's body next to hers and Ollie at her side. The three of them fit so well. Clara reached into her memory to find the last time she'd felt this comfortable, this at home. It'd been that Christmas morning, laying in the wrapping paper, her dad standing over her with his messy hair.

Fifteen years. So, so long.

She lapped up the sensation, a desert animal who'd stumbled onto an oasis. She knew it was part mirage, but didn't care right now.

"Are you cold?" Liam whispered.

"No. You?"

"Not at all." He adjusted to bring his arm around her and pull her as close as possible, his free hand reaching for her hand again. "Why did you wear my necklace all these years?" he asked quietly.

Clara felt the weight of it at the hollow of her neck. "Every time I took it off, I felt this itch of panic, like when you know you've forgotten something. I lost it once and tore my van apart, crying the whole time. I kept shaking my head and saying to myself, 'Why do you care so much?' Honestly, I never really understood why I kept wearing it. But it was one of the few things I had of this place. And I guess I needed that connection. To you, to the farm."

Liam nodded. "I still have all my dad's cowboy boots. They're stuffed in my closet. I snuck them out of my mom's room one day when she was at the store. I just needed something of his close to me. She must have noticed, but never said anything. I don't even wear them. They're just . . . there."

"Exactly. It's strange how we need things sometimes. Something tangible."

"And then sometimes, we have to get rid of things. I didn't keep anything from my marriage. Everything went in the trash."

Clara held her breath, the subject change unexpected, but she was eager to hear more. "Why not? What happened, if you don't mind my asking?"

Liam sighed. "When I met Kendra, she was this force of nature. Funny and full of energy. It was exciting and a change of pace from my normally calm life. When the dust settled after the wedding and life slipped back into its rhythms, she got bored. Bored with Hill Valley, bored with me. So . . . she found . . . *entertainment* elsewhere. A lot of it."

Clara's heart ached for him. "Liam, I'm so sorry. I had a boyfriend cheat once. It stings like you don't expect it to. It makes you doubt *yourself,* not just them. It's twisted and weird." Clara couldn't imagine a woman walking away from Liam to someone else.

"Yes, that's exactly what I felt. I seriously wondered if

there was something wrong with me. Which there wasn't. I didn't do anything wrong, except maybe ask her to marry me."

Clara laughed quietly. "We all make mistakes."

"Well, that's the worst one I ever made. Hands down."

"How long ago did it end?"

"A little over a year. She moved to San Francisco. We don't stay in touch."

"That's hard, even if it's better."

"I'm just relieved it ended. Especially now." He rubbed her upper arm. "Or I couldn't be here with you."

Liam hadn't planned to bring up Kendra, but he felt relieved it was out in the open. Clara's understanding soothed the old wound, a cool balm. Her body against his felt like a cure for every diseased thing in his life. He thought of some of the lyrics from the song he'd written for her. *Your face close to mine, your body melting with mine.*

Liam's chest ached.

But I can't even walk her home.

If I kiss her good night, she returns to another time. Like science fiction, like a deranged fairy tale.

Are we cursed?

Yet he felt compelled to make plans, to extend the time. As if their denial would open up some possibility. "I have a holiday dinner party tomorrow night," he said. "What do you think of meeting here for lunch? I'll bring the food."

"Sounds great." Her voice sounded sleepy.

Liam checked his watch. *How is it almost midnight already?*

"You should go home and sleep," he whispered, lips against her silky hair.

"I don't want to."

He smiled, a flash of heat moving through him. "I don't want you to, either, but I already kept you up most of last night. And it's freezing out here. If we fall asleep, we might wake up frozen to the ground. They'll have to chisel us off the stone." He tucked his chin down to look at her face.

Clara smiled. "It's not cold."

Liam brought his hand to her smooth cheek. "Your face is ice. Come on." He shifted, feeling a cold ache in his joints from sitting so long on the hard ground. With a groan, he pushed to his feet and then held out his hand to her. "We should have met in summertime."

"But winter is *our* time," she said, looking up at him.

He smiled, a pulse of warmth near his heart. "You're right. It is."

"Come on, Ollie," Clara whispered to the sleeping dog, who lifted her head, blinking up at Clara. "Time to go." Clara reached for Liam's outstretched hand, and he pulled her up. She stumbled a little, falling against him. "I can't feel my legs." She laughed and stomped her feet. "Okay, maybe it *is* too cold."

Liam laughed back, circled her with his arms, and held her close. "Remember the first time we hugged?"

"I remember the shock on your face," Clara said against his chest, her tone playful.

Liam laughed again. "It was a good shock." He held her tighter. A barn owl passed overhead, its wings nearly silent as they cut through the air. He watched its progress and then lowered his eyes to the well. "I wish I could ask the well to fix this somehow—make it so we aren't trapped here—but I don't dare."

Clara turned her head to gaze at the well. "Don't risk it. Who knows what it would do next?"

"It's only stone and dirt and air."

"Apparently not," Clara murmured. "Do you think it's done this before? Are we the first victims, or only the latest in a long line of very confused people?"

Liam frowned. "You'd think there'd be stories floating around if this wasn't the first. People would have talked and spread it around town."

"Great. Does that mean we're the special ones? The lucky freaks chosen for the weirdness?"

Liam smiled. "I guess so. Although, at this moment, I do feel pretty lucky. As cheesy as that sounds."

Clara lifted her gaze to him. "Me, too. I just wish . . ."

"Me, too." He rubbed her back. *I wish so many things right now.* Every moment with Clara had the thrill of possibility and the terror of the unknown. A jagged seesaw that lifted him up and dropped him low. Every time he said goodbye, it could be the last time.

In this moment, that fear made him bold.

Liam took Clara's face into his hands. He held her luminous gaze, studying the expression in her eyes. A spark of silver at her neck caught what little light there was from the moon. Her necklace. She reminded him of all things winter. The broad blue sky. The crisp smell of snow. Wood smoke and hot soups. Dark nights and brilliant-colored sunrises. The welcome rest after a long year. Hibernation. Rejuvenation.

Clara's hands slipped up his chest to rest over his heart. Could she feel the way it raced at her touch? Liam had never felt such a replete, pure desire. Not for Kendra or Lyla or any woman he'd held in his arms. He saw Clara's reciprocal longing flush her cheeks, the skin under his thumbs turning pink.

Liam lowered his lips to hers.

The brush of his mouth on hers was as soft as fresh snow. Her quick intake of breath pulled him back in to deepen the kiss. He refused to go too fast; he needed to savor this moment. To pull it out long, a taffy-stretch fight against time. Clara's arms slipped around his waist, inviting him closer. His arms pulled her close, the kiss heating their cold faces.

Your body melting against mine.

Losing some of his control, he tangled his hands in her dark hair, pulling strands free from her braid. Clara's cool, whisper-sigh on his lips nearly brought him to his knees. He moved his lips to the smooth skin at her neck, her head dropping back in invitation. Her hands slipped up to his face, drawing him back to her lips.

It's never been like this.

Liam knew if he didn't stop now, it'd be impossible.

Slowing the kiss, he brought his hands back to her hot face and pulled back enough to look at her. Breathless, he studied her eyes, drinking in the heat in her gaze. "If we don't stop," he whispered, "I'll start taking off your clothes, and it's *definitely* too cold for that."

Clara laughed, falling against him, her forehead to his chest. "That'd be an interesting case of frostbite. Which would be pretty awkward to explain to a doctor."

Liam laughed into her hair. "Way too awkward."

"I better go home." She lifted her head. "But I don't want to."

Liam smoothed her hair back from her face. "You know, I imagined kissing you when we were young."

Clara grinned. "You did?"

"After you hugged me—I was a teenage boy, after all. But . . . I could never have imagined it like that. That was . . ."

"Unexpected," she said in a sultry whisper.

"Most definitely."

"We're in it deep now." Her brow furrowed a little, her hands restless on his chest.

Liam nodded, unsure what to say, though he knew just what she was feeling. "Are you okay with that?"

Clara took a breath. "I want to be. This isn't your normal first kiss."

"No, it's not." They both turned to look at the well. "One day at a time," he added, remembering Lincoln's words earlier. "That's all we can do. See how things go."

Clara turned back to him. "Okay. Lunch tomorrow."

"Yes. I can't wait." Liam leaned down for one last kiss and then dropped his arms from around her waist. Clara stepped back, hesitated, and then turned.

"Come on, Ollie," she called, the dog following. Clara looked back over her shoulder.

Liam put his hands in his pockets to keep from reaching for her again.

"Good night, Liam," she said with a soft smile.

"Good night, Clara."

He watched her walk into the trees and disappear from his world.

A Winter Kiss

Hands pressed to her burning cheeks, Clara walked back to the blue house. She couldn't stop smiling. Liam's kiss had sent tendrils of surprise though her body. Sunrise-bright sparks of energy she'd never experienced. Everywhere he touched felt more alive, her senses amplified. Awakened. Liam made her feel awake for the first time.

She was impressed he'd had the control to stop; she'd been too swept up in his lips and arms to even realize she *could* stop. Even now, her body urged her to run back and jump into his arms.

I always want to run to him.

But . . .

Take it slow. This is not a normal boy meets girl moment.

Clara glanced over her shoulder, the pines shadowing the dirt path.

How is any of this happening?

Coming into the yard, Clara hurried up the back steps and into the house. The blessed heat made her sigh, only now realizing just how cold it'd really been outside. Much too cold to sit at a well until after midnight. Ollie shook herself vigorously and then went to her water bowl. Clara stripped off Lincoln's big coat and hung it on its hook. She rubbed her hands together. She knew she should sleep but felt much too energized.

Quickly, she brewed a cup of chamomile tea and headed upstairs. She changed into her pajamas and dove under the heavy quilt. Ollie found her place at the foot of the bed, almost instantly asleep. The stack of romance novels from Winnie was on the nightstand. Clara picked up the top one and settled in.

She'd only read a few sentences before she stopped to look up at the windows. Her euphoria morphed to anxiety. "Of all the men . . . I pick one who doesn't even exist in my world." Her stomach twisted. No one had ever kissed her like that. With such tender exploration but also fire-hot passion. Her body had never felt such a powerful flood of desire.

Good grief. What did we do?

She wanted to savor the pure joy of the kiss, but a muddled fear sullied it. Her mind took ahold of the silt and debris of worry and churned it around, a hundred bad outcomes floating to the surface.

Soon, Clara was curled onto her side, trying desperately not to cry.

Clara startled awake to the sound of knocking. It took her a moment to realize where she was. She'd fallen asleep, the old copy of *Dragonwyck* under her ribs. Ollie jerked alert as well, looking toward the hallway. Clara's first thought was, *It's Liam.* But, of course, it couldn't be.

Memories of his kiss filled her mind, potent and warm.

Memories of her quiet sobs of worry came swiftly behind.

The knocking came again.

Ollie jumped down and went racing into the hall. With a groan, neck stiff and head scrambled with thoughts of Liam, Clara pushed to her feet. She set the book on the nightstand, combed her hands back through her hair, and went down to the front door.

Winnie stood on the porch, a large coffee cup and white paper bag in hand.

"I bring caffeine," she announced with a gorgeous smile. She was dressed in well-fitted jeans, a black T-shirt, and her floral-print bomber jacket. Clara felt underdressed, still in her sleep shorts and the old hoodie she'd pulled on over her camisole. Ollie hopped at Winnie's feet, begging for attention. She leaned toward the dog. "Hello, trouble. Good to see you, too."

"What time is it?" Clara asked, squinting at the bright sun.

"Seven-thirty. Here, take this." Winnie held out the coffee cup.

Clara accepted the coffee, the smell helping to open her eyes all the way. "Thank you, Winnie. I—" She stopped short when she noticed a man hovering behind Winnie on the stairs.

Winnie stepped to the side. "Clara, this is Jad, the farm foreman. I'm just here to quickly make introductions. He can tell you all about how this place runs and what you'll need to do."

Jad, looking very much like a young Garth Brooks, goatee and all, came up the steps and tilted his tan cowboy hat. "Morning, ma'am." He wore a freshly ironed blue shirt under a black sport coat, crisp jeans, and cowboy boots.

Now she felt ridiculously underdressed. Had Jad gotten all dressed up at the crack of dawn just to meet her? And why hadn't Winnie given her any warning? "Good morning, Jad. Nice to meet you," Clara said.

Winnie lifted the white bag. "I also brought Hiran's cinnamon rolls. You're welcome."

Clara took the bag. "Thanks. Uh . . . Jad, come on in. I just need five minutes to get dressed."

Winnie cleared the way for Jad to step into the living room. He pulled off his hat. Winnie called out, "I gotta run. See you later, Clara. Thanks, Jad."

"Bye, Winnie," Clara said, a little flustered, as she shut the door with her foot. Jad stood awkwardly near the front windows, turning his hat in his hands. She gestured to the bag. "Do you want one of these?"

"No, thanks, ma'am. I had my breakfast."

"Jad, seriously, you can't call me ma'am. It's very polite, but it makes me feel eighty years old. Clara is just fine."

Jad smiled—he had a sweet, shy smile and dark blue eyes to go with his dark brown hair. His goatee had a touch of gray in it. "Sure thing . . . Clara." She could tell it was hard for him to say. His gaze flicked to her face and then back to his hat. Was he as young as he looked? His smooth skin and lean body made her think he wasn't much older than her, but his position on the farm and that touch of gray made her wonder if he was older. And hadn't Winnie mentioned him coming into her shop worried about Grandpa years ago?

"Give me five minutes. Have a seat. Ollie will keep you company," Clara said. The dog was already waiting at the foreman's side, looking up expectantly.

Jad ruffled the dog's head. "Of course. No rush."

Clara set her coffee and cinnamon rolls on the coffee table and then bolted up the stairs. She snatched a pair of skinny jeans and a gray sweatshirt from her bag, brushed her teeth, pulled her hair into a ponytail, threw on some mascara, and then hurried back to the living room.

Jad sat on the couch, Ollie by his side like an old friend. His hat sat upside down on the coffee table. "Sorry about that," she said, a little breathless from the rush. "Winnie didn't actually tell me you were coming this morning."

His eyes widened. "I'm so sorry. She told me it was all arranged. Do you want me to go?" He started to stand up.

"No, no." She flapped a hand to signal to him to sit down. "It's fine." Clara sat in one of the leather armchairs opposite the couch. She took the coffee cup and held it between her hands. She wasn't sure if she should take control of the conversation or let Jad. After a moment of silence, she started. "The first thing I want you to know is that I don't want to change anything."

A flicker of relief moved through his expression, his shoulders relaxing a bit. "I'm glad to hear that."

"I inherited this place, and I want to keep it in the family, but I don't claim any expertise. I'm going to rely on you a lot. Hope that's okay."

"Yes, ma'am—sorry." He smiled apologetically. "Clara. I . . . uh . . . normally, that'd be great news but . . ." His expression turned nervous.

Clara gripped her cup a little tighter. "But what? What's wrong?"

"Well, back in my hometown—Twin Falls, Idaho— there's this big apple orchard. My first job was on that orchard. The owner is retiring and . . . and I bought it."

Clara blinked quickly, her heart suddenly pounding. "So . . . you're quitting? You're here to *quit*?"

"Yes, ma'am. I'm sorry. I know the timing isn't great. But this is sort of a dream of mine, and our family is all there— mine and my wife's. It's the perfect opportunity for us."

"You're leaving," Clara said, an electric panic creeping into the edges of her awareness.

No foreman.

The farm has no foreman.

This only works if there's a foreman!

Jad went on. "I'll be around for a couple more weeks as

we arrange things. I can show you everything and get you going on training someone new. But then I'll need to go and focus on my own orchard."

"Okay," was all she could say.

What is happening?

He's leaving!

Jad shifted uncomfortably. "There's a young laborer who could take my spot. I wish he had a few more years' experience, though. Or I can put the word out. There's bound to be someone good who can take my place. Help you keep things going." His gaze dropped. "I'm really sorry, Clara. Lincoln was the best boss I ever had and a good friend. A great man. This farm is an outstanding operation. But . . . well, I have to move on. I'm really sorry about the timing."

Clara blinked, trying hard to keep her face neutral.

How will I find someone to run the farm?

Crap. Now Liz will be right.

I can't do this.

Liam had done this job—or in his time, *was* doing it. She so easily pictured him sitting on this couch, in this room, talking with her grandpa. Liam had probably been in the house a hundred times. She looked around the room, feeling his echo. Feeling his kiss and his hands.

She took a long gulp of the hot coffee, hoping the caffeine might fuel her brain to an easy solution.

What do I do now?

There's no one to run the farm.

I'll definitely need to stay to figure this out.

"Is there extra space in the barn?" Clara asked.

Jad frowned, confused. "What do you mean?"

"If I wanted to have an area to work on motorcycles?"

"Yes, there's plenty of space. You can shift some of the equipment around, move a few things out, if that helps."

"Okay. Good, good."

I can do that. I can start a garage here, be here.

Find a new foreman.

What if I can't find someone?

I know nothing about running the farm.

Clara rubbed at her forehead.

"Are you all right?" Jad asked hesitantly.

Clara dropped her hand. "Sorry, I'm just . . . panicking a little." She tried to smile. "I'm really happy for you, of course. But I just don't know anything about running the farm, and I wasn't planning on staying in Hill Valley."

"Oh. I'm sorry. Winnie made it sound like you were going to run things yourself. I'm sure we can find someone really good to take my place."

"Did Winnie know you were quitting?"

"No, ma'am. I wanted to tell you first."

Clara nodded.

I need a foreman, or this will never work.

The farm will fail.

But it has to be someone who knows this farm, these trees.

Not an outsider.

What am I going to do?

She squinted at Jad. "Well, thank you for telling me. I really am happy for you. I hope everything goes well with the orchard."

"If you have some time, I can show you around, start telling you what you'll need to know."

"Okay. Yes. We better get started."

Clara gulped down the rest of her coffee and set the cup down with a resolute tap. Then she followed Jad out the front door, her stomach churning with stress.

Liam walked out of the trees and headed for the white barn, the morning air frigid on his face. He buried his hands deep in his pockets and thought about Clara. About the supple texture of her lips, the weight of her body against his. He glanced over at the blue house, knowing she was there—in her time. He frowned and pushed his mind back to their kiss. Something he very much could understand.

He went into the barn, certain he could smell her citrusy perfume.

Lincoln was in his office, hunched over some papers. "Morning, sir," Liam said.

Lincoln swiveled his chair around. "Morning! How's Sally today?"

"Sitting in her bed, smoking." With a frustrated sigh, Liam leaned his shoulder into the doorjamb.

"Stress and bad habits—it's a vicious cycle." Lincoln shook his head. "I'm sorry, Liam."

Liam nodded. An hour ago, he'd quietly opened his mom's bedroom door to check on her and say he was headed to the farm. She wouldn't even look at him, her face half-hidden behind a haze of smoke, her eyes on the TV. He'd had the very distinct impression that her smoking was no longer about stress and grief, but about hastening the inevitable.

Don't think that.

Focus on work.

"Any word on that truck headed to Kansas?" Liam asked.

"It had to wait out some ice storms about a hundred miles out of Topeka, but it arrived early this morning."

"That's the last one, right?"

"Yep, all our trees got to their homes."

"It was a good year."

"Very good." Lincoln leaned back in his chair. "You sure you don't want to take today off, too? That tractor's oil change can certainly wait, and we can do spring planning anytime this month."

Liam folded his arms. "And sit at home? No, thanks. I'd rather be here."

Lincoln nodded thoughtfully. "I understand." He slapped his hands on his thighs and pushed to standing with a groan. "Getting old, Liam. Getting old!"

Liam looked away, the idea of Lincoln dead in Clara's time hitting him unexpectedly. This man was his second father, close friend, and boss. He didn't want to think of life without him. Liam looked up, and Lincoln had his astute gaze pinned to him. "Let's go get some coffee first, huh? Debbie's got a fresh pot waiting."

"Yes, sir. Sounds good."

Lincoln smiled, empathy in his expression.

After an hour with Jad, Clara needed to be anywhere else but the farm. Her head hurt badly from trying to absorb everything he had told her. Her worry churned, acid in her stomach. Every new thing Jad brought up was a new thing Clara realized she could fail at. In her mind, she saw each thing like dominoes stacked and then falling, failure after failure. Which would mean the end of the farm.

And it'll be my fault.

Jad talked more about the right person to replace him. It wouldn't be easy to find someone qualified. All Clara could think about was how much she wished Liam could do it.

Jad left in his truck with a stiff wave; Clara watched the dust settle in his wake.

Well, there goes my foreman.

And any chance of this working out.

Clara sighed and rubbed at her forehead, a headache

pulsing to life. Her attention turned to her motorcycle parked by the front porch. She looked down at Ollie. "Sorry, girl. I need a ride. You'll have to hang out alone for a bit."

Ollie trotted into the house behind Clara. The dog went right to the couch and laid down. "Good girl," Clara said, and then grabbed her keys and her helmet. The roar of the engine and the rush of the wind helped clear her head. She headed straight for Café Shanti. She needed the familiarity of a coffee shop and something to eat. She'd never gotten around to those cinnamon rolls.

The moment she stepped into the bright elegance, she felt her headache ease slightly. Hiran looked up from a table he was clearing. "Clara! Hello. How are you?"

Clara half-smiled. "Starving and stressed. What you got for that?"

Hiran laughed as he finished wiping the table. "Another bad day, huh?"

"My foreman just quit to become an orchardist. So yeah, not great."

"Jad is leaving?"

Clara blinked. For a moment, she forgot everyone knew each other. "Uh . . . yes. He bought an orchard in Twin Falls."

"Wow! Good for him." Hiran walked back, hands full of empty coffee mugs. "But not good for you. Sorry about that."

"Thanks."

"How about an incredible grilled cheese sandwich and a mocha?"

"Comfort food at its best. I like the way you think."

Hiran laughed. "Coming right up." He slipped into the back kitchen, leaving her alone. Clara set her helmet at her feet and leaned against the counter. She pulled her phone out to call Kiki. As she clicked over to her contacts, the door of the café opened. A bull of a man stepped in. Clean taupe cowboy hat, black work coat, jeans, and black boots. His beard was thick, just as she remembered it. The skin around his eyes was now deeply wrinkled, but his gaze as sharp as it'd always been.

Clara froze.

"Well, well, Clara Hill. How are you this fine winter day?" He stomped over to her and held out his hand.

"Hello, Mr. Barnes," she said in an even tone, quickly shaking his hand.

"We missed each other at the funeral. Very nice service. Your grandpa was a great man."

Clara pressed her teeth together, a hot anger rising in her throat.

Don't be rude. Don't be rude.

"Yes, he was," she said.

"I heard you inherited the farm. Congratulations."

There was something cunning and mocking in his tone. "Thanks. I heard that was a disappointment to you."

He grinned, a bit of surprise in his expression at her boldness. "Yes, I suppose it is. I'd love to expand my operation."

"That's a nice goal, but you'll have to do it with someone else's trees." Clara had faced a lot of big men in her career. Men who doubted her, underestimated her. She wasn't intimidated by Turner Barnes. But that didn't mean she actually wanted to have this conversation.

Turner folded his huge arms. "I heard you lost your foreman."

Clara silently swore. *How does he know that already?* "Yes. Jad is moving on to his own farm. I'm happy for him."

"Sure, sure. But that leaves you in a tough spot. And you haven't been here for fifteen years. Gonna be hard to run that farm all on your own."

Clara smiled. "That's true. But I can figure it out."

Turner laughed. "New farmers take about a decade to *figure things out*. Do you think you can keep the farm going that whole time?" He took a step closer. "There are so many possible fatal mistakes when you're working with growing things. I've heard of new farmers killing their entire crop with the wrong application of fertilizer."

Clara swallowed the knot in her throat. "How sad for them."

"Indeed. I wouldn't want that to happen at Hill Valley Farm. I want to help. What do you think of a partnership? You own the farm in name, keep it in the family, but I run the operation."

Clara bristled. She hated the way he talked to her like she was an ignorant child. "And I suppose you take all the profit? And run things *your* way, not my grandpa's way?"

"We'd work out something fair."

"Somehow, I doubt that."

His face turned hard. "You have no foreman and no experience. It'll be near impossible to find someone to run that place. No one will want to work for you."

Clara balled her hands into fists at her side.

What if he's right?

No! Don't listen to this bully.

"I appreciate your concern, Mr. Barnes." She said it coolly, which annoyed Turner enough to raise color on his cheeks.

"Working with me is your best option," he hissed. "Your only option, I think."

It's not my only option.

It can't be.

"My answer is no."

Hiran came from the kitchen, a plate in one hand and a large mug in another. He froze. "Hello, Mr. Barnes. Clara, everything okay?"

"Yes, Hiran," Clara said, hoping neither of them noticed she was shaking. "Everything is fine."

Turner's jaw worked for a moment, and then his expression turned smooth. "You know, I'm starting to believe those rumors."

Clara braced. "I don't know what you mean."

Turner unfolded his arms, casually putting his hands in his pockets. "Just one of those silly things that goes around the farming community. But you wouldn't know about that, would you?"

Hiran stepped forward, setting the food on the counter. Clara gently shook her head, signaling to him that she could handle it.

I can handle this. I can.

"I'm sure you'd like to order, Mr. Barnes." Clara moved to pick up her food.

"You don't want to know the rumor about your own farm?"

His tone made her want to scream—and punch his wide face. "Fine. What is this rumor?"

Turner smiled. "That Hill Valley Farm is cursed."

A chill went through her as she instantly thought of Liam and the wishing well. She tried to hide her shock with a scoff and a roll of her eyes. "Mr. Barnes, I really don't—"

"It started with the man who died at the old well."

All the warmth drained from Clara's body. "What?" she hissed.

"Yeah, way back in Willis's time. The stone mason who worked on the well. He was working alone one day, and somehow must have fallen in. They found all his tools and his hat at the bottom of the well, but never found his body."

Clara let go of the breath she was holding. *He's just trying to rattle you. Don't let him.* "That sounds like an urban legend to me."

Turner shrugged casually. "Maybe. But then there was the fire that killed two people in the '80s, Debbie's cancer, Lincoln's cancer. And, of course, your parents."

Clara lost her control. She stepped forward, looking up at Turner Barnes. "Don't!" she said forcefully. "Don't you dare turn my parents' deaths into a cheap story."

Turner didn't budge. "Come to think of it, there was also Jim Cooper. He was Lincoln's best friend. And it was his son and wife that died years later."

A wave of nausea contorted Clara's stomach. She stumbled back.

Hiran said firmly, "I think that's enough, Mr. Barnes. "Why don't I take your order, and you let Clara eat hers?"

Clara swallowed bile. "Wait! You mean Liam and his mother? What happened?"

Turner frowned, a little confused at her question. "They died in a fire. That old cottage—they lived there. A *lot* of death tied to Hill Valley Farm."

Clara had to reach out for the edge of the counter to keep from collapsing to the floor. Hiran reached out to put a steady hand on her back. "Clara, are you all right?"

She shook her head. "I have to go. Right now." Her mind buzzed in a strange way, and all she could think about was getting to the well. She had to see Liam this instant to make sure he was okay.

Liam dies. In a fire.

When?

Her head snapped up. "When exactly? When did the fire happen?"

Turner scoffed and threw his hand out in a dismissive gesture. "Way back in the '80s."

Her vision went black; she smelled smoke.

Liam. No.

She scooped up her helmet and raced to the door. Hiran called out, "What's wrong?"

"Sorry, Hiran!" was all she said as she flung open the door and ran for her bike.

No, no, no. That can't be right.

Turner was just being mean.

But she'd seen the burned-out ruins of the cottage herself. She sat on her motorcycle. Pressing a hand to her forehead, Clara tried to stop the searing panic.

What if the fire is today, tomorrow?

I have no way to get to him.

I need to . . . tell him. Warn him.

Can I do that? Messing with time and all that?

Ugh. That's TV, not real life.

"Clara?" Hiran said from the café's door. "Are you okay?"

She flinched. "Sorry. I just need to go."

"Of course. Are you okay to drive?" He looked worriedly at the bike. "You shouldn't listen to Turner. He's a bitter, old bully."

"I know. It's not that. I just . . . gotta go." She pulled on her helmet, ending the conversation. Hiran frowned, concerned, but waved his goodbye.

The engine roared as Clara pushed the bike to top speed. She thundered up the driveway of the blue house. Ollie came running from around the back of the house. Clara slowed down enough to tell Ollie to follow her. Then she rode her bike into the trees, her panic visceral and desperate. Skidding to a stop at the well, she turned in all directions.

Of course, he's not here!

She yanked off her helmet. "Liam?" Clara yelled. "LIAM!" She went to his side of the trees and yelled a few more times, her voice cracking with the force she put behind it. She turned back to the well, ready to kick and scream. Clara took a shuddering breath and went to the well to peer into its black mouth.

Did a man really die down there?

And did it start something . . . bad?

No. Not possible.

Grandpa never said anything about a man dying in the well.

But there is something about it . . .

"Liam, can you hear me?" Her voice echoed weakly against the stone. She swore. "Bring him to me! Right now. Don't you dare make this thing any more twisted than it already is. You can't bring him into my life and then take him away. *You can't!*"

Clara leaned farther into the well, listening, waiting to feel something. Some sign it had listened. "Come on!" She slapped her hands down on the stones and then drew back.

Ollie let out a short bark. Clara looked down at the anxious dog. She knelt and took Ollie's face into her hands. "Sorry, girl. It's okay. It's fine. Liam will be here in a couple of hours. He'll be fine. I'll . . ."

What do I do?

I can't just tell him he's going to die in a fire.

Can I? Should I?

The struggle had her dropping to the ground, to sit in the cold dirt. Ollie sat beside her, close and attentive. "I don't think I like how much I care so soon. All of this feels . . . dangerous." She let out a long sigh that did little to relieve the pressure in her chest. "Maybe Turner was wrong. He was just trying to hurt me, to make me angry. Force me to give him the farm. But what if he's right? What am I supposed to do?" Clara shook her head. She imagined Liam trapped in a room, flames crawling up the walls. His sweat-drenched fear. She pressed a hand to her mouth, suddenly nauseated. Ollie licked her other hand. "In 2019—right now—he's dead," she whispered. Bile stung the back of her throat.

Clara gazed toward Liam's trees, willing him to walk into the clearing. She took three slow breaths.

Go to the library. Dig up a newspaper, find the truth.

But if I leave, he might come.

As much as she needed to know the truth, she needed to see him more. She needed to run at him and throw her arms around his neck. Feel him solid and real. Alive. Clara walked around the well, calling his name again. Then she walked onto his side of the clearing, hurrying to get to the cottage. Once she cleared the trees, she found exactly what she expected, but dreaded. The burned-down ruins of the cottage. The old rock fireplace standing alone in the rubble. Tears flooded her eyes.

Oh my gosh. No.

Liam lived here.

And died here.

She shuddered and turned away, unable to look at the black wood and brown ivy choking the ruins. Running, she went back to the clearing. She stopped at the well, both hands on her head, pressing into her temples.

Her face stung with the cold.

I can't sit here like this for hours.

I really will get frostbite.

"Let's go, Ollie," Clara called to the dog, who was sniffing the tree line on Liam's side. "Back to the house for one minute. Then . . . we wait for him."

She rode her Harley back to the house. Tearing through the drawers and closets, she found two thick quilts and a box of matches. Clara piled everything in the mudroom. She filled a large baggie with food for Ollie, grabbed water and a bowl. Threw the bag of cinnamon rolls on the pile—she had to eat at some point today.

She pursed her lips, glaring at the pile. "How am I going to get all this to the clearing?" Clara looked at Ollie, thinking. When the idea hit her, she smiled. "Let's hurry."

Debbie Hill checked the basket one more time. "Okay, kiddo. There're two roast beef sandwiches, pickled veggies, those potato chips I made last week, and a bunch of ginger snaps. Which will also be featured at the party tonight. Sound good?"

Liam smiled at her. She had on her favorite rose-print apron and her signature wide-mouth smile. "You didn't have to do this, you know? You're busy with tonight."

"Excuse me! You said you were having lunch with a woman. A lunch *date*! And you—foolish man—were going to pick up that lame food from the diner. I. Don't. Think. So. You want her to like you, right?" She shoved the blue gingham-lined basket at him with a triumphant grin.

"Of course I do. Getting her addicted to your food is a good strategy. It's kept me coming around for years." Liam saw Debbie differently now—this was Clara's grandma. He could see a little resemblance in the eyes, the oval face. The vibrancy of her personality.

She swatted his shoulder. "It won't be my food she keeps coming back for, you shameless suck-up. Now, get out. Can't be late."

"Yes, ma'am."

"And you better come back and tell me how it goes."

"Yes, ma'am." Liam went out the back door. "Thanks again. See you tonight."

"If it goes well, bring her along!" Debbie smiled and waved him off, already headed back to her party preparations.

Bring Clara? I wish, but that's not possible.

182

Debbie's house, Clara's house.

Do I tell Clara her grandma made this food?

Will that be a comfort or painful?

Liam paused at the bottom of the back steps, looking through the trees.

This blurred line of our lives, even though we're decades apart, is so confusing.

Was it this connection, this weaving of their lives, that had brought them together? Is that why the well had breached time? Somehow, it had discovered the existing link and opened the door?

Liam shook his head. It was pointless to try to find reason or explanation. He hurried toward the well. All that mattered now was being with Clara.

Crossing the Bridge

Ollie heard Liam first and went tearing into the trees. Clara smiled to herself. *Guess the dog fell for him as fast as I did.* She stood, the anxiety of the last few hours churning in her stomach. She stepped around the fire she'd built just as Liam came through the trees. The relief of seeing him launched her into his arms.

Liam's free arm came around her back. "Hey!" he said. When she held on tighter, he gently dropped the basket to the ground and wrapped her close. "What's wrong?"

She pressed her eyes shut, fighting tears. *Stop it! He's fine.* "I just . . . had a bad feeling."

"I'm here," he whispered. "It's okay."

Clara wrestled with the idea of telling him about the fire. It felt wrong to say anything, but dangerous not to say anything. How did she tell him without the facts? *Turner could be wrong. Please let Turner be wrong.* She buried her face in Liam's neck. He smelled of pine and ginger. "I'm so glad you're here."

"Me, too." He kissed her forehead. "Did something happen?"

"It was a bad morning. And then I just . . . suddenly worried you wouldn't be able to come back."

"I know. I had that same thought." He rubbed her back. "Why was it a bad morning?"

Clara pulled back to look at him. "My foreman quit. He bought an orchard in Idaho. And then I ran into Turner Barnes at the café. He was . . . a jerk. To say the least."

Liam scowled. "Yeah, that sounds like a bad morning. I'm so sorry. I can't believe your foreman quit."

"Me, either. I don't know what I'm going to do now."

"Ugh. I want to help so much. But it's not like I can with our little time problem."

Clara smiled. "I'm just glad you're here. That helps a ton." She hugged him again, reassuring herself once more that he was alive and okay.

Looking over her shoulder, Liam said, "Wait—is that a compact tractor wagon attached to your Harley?"

Clara pulled back to laugh at the expression on his face. "Yep. I had to haul the firewood, blankets, and everything. I noticed it in the barn yesterday. It wasn't hard to rig it for the short drive through the trees."

"You rode your Harley through the pines?" Liam laughed. "Really nice bike, by the way. Motorcycles are pretty incredible in 2019."

Clara grinned. "Thanks! What'd you bring?" She nodded at the basket.

Liam released her to go pick it up. "Umm . . . your grandma made us lunch." He winced slightly, waiting for her reaction.

Clara blinked quickly. "Really? Everyone said she was an amazing cook. She died when I was little; I don't really remember her."

"She is amazing, at everything. I mentioned our lunch— or that I had a lunch date—and she insisted."

A warmth spread in Clara's chest. "Well, it's totally strange that my dead grandma made lunch, but I'm so excited to try her food."

"Then let's eat. Great idea to make a fire." Liam crossed over to sit on the blanket at the fire's edge. Clara joined him, followed by Ollie. Liam lifted out the wax paper-wrapped sandwiches, a big mason jar of veggies, and a white tea towel filled with cookies. Ollie gave him some puppy dog eyes, and he tossed her a cookie.

"Sucker," Clara teased him.

"I know. But who can resist that face?"

"Not me." Clara unwrapped her sandwich and tossed Ollie a loose piece of roast beef. "Good grief. Did Debbie *make* this bread? It's incredible."

"She's a master," Liam answered, mouth half-full. "She's been pushing food into my hands for fifteen years."

"That's nice. I should learn how to cook. I wonder if her recipes are still around."

"I bet they are. Lincoln wouldn't get rid of those. She keeps them in a small wooden box. It has roses painted on it."

"Of course it does. She loved her roses. I'll look for it."

They ate in contented silence, chewing and watching the fire burn.

"How's your mom today?" Clara asked after several minutes.

Liam frowned. "Trying to bring on her death by smoking herself into oblivion."

"Oh, no. I can't even imagine the mental toll cancer would take. It's hard to blame her." She thought of Debbie and Lincoln, both cancer victims.

There's a lot of death at Hill Valley Farm.

Clara forced back Turner's words and smiled at Liam.

Liam sighed. "I don't blame her. I just wish there was something more I could do."

"I know. Hardest part of relationships is not being able to help. She has to want to do it herself."

"I think the window for that has closed."

Clara sighed, wishing there was something she could do. She decided to change the subject to get his mind off it. "What did you say you have tonight? A party?"

"Yeah." Liam brushed crumbs from his jeans. "It's actually the Hill Valley Farm annual party. Debbie and Lincoln host it every year."

Clara blinked, memories coming of a festive crowd smashed into the blue house. Christmas music and piles of food. "I remember those."

Liam nodded. "Sorry—I know this is weird. How our lives intersect."

"Even with so much time between us." She sighed. "I was thinking about that earlier. These trees, my family. Your family. It's all so connected."

And there's been so much tragedy for us all.

Are we cursed, like Turner said?

He turned to fully face her. "I was wondering if that's why the well brought us together."

"Maybe. Turner told me today that a man died in the well. The stone mason. Have you ever heard that?"

Liam frowned. "No. Never. Why would he tell you that?"

"He thought I should know there's a rumor that the farm is cursed."

Liam's eyes went wide, and then he laughed. "Seriously? He said that. Good grief. He'll say anything to get his hands on the farm, won't he? That's ridiculous."

"Yes, it is." Clara thought of all the deaths he'd listed. "But isn't it weird, everything that has happened to our families? Seems like some serious bad luck."

Liam frowned. "True, but I don't think that qualifies as a curse. Just life." He leaned toward her. "Turner was just being a jerk, Clara. We're not cursed."

187

Clara looked down. "I know, but . . . it kind of feels like it. Just look at us! Stuck at this well, divided by time."

Liam took her hand. "Hey, look at me."

Reluctantly, Clara lifted her head to meet his affectionate gaze. "What?"

"We're together. That's a gift. Sure, it's kind of a broken gift, but still . . . We're here."

She smiled. "Yeah, true. Sorry—Turner kind of got to me."

"He's an intimidating guy—hard not to. What else did he say?"

"Somehow, he knew that Jad is leaving in a couple weeks. Turner offered me a partnership. I'd own it in name, he'd run it."

Liam's brow furrowed. "Are you considering it?"

"No way! But he's influential. What if he makes it impossible for me to find anyone to replace Jad? He used that rumor like a threat. Like something he'd use to make life hard for me."

"No one will believe that—no one you'd want working for you, anyway. And he'll just look like an idiot if he tries that." He shook his head. "I could recommend a few guys—*if* we lived in the same decade."

"If we lived in the same decade, it'd be you." Clara touched his face.

Liam closed his eyes and leaned forward into her touch. "Yes, it would." He gave her a soft kiss. "What can I do to help?"

"I don't know yet. I need to let it sink in. I don't want this to eat up all our time today."

"Okay. Well, when you're ready, I can tell you everything you need to look for in a foreman."

"Good. Thanks. Does he have to have hat hair?" Clara

pulled off his baseball cap and ran her hand over his easy-going hair. Something she'd wanted to do from the beginning.

Liam grinned. "Of course he does."

"This is great hair," Clara said as she let it slip through her fingers, heat growing in her belly.

In a swift, easy movement, Liam pulled her into his lap, his lips meeting hers with a delicious fierceness Clara was happy to match. She kept her hands in his hair at the base of his skull as his explored her waist and hips. Everything she'd felt during their first kiss was even more intense the second time. Heightened, fresh craving. Which surprised her so much, she gasped against Liam's mouth.

We have the fire and blankets this time.

It's not freezing.

How far should we take this?

Making the decision for them, Ollie pressed her head between them. Clara laughed, pulling back. "Ollie! Rude!"

Liam put his hand on the dog's head. "Feeling left out?" He shook his head, meeting Clara's gaze, desire in his eyes. "Maybe it's good she interrupted us."

"Maybe. Although . . ." Clara leaned in for another kiss. Liam tried to pull her close again, but Ollie wedged her face between them once more.

"Ollie, seriously!" Clara laughed.

Liam touched Clara's face. "I guess she's a good chaperone."

Clara rolled her eyes, tousling Ollie's head.

"So," he said, "that bike looks fast."

Clara appreciated the segue. It was much too soon to take things too far between them. *Even if I do feel everything for him already.* "It is fast. Sometimes too fast—hard not to get a ticket."

"I need to get mine up and running. I haven't ridden in so long."

"Wanna give it try?" Clara smiled when his eyes went wide. "I can take the wagon off. You can take it up and down a few rows. Not the full experience, but you'll at least get an idea of how it rides."

"Really?" Liam asked, little boy eagerness filling his eyes.

"Yes!" Clara laughed as she stood to cross over to the bike. She removed the rigging for the wagon while Liam looked the bike over. "It's really easy to start. Ignition there," she instructed. "And clutch there. Sit on it. Go ahead."

"Are you sure?" Liam said, one hand on a handlebar.

"Oh my gosh! Yes. Are you scared or something? I'm not one of those riders who protects her motorcycle like it's porcelain. Bikes are meant to be ridden."

Liam half-smiled and shook his head. "Okay. If you insist . . ." He slung his leg over the bike and sat. Clara nearly sighed out loud at how sexy he looked on her Harley. Liam ran his hand over the smooth gas can, tracing the blue pinstriping. He turned the ignition, and his entire expression lit up. She fell for him even harder.

They grinned at each other for a moment, the loud growl of the engine filling the clearing. "Get on," Liam said.

Clara laughed, all too eager to sit behind him, body to body. She stepped forward, but stopped short. "Wait. What will happen if we leave the clearing?"

Liam frowned. "Good point. If I drive that way—" he pointed to his side —"will you just disappear?"

"Or get pulled off the bike and thrown back into the clearing?" Clara scrunched up her face. *I want to ride with him.* She stepped close, put a hand on Liam's shoulder, and settled into place behind him. She wrapped her arms around his waist, lean and solid. "Let's find out."

Liam put his arm on top of hers. "You sure?"

"No, but do it anyway."

He took a thoughtful breath and then nodded. His hands went to the handlebars. "Hold on tight."

She tightened her arms, pressed her cheek to his back, and closed her eyes. Ollie barked, sad to be left out. "Ollie, stay. It's okay. Stay," Clara called out. Ollie huffed but sat on her haunches. Liam moved the bike forward slowly. He went once around the clearing. "Here we go," he said tensely as he came around a second time, bike pointed to his side of the clearing. He added a little speed and drove into the trees.

Clara expected her arms to be empty at any moment and the bike to crash into the pines, driverless. But after a full minute, they were still racing down the row and Liam was still in her arms. She lifted her head and looked over his shoulder. "Liam?"

He got to the end of the row and stopped. She followed his gaze. "That's my house," he said quietly.

Clara's heart stopped for a split second. "The cottage." The cottage had wide planking, painted white, a yellow door, and a hedge of winterberries, the leaves gone and the berries bright Christmas red.

He looked at her. "What's wrong?"

At some point, it burns down. Liam dies there.

No, no.

Clara's stomach revolted at the idea; she pressed her teeth together.

Turner isn't wrong. Do I tell Liam?

She managed to say only, "I used to play there sometimes. It . . . doesn't look like that in 2019."

"This is 1989?" Liam frowned.

"Yes," she breathed.

"What does it look like in 2019? I guess I don't live there anymore?"

Clara shook her head; that was all she could manage.

191

"I hadn't thought of this yet," he said slowly, "but if Jad was the foreman and not me, where am I in 2019? I'd only be fifty-seven. Not old enough to retire. I should . . . still . . . be there. But I'm not." He blinked quickly, eyes moving to the trees. "Clara?"

You're dead. Clara's stomach twisted painfully. She shook her head again. "I don't know," she answered, unable to tell him what she knew. *Not until I know more.*

Liam's jaw flexed. "Hold on," he said as he turned the bike.

He raced through the trees, bouncing out into the clearing and plunging into the trees on her side. "Go to the blue house," she said. "We have to make sure."

Liam went up a gear, the pines whooshing past.

He slowed at the edge of the trees, the blue house coming into view. Looking over his shoulder, they gave each other a questioning look.

What's happening?

How is this working?

"Stop the bike," Clara said into his ear. Liam braked and shut down the engine. For a moment, they sat stone-still and looked at the house. "Is it yours or mine?" Clara asked.

Liam peered at the house. "Looks the same. Come on." He turned, took her hand, and they dismounted the motorcycle. Clara clung to his hand, her heart banging against her ribs.

"We went to 1989 together," she whispered. "How did that happen?"

"I don't know."

They went up the back steps. Clara had to remind herself to breathe. "Do we knock? If it's 1989 . . . my grandma will be in there. Grandpa Lincoln." Gray spots flashed in her vision. "Liam! The dog door!"

They both braced. "My blue house doesn't have a dog door," Liam said.

Clara reached out and turned the knob. They exchanged a look and then went inside. Ollie's food and water bowl sat on the floor. Clara kept a hold on Liam's arm. "It's mine. It *my* blue house."

"We're in 2019 now? How is this working?"

Clara guided him into the kitchen. Her phone and laptop were on the kitchen table. "We tested it. Before, when we walked into the trees and lost each other. Why did it work this time?"

Liam ran a hand through his wind-messy hair. "The bike?"

"My Harley is awesome, but it's not . . . *magical.*" She almost choked on the word. "That's all the well, isn't it? Do you think it was because we were touching? Because I was holding on to you?"

"That seems too simple. But . . . maybe?" He looked around the kitchen. "If that were the case, shouldn't we still be in 1989? It looks pretty much the same. You're *sure* this is your house?"

Clara pointed to the table. "Yes."

"What are those?"

"My phone and computer."

Liam's eyes pulled wide. "Seriously? But computers are big, bulky."

"Not anymore." She pulled him to the living room. Her teacup from the other night was still on the side table. "How? How is this possible?" she repeated, thinking of Liam's cottage and fire consuming it.

Liam, wide-eyed, inspected the room. "This is . . ." His voice trailed off. "Where's your Christmas tree?"

Clara blinked. "*That's* an important question right now?"

"This is the blue farmhouse on Hill Valley Christmas Tree Farm. Every room *always* has a tree from Thanksgiving until New Year's. I've never seen this room in December without a massive tree."

Clara scoffed. "I . . . don't know. I guess Grandpa was too sick. I didn't even think about it."

"Well, I can fix that right now." Liam turned and headed back through the kitchen.

Clara raced after him. "Liam! What about you being here, in my time? And going to 1989?"

"I don't have any idea," he called over his shoulder. "I can't explain *any* of this, and it's pissing me off. But I can cut down a tree and help you decorate it."

"Seriously?"

"Seriously."

Clara caught up to him and latched onto his arm. "Liam, wait." He met her eyes. "We can't just ignore this and decorate a tree."

"What else are we supposed to do?" His voice was tender, edged with a desperation that took her breath. Clara thought of his death, of the precarious situation they were in. "We don't know how much time we have," he added.

The way he seemed to read her thoughts sent a chill down her spine. "You're right. I know."

"We may walk back into the clearing and never get this chance again. Maybe it's a weird fluke." A sound in the trees made them both turn. Ollie came bounding out of the pines toward them.

Clara held out her hand to the dog. Ollie licked it and stood looking between them. "'Live in the moment' takes on a whole new meaning," Clara said, her chest aching. "But what if you can't get back?"

Liam stepped close, putting his hands on her shoulders.

"Let's worry about that later. I have a few hours before I need to be back." He slid his hands down her arms to rest on her hips. He leaned down to kiss her, his lips cool from the winter air. She drew out the tender kiss, looping her arms around his neck. The sensations in her body immediately took over, silencing her agitated brain. He moved his lips to her neck, and the world disappeared.

She'd dreamed of him here, and now he was. The *how* of it suddenly seemed unimportant. The consequences worth dealing with afterward.

Gradually, sensuously, the kiss ended. Liam dropped his forehead to hers. After he caught his breath, he said, "Or we could do that for the next few hours."

Clara laughed. "Too late. Now, all I want is a big, beautiful Christmas tree."

Liam grinned. "Let's go find it."

A Tree for the Blue House

Saw in one hand, Clara's hand in the other, Liam led her to the far corner of the farm. "The trees for the house always come from the heritage stock. From the descendants of the very first trees."

"Grandpa Willis's trees—that's right. I remember."

Liam smiled, taking in a full breath of December air. He'd walked this land so many times, but having Clara at his side made him feel as if something had been missing, and now, he'd found it. He wanted to always walk the trees with her small hand in his, to kiss her in the rows between the pines, to cut down a tree for her. For them. For the house they shared.

Whoa. Don't get ahead of yourself.

This dreamy moment may end in some kind of twisted nightmare.

This isn't normal. Not at all.

Liam looked over his shoulder. Clara's hazel eyes, more green than brown right now, were wide with wonder. "I can't believe my family created all this. They took a few trees and built a life, a business. It's just . . . I never really understood the scope of that before."

"And now, it's yours."

She frowned slightly. "Now, it's mine."

He heard the struggle in her voice. How hard it must be to be handed a new life, one that included so much pain and hurt. How hard it must be to think of leaving her current life to step into this one. If someone told him he had to leave Hill Valley and become a stockbroker in New York, he'd be devastated. He'd be clueless and afraid.

Is that how she feels?

"You've always traveled for your work?" he asked.

"Yep. Since school in Florida. About five years now. All over the country."

"That must be fascinating, seeing all those places."

"It is, but life on the road can be exhausting. I didn't realize that until I came here. Slept in a real bed, took a shower that I didn't have to wear shower shoes in. Had a homecooked meal. I love what I do, but . . ." Clara sighed. "I don't know."

A spark of hope kindled in Liam's chest. *She wants to stay.* "It'd be a big change, to stay in one place."

"It would." They climbed a short hill. "But your idea about my own garage—that was a total light bulb. I mean, I've dreamed about it in a lazy, 'that will never happen' kind of way. It just takes so much money and time up front. Finding a place, buying equipment, building clientele. But maybe here . . ."

"I think you could figure it out. If people bring their bikes to you at other garages, they'll happily bring them to your own." Liam stopped them at the top of the hill, the border of the heritage trees. "Welcome to Legacy Acres. Not an official name, but Lincoln liked to call it that."

The hill gave way to a sprawling hollow, the curves of the land supporting the rows of Scots pines. The winter sun deepened the green of the evergreen boughs. Birds called out from overhead, swooping down into the branches to rest. "It's beautiful," Clara said. "They should film Hallmark movies here."

"My mom loves Hallmark Hall of Fame. Hey, that could

actually be a good revenue stream for the farm. Or some seed money for that garage of yours."

Clara scoff-laughed. "I was joking but . . . maybe." She shrugged.

Liam nodded, deciding he'd nudged enough on the idea of her staying in Hill Valley. "I like to imagine old Willis Hill out here, a big, old, burly gray beard, sweat-stained hat, hoe in hand," he said. "Standing right here and beaming down on his young trees with pride."

Clara laughed. "I'm sure he did. I saw a picture once—he *did* have a pretty gnarly beard."

Liam laughed back. He ran a hand over his close-shaven beard. "Should I let mine grow out? Do the Willis look?"

Clara shook her head. "No way." She brought her hand to his face and ran her palm over the stubble. "I like it just as it is."

Liam let the heat from her touch sweep through his body. He put an arm around her waist. "How tall do you want your tree, Clara Hill? The living room can take a ten-footer."

Clara's gaze moved over the trees. She lifted a hand. "I want that one, Liam Cooper. Not too short, not too tall. Perfect shape."

"Excellent choice." Liam released her and took his gloves from his back pocket. "Come spot the tree."

"Spot the tree?"

"I'll saw at the base. You make sure it doesn't fall on top of me." He smiled and headed down to her tree.

Twenty minutes later, Liam dragged the tree through the front door of the blue house. Clara held the door open. He dropped the tree at her feet and stopped to kiss her. He moved to touch her, but then remembered his pine sap-covered gloves. Ollie came leaping over the tree and started pawing at Liam for attention.

Clara gave a quiet laugh against his lips. "Someone is jealous again," she said. "Ollie, you can*not* do that every time we kiss."

Liam gently nudged the dog with his knee. "A little busy here, Ollie." The dog took the movement as an invite and wagged her tail excitedly.

Clara smiled up at him, her cheeks rosy from the cold. "You smell like Christmas," she said.

"So do you," he replied, kissing her once more. "Where do you think the tree stand is?" He pulled off his gloves and scratched Ollie behind her ears.

Clara shrugged. "It used to be in the basement, with all the decorations."

"Okay. Let's start there."

Johnny Mathis on the record player. The tree filling the room with its blissful scent. Liam stringing lights and swearing under his breath at all the sap. Clara stood behind him, holding the slack of the light strand and laughing at his frustration.

She couldn't imagine a more perfect moment.

"I'm going to be covered in it," Liam hissed. "Stop laughing, or I'll kiss you again and not resist touching you with these gloves. We'll be stuck together—permanently."

"I'm sorry! Also, I'm not sure that's really a threat," Clara said, holding back a laugh. "You have a talent for salty swearing. I'm impressed."

Liam laughed. "You can thank my cowboy, rodeo champ father for that. I knew every swear word by the time I was two." Liam moved around back, carefully winding the lights around the branches.

"My mom had that gift—I remember several choice

phrases mumbled behind my dad's back," Clara said. "But she would always yell at my dad and grandpa anytime they swore in front of me. It was pretty funny." Clara realized this was one of the first times she'd openly reminisced about her parents. She'd spent far too long remembering the tragedy but not the life. Not the good. She looked at Liam. "My dad did the lights this way."

"Of course he did," Liam answered, hidden behind the tree.

"But you could just loop the lights around and call it good, right?"

Liam dropped his head to the side to see her past the tree. "Excuse me? That's a solid no. Lights have to be done *right*. They have to complement the tree, from the surface into the trunk. Otherwise, you don't get that *glow*."

Clara smiled. "The men around here really have a thing for Christmas trees."

"Comes with the job." He plunged back into the boughs.

Clara's chest constricted.

He belongs here.

I belong here.

We belong together.

The vision of Liam trapped in a burning room filled her head. She flinched, crunching the lights in her hand.

"A little more slack, please," Liam said, startling her. She let out some of the strand, quickly checking to make sure she hadn't broken any lights. Liam stopped to look at her. "You okay?"

Clara tried to smile. "Yeah, of course. The . . . weirdness of all this just kind of hit me again."

His expression sobered. "I know."

"I don't want this to end."

"Me, either."

Clara leaned into the tree to kiss him, touch his face, assuring herself he was real and alive and safe. A sting of agony moved over his face. "We'll figure it out," he whispered. "I don't know how, but . . . we will. I promise. We are *not* cursed."

Clara nodded, his tender conviction bringing tears to her eyes. She blinked it back. "I think we need some hot chocolate."

"Absolutely." Liam smiled sweetly. "I'm almost done. Thank goodness."

"I'll go start it."

"Do you know how to make hot chocolate?" There was a tease in his tone.

"Rude! I may not be Grandma Debbie, but I can manage hot chocolate." She tossed a stocking at him.

Liam laughed, dodging the knitted projectile. "Just checking. You did mention you can't cook."

"But I'm not incompetent—" The back door opened. Liam and Clara froze.

"Clara? You here?" Winnie called, her footsteps coming toward the living room.

"She knows me," Liam hissed, his expression troubled.

Clara's breath stopped. She looked from him to the front door. "The barn. Hurry."

Liam slipped out the front door just as Winnie came into the living room. "There you are! Oh! And you're putting up a tree. Lincoln would be so happy."

Clara tried to smile. "Hey, Winnie."

"Were you just talking to someone?" Her gaze moved around the room.

"Ollie." Clara gestured to the dog, who was fast asleep on the couch. She frowned.

Winnie stepped close to the tree and peered into the branches. "Doing the lights right. Nice work."

"Thanks. So . . . what's up?"

"Oh! Jad told me his news. I had *no* idea! I can't believe it. He said you seemed pretty upset. I came to see if you're okay."

"I'm okay. Disappointed and frustrated, but okay." Clara picked up a box of ornaments to keep her shaking hands busy.

"I also heard about the Turner Barnes run-in."

Clara scoffed. "News really does travel at light speed in small towns."

Winnie folded her arms. "Hiran said it was pretty bad."

"It was fine. I know how to stand up to men like Turner Barnes."

"I'm sure you do." Winnie gave a little smile. She looked at the tree. "You also seem to be able to cut down and haul an eight-foot tree into the house. By yourself. That's not easy—trees are heavy and awkward."

Clara blinked. "I used my bike to tow it. Easy enough."

Winnie nodded. "Smart. I like it."

"I was just going to make some hot chocolate. Can you stay?"

Please say no.

"No, thanks. I gotta get back to the shop." She squinted at Clara. "You sure you're all right? You seem a bit jumpy."

Clara gave her a smooth smile. "Of course. Bad day, but all good now. Thanks for checking on me." *Change the subject!* "I started *Dragonwyck.* It's fantastic."

"Isn't it?" Winnie kept her searching gaze on Clara's face, and Clara felt like the older woman could read her every thought. "Well, I'll let you get back to the tree. Can't wait to see the finished product."

"Thanks, Winnie." Clara followed her to the back door.

As Winnie went down the steps, she called back, "When you're ready to talk about the man you're hiding, I'd love to

202

listen." She waved over her shoulder. "Don't let him forget his gloves sitting on the coffee table."

Clara blinked quickly. "Those are my gloves," she hurried to spit out.

"No, they're not. His coat is on the chair, too. Have a nice evening, Clara!"

Clara's jaw dropped, and then she laughed, shaking her head. As she watched Winnie disappear around the house, she realized something.

Winnie knew Liam.

Which means she knows what happened to him.

Winnie knows.

Clara looked back into the kitchen. She needed to know what happened, mostly *when* it happened. But right now, being with Liam was the priority. As soon as he went back to his time, she'd talk to Winnie.

Liam and Clara sat shoulder to shoulder on the couch, all the lights off except the tree. He held her hand, enjoying the ease of the moment.

"You were right about the lights," she said quietly. "It glows. It's . . . ethereal."

"Of course it does. I *am* an expert." He turned to kiss her temple. A pensiveness had come over her since Winnie left. She'd withdrawn a bit, as if thinking about something seriously. Was it just their odd situation, or something more? Liam got the feeling it was more. Maybe her foreman quitting and her future.

He checked his watch. If he didn't leave in five minutes, he'd be late for the annual Hill Valley Farm Christmas party. But how could he leave this perfect moment? He debated on staying instead of going. Would missing it be a big deal? He could blame it on his mom. However, his loyalty to Lincoln pulled him hard toward going.

But what if this chance never comes again?

Liam looked around the living room, fully decorated now. The shimmering tree and sparkling glass ornaments. Stockings hung on the fireplace, framed by a garland of boughs Clara had made from the tree's trimmings. Soft, lilting Christmas music on the stereo. If it started snowing, it really would be perfect. His gaze moved to the twilight windows and the clear skies over the trees.

He took a slow breath. "I'm supposed to go to that dinner."

Clara blinked up at him. "Oh, right. Are you late?"

"I don't want to go."

She gave a tender smile. "I don't want you to, either. But can you miss it? Lincoln and Debbie will want you there, I'm sure."

"I should go. I should also check in on my mom."

"Then go. We can try this again tomorrow. Maybe we'll get lucky, and the bike really is some magical portal into each other's lives."

Liam smiled and reached out to touch her face. "That sounds so weird."

"I know!" Clara leaned into his touch. "I'll drive you back to the clearing."

He sighed. "All right." They stood, both looking at the tree. "We did a really good job."

"We did. Thank you for thinking of it. This really feels like home now." Clara stepped into his arms. "Christmas in Hill Valley. I never thought I'd be here again."

"I'm so glad you are." He held on for an extra moment.

"And we got to sit on the couch, in the warm house, and not the freezing cold ground at the well."

Liam laughed. "That was a nice change."

Clara lifted to her toes to kiss him. A gentle goodbye.

They headed outside. This time, he rode on the back seat, his arms around her middle. Clara drove slowly back through the trees, the motorcycle headlights throwing strange, jagged shadows across the trees. Coming to a stop near the well, Clara put her hand on his thigh. Her fire had died out completely, Debbie's basket still sitting beside it.

"Meet me tomorrow?" she whispered.

"Yes. I have the day off. Is sunrise too early?" He smiled.

Clara smiled back. "Nope. I'll be here. Promise you will be, too?"

Liam frowned at the concern in her voice. "Of course, I'll be here." Clara nodded and took a quick breath. Liam reached out to kiss her once more. "I'll be here," he repeated as he got off the bike.

Clara nodded again. "Good night, Liam."

"Good night, Clara." He picked up the basket.

"I'll wait a few minutes—in case you get to your side, and it's not 1989." She winced.

"I'm sure it'll be fine."

What if it's not?

What if I'm stuck here?

I'd be with Clara, but my mom would be all alone.

His chest tightened. "I'll see you soon." He plunged his hands into his pockets against the cold and forced himself to walk forward. He felt Clara's worried gaze on his back as he went into the trees.

Is it 1989 yet?

Everything felt the same, smelled the same.

Liam quickened his pace.

Please let it be 1989. Mom needs me.

The light in the window of the cottage allowed him to

breathe again. He jogged to the door and ducked inside. "Mom?" The house was quiet. He went down the hall to her room and knocked. When she called to come in, he opened the door. The TV was on, but barely audible, and she was sunk deep inside her bed. Her ash tray was full of fresh ashes. He held back his reproach.

"You doing okay? Sorry I was gone so long. I was with Clara." He hoped that news would snag her interest.

"I'm fine," she murmured; no acknowledgement of his good news.

"Did you eat anything?"

She shrugged, eyes on the TV.

Liam pressed his jaw together. "I'll get you some toast and a banana. And then I can bring you something from the party. I assume you don't want to go."

"I don't."

"Okay. That's fine." Liam waited to see if she'd say anything else. When she didn't, he went to the kitchen to make the toast.

Clara waited a good fifteen minutes before she turned the bike and headed back into the trees. Instead of going home, she sped past the house and out onto the road, driving way too fast, especially without a helmet.

Please be at the bookshop, Winnie.

We need to talk.

She skidded to a stop outside Pages on Main, relieved the lights were still on. She thrust down the kickstand and ran inside. Winnie sat at the cash register, reading a thick paperback. Her head jerked up. "Clara? What's wrong?"

"I need to talk to you. Please."

Winnie set down her book. "This about the guy?"

"Yes."

Winnie nodded once, stood, and came to the front door. She turned the deadbolt with a resolute click. Flipped the "open" sign to "closed." "Let's sit." She gestured to the interior of the store.

Clara followed, heart pounding and mind racing. She stopped short when Winnie dropped down onto the giant stuffed octopus in the kids' section. Clara frowned.

Winnie rolled her eyes. "Just sit. It's comforting. Even when you're approaching thirty or ninety."

Clara dropped onto one of the soft, thick tentacles. She looked at Winnie, and her throat went dry.

Winnie widened her eyes, waiting. "Go ahead."

Clara swallowed. "I'm trying. This is . . . I don't know how to ask this or say this or . . ."

"Just start." Winnie folded her arms, eyes pinched in concentration.

"I think you're the only person who will listen to me and not think I'm crazy." Clara squeezed her hands into fists.

"Great way to start." Winnie gave her an encouraging smile. "What's so crazy?"

"Do you remember Liam Cooper?"

Winnie blinked in surprise. "Yes . . . Lincoln's foreman back in the eighties. A really great guy."

"Can you tell me how he died?"

Winnie's eyes went wider. "Uh . . . okay. Not what I expected." She huffed out a breath. "His mother liked to smoke—a lot. She was in treatment for lung cancer, in fact. But didn't quit. One night, she fell asleep with a butt in her hand. The house caught on fire. Liam tried to save her. They both died. It was . . . so terrible." Winnie shuddered. "That poor family. And after Jim's accident. Jim was Liam's dad. He—"

"I know." Clara closed her eyes, an icy wave of horror crashing over her. She shook her head, tears rolling down her cheeks.

No. Not that. Please not that.

Winnie leaned forward. "Clara, why are you so upset? That was decades ago. How do you know about Jim Cooper?"

"It wasn't decades ago. At least, not for him. Not for me."

Winnie frowned deeply. "What do you mean? That doesn't make any sense."

Clara took a shaky breath and then dove into the best explanation she could about Liam and the wishing well. Winnie sat incredibly still, listening intently the whole time. "Liam was with me today," Clara finished. "He cut down that tree. We decorated it together. And . . . I think I'm falling in love with him."

For a long time, Winnie didn't say anything. She sat, a statue, the bright orange and red of the octopus suddenly feeling out of place, garish, and not at all comforting. Clara shifted, nervous. A clock somewhere clicked loudly; the heater turned on with a loud kick.

"Winnie?" Clara whispered.

Winnie startled slightly. "Liam was such a good reader. He was in here *every* week. I'd let him borrow books when I knew his mom couldn't afford it. He always brought them back on time and in pristine condition." She blinked quickly and then focused on Clara. "You were friends as kids? Right before your parents' accident."

"Yes. That day was the last time I saw him until the day of Grandpa's funeral. He works for Lincoln—in his time."

"I know. Lincoln talked about him often, even long after the fire. Best foreman he ever had. They were close. Because of Liam's dad. Lincoln and Jim were best friends."

Clara nodded. "I don't want him to die, Winnie."

The words made her flinch. "But . . . he already *is* dead, Clara."

"No." Clara shook her head. "That's what I'm saying. He's not. I know—time paradox—it doesn't make sense. But it's real. He's real."

"You promise you're not making this up?"

"Of course not."

Winnie sighed. "That old well. I knew there was something about it. But this . . ."

"I know. Do you remember when the fire happened? What year?"

Winnie closed her eyes. "It was Christmas time. The night of the Hill Valley Farm Christmas party." She opened her eyes. "Lincoln and Debbie always threw these great parties for their farm staff. A celebration of the season and the successful end of a harvest."

"I know. He's—there now." Clara's throat closed down. "Wait—it could be now? Or, 1989? Liam is going to that party tonight. What year, Winnie? Please!"

Winnie bit her bottom lip. "I'm trying to remember. The years blend."

"Unblend them!" Clara leaned forward, her whole body ready to spring into action.

Winnie pursed her lips. "Easier said than done. Let's go check the city archives." She looked at her neon green, plastic watch. "Library closes in ten minutes."

Clara jumped up. "I have my bike. We can be there in two."

Winnie grunted as she stood. She grinned. "I was hoping for a ride on that thing."

Fueled by a panic she couldn't calm, Clara drove a little on the reckless side. Winnie didn't mind at all, laughing and cheering with each turn and acceleration. But Clara couldn't find any joy in the speed, only a mad need to save Liam. Some instinct told her they were running out of time. It couldn't be a coincidence that he was going to that party tonight.

It just can't.

What do I do if it's tonight?

Clara parked the motorcycle. They plowed through the double doors of the old stone library building. The librarian at the circulation desk jerked her head up at the loud intrusion. Winnie called out, "Sorry, Rue, last-minute library emergency."

The tall, stately woman with round glasses scowled. "Winnie, we close in five minutes, and there's no such thing as a library emergency."

"I know. We just need to check the *Hill Valley News* archives. We can be quick since you did such a fine job of digitizing those." Winnie's tone was sweetly flattering. Clara smiled to herself. Winnie knew just what to say to everyone.

Rue's scowl turned to a half-smile. "All right, then, but please hurry."

"Of course!" Winnie called out. They were already several feet behind the desk, moving toward the archive room at the back of the library. Winnie opened a door. "In here. Boot up the computer."

Clara flung herself into the rolling chair at the first computer she saw; it was at least ten years old, clunky. She shook the mouse. A search page blinked to life. Clara started typing.

Liam Cooper, fire

She bit her bottom lip as she clicked the search button. Winnie put her hand on Clara's shoulder. Part of Clara wanted to turn off the screen before she could see the truth. She didn't want to see black-and-white proof that Liam would die—had died.

"Is it stuck?" Winnie whispered.

Clara frowned, watching the mouse icon spin and spin and spin. "Come on, you old piece of—"

The search results filled the screen—the top result, *Cooper Family Dies in House Fire.* Clara froze, her breath turning to ash in her lungs. *We are cursed.* Her hand hovered above the mouse, unable to click on the link to the full article. She stared at the date of the article: December 7, 1989.

"Clara," Winnie breathed, "tomorrow is December seventh. The fire—"

Clara forced herself to click the link. She needed the details. The short article filled the screen. She blinked the sheen of tears away, bringing the words into focus.

> *Our community lost two long-time members last night. Sally Cooper and son Liam Cooper, foreman at Hill Valley Christmas Tree Farm, died in a fire at their home. We do not have all the details yet, but it appears Liam was attending the annual Hill Valley Farm Christmas party right before the fire. Sally did not attend and was at home. Chief Beck Jensen's preliminary investigation points to a cigarette as the cause of the fire. We all know Sally has smoked for decades. She was also recently diagnosed with advanced lung cancer and was receiving treatment. Jensen said it appeared that Liam came home from the party and tried to save his mother. We will continue to update the community as we receive more details from Chief Beck. Our hearts and prayers go out to all who were close to the Coopers, especially the Hill family.*

Winnie and Clara sat in horrified silence for a bleak moment. Clara's entire body trembled, ice replacing her blood.

We are cursed. No doubt.

Finally, Winnie dared to say, "The fire . . . it's . . ."

"Tonight," Clara said slowly. "The fire happens tonight."

Defying Time

Liam stood inside the tree line, looking at the blue house of his time. All the windows were gold from the warm lights within, each one with a flickering Christmas candle on the windowsill and a wreath hung above it. White lights followed the roof line and outlined the shape of the house. The hum of voices drifted on the air, mingling with the smell of roasted meat and spices.

This night had always been one of his favorites of the Christmas season, but tonight felt different. He couldn't shake the prickly feeling that he shouldn't be here. His mom had fallen into a dark place. Clara was far, far away, in a way that strained his brain and broke his heart. He'd forgotten to get flowers for Debbie. Looking at his empty hands, he felt guilty, frustrated.

Just go to the dinner. Debbie doesn't care.

Mom is fine.

Clara will be at the well at sunrise.

Liam took a long breath and then forced himself to walk around the house and up the front steps. The front door was open, the sound of voices and loud music intoxicating as it rolled out of the house. All Liam could think about was his day with Clara, in this house, filling it with Christmas. Kissing her, holding her.

I don't belong here. I belong with her.

Liam started to turn around, but Lincoln called out to him, "Get in out of the cold, Liam." He stepped out the door and gestured to his foreman. "Someone has to help eat the mountain of food Debbie prepared."

Liam forced a smile. "I'm happy to help with that."

Lincoln laughed. He wore a clean white shirt, no tie, and slacks. It was the only time he ever wore slacks. It was the only time Liam wore slacks. He brushed at his black pants as he climbed the steps. In Lincoln's grip was a half-full tumbler. He raised it to Liam. "Good man! I'll get you one of these to make things go a little smoother. I know you're not much for socializing. Neither am I." He laughed. "Which is why this is my second drink!"

Liam had to smile. His chest ached a little, wishing Clara could have had more time with her grandpa. It wasn't fair that Liam knew him better than she did. "Yes, sir. I'll take two as well. Put one in each hand."

Lincoln laughed harder as he clapped Liam on the back and ushered him into the joy-filled house.

"Clara! Wait!"

Clara ran down the stairs of the library and jumped on her bike.

Winnie hurried after her, wincing as she pounded down the stairs, her old joints protesting. "What are you going to do?"

The motorcycle engine growled to life. "I have no idea!"

Winnie stopped at the bike, a hand on the handlebar. "But . . . you can't get to him."

Clara rubbed her forehead, shook her head. "I know, I know. But I have to try something. Maybe the well will . . ."

If I ask the well, will it let me go there?

Winnie frowned. "You think the well will let you go to . . . 1989?"

Clara revved the engine. She didn't have time to talk about this. "It has to. Do you want a ride back?"

Winnie shook her head. "Good luck, honey. I'll walk back. I'm here when you need me."

"Thanks, Winnie." Tears misted Clara's eyes. She was so grateful that Winnie believed her and supported her after only a short time of knowing her.

Clara backed up the bike and turned it into the road.

Debbie had Liam join her in the kitchen. "Now, you tell me about this girl, Liam Cooper." He sat at the counter eating, while she bustled around the food. They should be out with the group, but it seemed they both needed the quiet moment.

Liam chewed, the roast beef juicy and perfectly seasoned. Debbie went to the stove, dipped a ladle into a pot, and then drizzled extra gravy over his meat.

"Her name is Clara," Liam offered between bites. His face felt hot, his head gauzy from the Moscow mules Lincoln kept putting in his hand.

"Pretty name. She from around here?"

Liam swallowed. *Actually, right here.* "No, just visiting."

"Hmm. That can be tricky." She took a knife from a drawer. "Wait! Why does that name sound familiar? Why do I feel like you've sat right there and talked about Clara before?"

Liam shook his head, unsure what she meant.

"Oh! I remember. Another Christmas, a long time ago. You were a teenager. You came asking if we knew someone named Clara. Liam, is this the same girl?"

He knew instantly what moment she'd been talking about. The first time he'd tried to find Clara. That Christmas afternoon. "Wow. Yes. I can't believe you remember that. We were friends as kids, for a short time." *Also, she's your granddaughter.*

"That's so great. Childhood sweethearts!" Debbie nodded as she pulled a loaf of bread onto a cutting board. "But she's just visiting?"

"Right."

"That's tough."

You have no idea. "Yes. Not sure what to do about it."

"What does she do?"

"She's a motorcycle mechanic. Specializes in restoring vintage bikes."

Debbie stopped mid-slice of the bread. Her jaw dropped, and then she laughed out loud. "Seriously?"

"Yes, ma'am."

"Well, she *must* be amazing. A woman in that line of work. Oh! I like her!"

Liam grinned. "Me, too."

"Is she helping you with that piece of junk you got in your garage?"

"Yeah. Well, she's offered to."

Debbie studied his face, her keen gaze seeing much more than he was saying. "You like her a lot. In fact, you're falling for her." She pointed her knife at him.

Liam blushed, looking down at his loaded plate. "I am, yes."

Debbie put down her knife, her expression changing. "She the first since Kendra?"

"Yes, ma'am."

"That's a big deal."

"Yes. It is." Liam nodded, meeting her understanding gaze. He wanted so badly to tell her everything, ask her advice. Debbie's honesty could solve so many problems. He wanted to tell her all about her granddaughter, so Debbie would know her.

"Don't let what happened with Kendra ruin this. Okay? Sometimes, it's hard to move on. The past clouds our judgement, casts a shadow over new, good things."

Liam nodded. "I'm working on that. Clara makes it easier."

"You think she feels the same?" Debbie put the sliced bread on a platter.

Liam thought of Clara's hug at the well this afternoon, the way she'd held on so tight. "I sure hope so," he said solemnly.

Debbie nodded, opening her mouth as if to say something else, but Lincoln burst into the kitchen. "What are you two doing in *here*? The party is out *there*!" He flung his hand toward the living room.

Debbie grinned. "Lincoln Hill, you are *drunk*."

"I am not!" He gave her a sloppy smile, and Debbie laughed loudly.

"Liam, what do you think?" she asked.

Liam stood up from the counter. "Definitely drunk."

Lincoln laughed heartily. "Well, it *is* a party. Come join me, woman!" He scooped her into his arms, and Debbie squealed and laughed.

Liam smiled, his chest warm. *I want that with Clara.*

Lincoln released his wife and summoned Liam. "Let's go, Cooper. I think it's time for some dancing."

Liam shook his head but followed his boss with a smile.

Clara skidded to a stop at the back of the house. "Ollie!" The dog came charging out of the dog door. "Good girl! The well." Clara jerked her head in that direction, and Ollie took off. Clara followed on her bike.

The night was crow-black now, the sky thick with stars. Uncaring, glacial winter air slapped Clara in the face. Her chant to the well started to loop in her head.

Send me to Liam.

Let me save him.

Send me, save him.

Pushing the bike much too fast for the close quarters of the trees, Clara arrived at the clearing in only moments, Ollie a second behind her. Clara parked the motorcycle and ran to the well. Dropping to her knees, she leaned over the edge into the dark hole.

"I wish to save Liam and his mom. I have to! Please let me save them. Please!" Clara held her breath, waiting, as if something might happen or change. Maybe a feeling that told her the wish had worked. But the well sat quiet, the night cold. Ollie, paws on the edge of the well, barked at the expanse below. Clara put her hand on the dog. "Good girl. Let's go see if it worked."

Please let this work.

Whatever you are, wishing well, please help me.

Clara bulleted down Liam's side of the well, the trees a black blur in her peripheral vision. She felt sick with worry and fear, anxious to act. The trees stopped, and the bike roared out into the open. Clara braked hard; Ollie came up behind her.

Clara stared at the cottage in front of her.

Ollie barked twice.

Clara closed her eyes and then opened them again. Just to be sure she could trust her sight.

Ollie pushed her head into Clara's leg.

Clara let out a mournful sob, the site of the burned cottage of 2019 blurring behind her angry tears.

"You sure you won't stay longer?" Debbie asked as she handed him a basket full of food to take home to Sally.

"I shouldn't," Liam said, accepting the load of goodies. "She's had a really rough couple of days. And I've already left her alone too much today."

"I understand. Poor thing. It's just not fair. So glad she has you for a son."

"Thank you for everything, Debbie," Liam said, feeling blissfully buzzed from the drinks, food, and company.

Lincoln came through the kitchen to join them at the back door. "Leaving us so soon? The night is young, Liam!"

Debbie swatted Lincoln's shoulder. "He's being a good son and going home to Sally."

Lincoln hummed his understanding. "Of course. Give her our best."

"I will. Thanks." Liam stepped out onto the porch, Debbie and Lincoln following. Seated on the porch steps, they found Randy and Grace, wrapped in a blanket and snuggled close.

"Well, this is where you two snuck off to," Lincoln said.

Randy, young and handsome, looked up at Liam. "Grace likes to look at the trees in the moonlight. Even though it's freezing."

"I don't blame her. It's a beautiful night," Liam said. His heart constricted thinking of their future, their daughter. Of the accident and the damage it would leave in its wake. He looked at the four people who had been most important to Clara, and who were all gone now for her. He wished he could have brought her here to see them, to know them like this, even if only for a moment.

"You going home, Liam?" Grace asked, her voice low and sleepy.

"Yeah. That's enough for me. You all have a good night. Thanks again."

"Good night, Liam," Debbie said. "You let me know if you need anything. And you keep me updated about Clara."

"Who's Clara?" Grace asked, her face lighting up. "That's a pretty name."

Liam lost his breath for a moment. Debbie stepped in. "She's the girl Liam is falling in love with. She sounds amazing."

Liam smiled, his chest warming. "Yes, she certainly is. She reminds me of you, Grace, and Debbie."

Grace smiled. "Then I know we'll like her."

"Bring her by sometime," Randy said.

If only I could.

Liam nodded. "Good night, everyone." He waved as he walked down the steps and headed into the trees.

Clara flung herself back onto the well, tears streaming down her face. "Please," she yelled. "Isn't this why you brought him into my life again? So I could save him? It has to be. Let me go to him!" She slapped the stone so hard, her palms stung. "I couldn't save my parents or Grandpa, so you *have* to let me save Liam and his mom. It's too terrible not to." She slapped it again. "You can't do this to us!"

Ollie barked down into the well, imitating Clara's desperate, clipped words.

"I want to stay here. I love this place. I miss it. I need it." Clara sobbed, realizing just how true it was. "But I can't stay without Liam. I can't stay here if he dies, too. It will break me." She paused to take a breath, gain a modicum of control. "Please. I wish to save Liam, save the farm, and save . . . myself."

Exhausted and fighting a mountain of defeat, Clara collapsed onto the dirt and laid her head on the side of the well. The stone should have been freezing, but it was warm against her cheek. She pulled back and touched it again to make sure. Clara's breath caught in her chest. "Why . . ." She jumped to her feet and back onto her bike, Ollie following close behind, and they raced to the cottage.

Clara jerked to a stop.

The cottage sat whole and quiet under the winter moon.

A tendril of smoke coming from under the front door.

Fighting Fire

Liam staggered a bit as he walked, annoyed he'd let himself drink so much, though he was still smiling from the glow of the evening. He was certain he smelled snow. Stopping, he gazed up at the clear, obsidian sky. He inhaled deeply, the sharp scent of coming snow so strong. He frowned, confused, and then kept walking.

Soon, another smell caught his attention.

Smoke.

Thick, acrid smoke.

Liam dropped the basket of food and sprinted the rest of the way through the trees, stumbling and cutting his hands on the pine branches several times.

Mom. Her cigarettes.

No, no, no.

Please, no.

Movement above the trees caught his attention: a massive black plume clawing upward. Liam ran faster, his clumsiness vanishing. He tore out of the trees and instantly fell back, the heat like a brick wall. For a moment, he couldn't process the sight before him.

The cottage fully engulfed in furious flames.

The old, dry wood the perfect fuel, feeding it.

Liam put his arm over his eyes and started to run to the

side of the house. If he could get around to the back, maybe he could get in and save his mother.

Tears from his fear and the smoke made it almost impossible to see. For a split second, he thought he saw a figure near the edge of the property, near his mom's old vegetable garden. He turned away, looking for a way into the house.

The fire was so loud, raging and consuming.

Glass breaking, the structure collapsing.

Is someone calling my name?

Mom!

He plunged for the back door, despite the outpouring of black smoke.

Someone grabbed his arm and yanked him backward. He stumbled, coughing, his eyes so full of smoke and tears that for a moment, he couldn't see who had him.

"Liam! Stop! She's safe!"

Liam's eyes focused, but he doubted what they saw. "Clara!" She kept pulling him away from the fire until he fell to the ground at the boundary of the garden. Clara put her face close to his.

How is she here?

Is this real?

"Are you okay?" she asked, panting.

"Clara—how—" Liam coughed violently. "My mom—" He moved to get up and race back to the house.

Clara pushed him back down. "Stop! She's safe. Liam, look." Clara pointed beyond the garden to a small hill. Sally sat, huddled with her knees to her chest, eyes wide and trained on the fire, her white cast glowing in the darkness.

Liam scrambled up, tripping, but righting himself with Clara's help. They moved to where Sally sat. Liam dropped to his knees beside her. "Mom?"

Sally didn't answer. Streaks of tears left jagged trails down her smoke-stained cheeks.

Liam put a hand on her arm. "Mom, are you okay?"

"I fell asleep," she said, almost too quiet to hear over the raging fire. "The cigarette fell on the floor. I—" She lifted her red-rimmed eyes to Clara, blinking quickly.

Liam looked at Clara for an explanation. She lowered to her knees beside him. Liam realized that Ollie was there, too, on the other side of Sally, allowing the woman to lean into her. Clara took Liam's hand. "I pulled her out before it got too bad. Luckily, the fire started on the opposite side of the bed than the door. We had a way out."

"But . . . *how*? How are you here?" Liam touched her ash-smudged cheek.

Clara shook her head. "When I talked to Turner today, he listed everyone who has died that was connected to our farm. You and Sally were on that list." She shook her head and closed her eyes. "I thought he was lying, but in 2019, the cottage is in ruins, burned to the earth. I went to Winnie, and we found an article in the newspaper. From 1989, from tonight. It confirmed everything. I panicked. No, that's not the word. I was *terrified*. I begged and begged the well to let me save you and your mom. And . . ." She shrugged, looking at Sally.

"She saved me, Liam," his mom said, reaching for Clara's other hand.

Liam shook his head. "But . . ."

"I don't know how," Clara said softly. "Maybe the well is magic, maybe the ghost of that stonemason is manipulating all this. It doesn't matter. I'm just so glad it worked. Or you would have gone into that house to save her and died. Both of you should have died."

A shudder moved down Liam's spine, a wave of cold

spreading through him. He pulled Clara and his mom into a desperate hug, needing to hold on to both of them. They all started crying again, their soft sniffles drowned out by the fire's crackles and hisses.

"I'm so sorry," Sally sobbed. "I know better. I—"

"Stop, Mom. Stop," Liam begged. "We're safe. It's okay."

"But the house. Our little house!"

"We'll figure it out." Liam sat back, clinging to their hands. "Clara, thank you." A horrible thought hit him. "What if you can't get back?"

Clara shook her head. "It doesn't matter. You're safe. We're together."

"But . . ."

Clara only shrugged. "I couldn't let you die. I couldn't."

"But we were *supposed* to die."

"No! That well brought us together for a reason, and it wasn't so I could lose someone else. I could *not* accept that. There's been too much death—like Turner said. I couldn't let us be cursed anymore." Her chest hitched with more sobs. "Liam, I love you. I know it's too soon, but I'm so sure of it. Sure enough to time travel, I guess." She smiled, shrugged.

Liam laughed quietly, his heart swelling with joy. He put a gentle hand on her neck and pulled her close to kiss her. Any doubt about his feelings for her or their future evaporated. "I love you, Clara. I always have. From that first moment you came running into the clearing, I wanted you in my life. That well brought us together, and now it looks like it will help us stay together."

"It better." Clara pressed her hand to his face, kissing him again. "I want to stay in Hill Valley. I want to be a part of my family's legacy and be with you. Whether that's in 1989 or 2019—it doesn't matter. I don't know what the well will do to us next, but I know we can figure it out."

"We can," Liam said, wiping tears from her dirty face. "We will."

"This is very sweet, but—" Sally coughed. "I think something is wrong with me. I thought I heard Clara say she time traveled. Did I hit my head?"

Liam and Clara shared a look. Liam turned to his mom, hoping she would believe him. "No, you're fine, Mom. It's going to sound impossible, but . . . Clara is from the future." Liam grimaced.

Sally blinked, looking between them. "You better tell me more."

Liam launched into a quick version of their story; Clara still had a hard time believing it even as she sat in 1989. Sally's eyes grew wider with each incredible detail. He finished by saying, "Clara came an extra-long way to save us tonight."

Sally shook her head. "But *how*?"

Clara smiled. "We have no idea."

Sally sighed. "I just . . . didn't know that kind of thing was possible, or real. But that old well—there's definitely something about it."

Clara and Liam shared another look. "What do you mean?" he asked.

Sally sighed. "It started when I went there the night after Jim died."

Liam startled. "You did? You went to the well?"

Sally nodded. "You'd finally calmed down enough to sleep. I left you on the couch and went for a walk. The house was so hot and stifling with the loss. I walked in the trees, not really going anywhere, and ended up in the clearing. I stood at the edge looking down into the well, feeling that gaping blackness match the hole inside me, and . . . I asked it for help—not for me, but for you, Liam. I didn't know why I felt compelled to say anything. I felt stupid, actually, but also . . ." She shrugged. "I don't know. I said, 'Please help Liam be okay without his dad.' And then I felt this . . . peace. It was short-lived, but it was there. A tiny moment of hope in all the darkness. Every year on the anniversary of your dad's death, I go back. I sit on the stones and smoke a cigarette and say the same thing."

Clara put her hand on Liam's arm, new tears misting her eyes. He nodded reverently and then said, "Maybe this all started with you, Mom. Maybe it was *your* wishes, not ours, that brought us together."

Clara moved her gaze back to the burning cottage. Goose bumps rose on her arms. "Maybe it was *all* our wishes."

For a long time, they watched the cottage collapse and scorch, holding tight to each other, Liam in the middle of Clara and Sally, Ollie still at Sally's side. Clara's mind and body felt wasted, hollow. Yet, her heart felt light and content. She leaned her head onto Liam's shoulder.

"What do we do now?" Sally asked, and then coughed for a moment. When Liam leaned toward her, she waved him away. "I'm okay." She cleared her throat. "What do you do after you were supposed to die and didn't?"

Liam sighed and shook his head. "I have no idea. We've changed time."

"I know," Clara said. "I broke the first rule of time travel: Don't change history."

Liam laughed quietly. "But if the well sent you here, I can't believe that was breaking any real rules."

Clara nodded. "Maybe. If there actually are any rules. Who knows?"

Liam turned his head to kiss Clara's hair. "I can rebuild the cottage, or we can buy a house in town. I'm not worried about that. And, Mom," he turned to her, "we have to get you to a doctor. That smoke in your weak lungs could have done some serious damage."

"I'm fine, Liam."

"No, you're not."

"Well, I can promise you one thing," Sally started and then paused to cough. "I'm quitting smoking—for real this time. No more cigarettes. I don't think I can even look at one."

Liam scoffed and then laughed. "And it only took burning down the house. I should have tried that years ago."

Sally weakly punched his shoulder. They laughed together. Clara marveled at how good it felt, sitting on this hill, laughing with Liam and Sally, despite all the bad around them.

Clara said, "As nice as this hill is with the firelight ambiance—" Liam and Sally laughed again— "we can't stay here all night. What should we do?"

Liam nodded. "I say we head to the Hills'. It's close and warm; I know they will take us in. But what do you think, Clara? Your family is there. Would you rather try to go back to your time?"

Clara stiffened. *My parents, my grandparents.* "I guess we'll see what happens when we try. I don't want to leave you."

"I know that will be strange, if we stay in 1989. We could go to Winnie's instead?"

"No, let's try the blue house." Sparks of nervous energy popped in Clara's blood.

Liam nodded. "Mom, you okay if I carry you?"

"Yes. Let's go. I'm getting cold sitting here in these old jammies."

Clara and Liam helped Sally to her feet, and then Liam scooped her into his solid arms. "My bike is at the edge of the trees," Clara said. "I can give you a ride back, Sally."

"On a bike?"

"Sorry—motorcycle."

Sally smiled, glancing at her son. "She likes motorcycles, like you."

"Clara is actually an expert. I'm just an admirer."

They skirted the burning house, the flames smaller, losing strength. Sally's attention stayed on it as long as possible, the pain evident in her expression. Clara couldn't imagine the agony of watching the blue house burn. "I'm sorry we couldn't save the cottage, Sally."

"Me, too. My fault. It will always be my fault."

"It's time for a new start, Mom. It's okay," Liam said.

Sally sighed, nodding. "New start. Sounds good."

They came to the motorcycle. Liam helped Sally onto the back. "Just hold onto Clara."

"I'll go slow," Clara added.

"Okay. I guess it's a little like riding a horse. I used to do that every day."

Clara smiled. "A little. It's not far."

"I'll walk behind with the dog," Liam said.

"What if . . ." Clara felt a sudden stab of worry.

"We will stay together," Liam said, reading her thoughts. "I know it."

She nodded and started the bike. They moved into the trees. Clara could hardly tell Sally was there; she weighed barely anything.

Let us stay together.

Whatever time—I don't care.

Just let us stay together.

They moved slowly through the clearing, glancing at the well, and then into the trees on the other side. Clara held her breath and checked over her shoulder. Liam and Ollie were still there.

Stay with me.

229

They came out of the trees. The air smelled of coming snow. Clara stopped her Harley near the back porch and looked up at the sky. Clear and velvet black.

"It smells like snow," Sally said.

Clara nodded. "But no clouds."

"That's weird. Liam, you smell that?"

He and Ollie stopped beside them. "Snow. But totally clear skies," Liam said. He frowned and then moved to help Sally off the bike. Clara waited and then dismounted, her eyes on the blue house.

Which one is it?

Which time are we in?

She looked at Liam and saw the same question in his gaze. He shook his head. Supporting Sally, they went to the back door. Ollie hurried past them and through the dog door. "Liam!" Clara gasped.

"It's *your* house," he breathed.

"Wait—we're in 2019?" Sally asked, looking at the back door with disbelief.

Clara went to open the door, oddly disappointed when it wasn't the home of her young grandparents and parents, but her own quiet, dark house. She flipped on the kitchen lights. "It's 2019," she murmured.

Liam helped his mother to a chair at the table. "I'll get you some water," he told her.

Clara handed him three glasses from the cupboard, and they went to the sink. "How are we in my time?" she asked, pulse racing with confusion.

Liam shook his head. "More importantly, why? I need to go check the cottage."

"Take the bike." Clara handed him the key. He gulped down some water. Clara took a glass to Sally.

"Mom, I'll be right back. I'm going to check if I can get back to 1989."

Sally nodded, bringing her glass to her lips. Clara settled into a chair as Liam went out the door. Sally set her cup down. "This house looks the same."

Clara nodded. "Grandpa kept it up beautifully."

"He sure did. I can't believe Lincoln is dead." Sally sighed. "And that this is 2019. I just . . ."

"I know." Clara bit her bottom lip and anxiously watched the back door.

Liam sat on the bike, listening to the chug of the engine as he stared at the wishing well. "What comes next?" he whispered. He decided to leave the motorcycle in the clearing, in case it somehow tied him to 2019.

Slowly, his steps made cautious by what could be, Liam walked into the trees on his side of the well. "'How time disappears under the pines,'" he sang softly, the lyric from Clara's song looping in his head.

When he smelled smoke, Liam stopped. He stood just inside the tree line. The cottage was smoldering, only a few weak, meandering flames left. The fire department had arrived. Men with axes dug in the outer rubble. The air smelled of wet wood and ash.

Liam held his breath.

Lincoln and Randy stood near Liam's truck at the end of the driveway. Liam couldn't make out their expressions in the dark, but Lincoln kept rubbing at his face, pacing forward, and then turning back. Randy spoke to his father; Lincoln nodded or shook his head.

What do I do?

A loud part of Liam wanted to go to Lincoln and explain everything. Take away the pain and hurt of his and Sally's assumed deaths.

We're fine.

Everything is good.

Your granddaughter came from the future and saved us.

Also, I'm in love with her.

Liam huffed out a frustrated breath.

One of the firefighters came over to talk to Lincoln and Randy. Lincoln shook his head, gesturing wildly. Randy put his hand on his dad's shoulder. Lincoln turned away.

Hot tears stung Liam's eyes. He glanced back toward the well, the blue house, Clara, and 2019.

They think we're dead.

What do I do?

Liam saw two options. Walk out and tell Lincoln they were fine. Make up a story about escaping the flames. Find a way to live in both timelines, his and Clara's. Live with the constant worry that the well would shut the door on them.

Or . . .

Walk back to the blue house and be with Clara in 2019.

I have to choose.

Liam gave the cottage and Lincoln one more look.

Goodbye, Lincoln. Thank you for everything.

Liam walked back to the clearing to stand over the well. "I choose Clara. Shut the door." He put his hand on the stone and felt an odd pulse of warmth from what should have been freezing rock. A peace settled over his heart. He knew without walking back that the other side of the well was now 2019.

His 1989 timeline was over.

We changed time.

The future presented a whole new life. With Clara, on the farm he loved. In a world where cancer treatment had to be better.

He leaned closer to the well. "Thank you," he whispered.

Liam drove fast back to the house. He took the stairs to

the back door two at a time. Clara and his mom sat talking at the table. Clara jumped up. "So 1989?" she asked.

He sliced across the room and pulled her into his arms, lifting her feet off the ground. "Nope. It's 2019 on both sides."

"What . . ." Clara said, hugging him back with the same intense tenderness.

Liam set her down. "We were supposed to die," he said, his excitement growing, which seemed odd considering what he'd just told her.

"Okay," Clara started, her brow pulled down in confusion, "but you couldn't get back to 1989? We were just there."

"We can't go back?" Sally asked. "You mean . . ."

"I *did* go back, but we don't belong there anymore," Liam said, looking between them. He took Clara's hands in his. "I choose you, Clara. I want to be here with you."

Clara laughed hesitantly. "I don't understand. It was 1989, but now it's not?"

"We can't live in both timelines. They consider us dead in 1989. Who are we to argue with that when it allows us to be together? Here. In 2019."

Everyone fell silent for a moment.

"Don't you see?" Liam asked, walking over to his mom. "We couldn't stay in 1989, because we were supposed to die. But we're here, with Clara, on the farm. And modern medicine may have better ways to help you."

"But . . ." Sally blinked. "A fresh start. A *serious* new start."

"Exactly!" Liam said. "It's amazing. Are you okay with that, Mom?"

Sally took a big breath. "Yes, I am."

Clara put a hand on her chest. "What did you do, Liam?"

"I told the well that I choose you. I want a life with you."

Her eyes misted. "And what happened?"

"It shut the door to 1989 and allowed me to come home to you." Liam reached out for her hand. "How's that for a wish granted?"

First Snow

Clara's pulse sprinted. "But your life, your job . . ."

Liam kissed her once, gently. "My life there ended with that fire. Now my life with you begins. Think about it—we wanted a way to be together. This is it."

The possibilities exploded in her head. "We can run the farm together?"

"Absolutely. Say hello to your new foreman."

"Co-owner, not foreman."

"Sounds good to me."

"I can open my garage?"

"Yes."

"We can live in the blue house and have a thousand amazing Christmases together. With the trees and the snow."

"Yes, please."

Clara clasped her hands together. "That sounds . . . like everything I always dreamed of as a kid and stopped letting myself imagine after my parents died. Like everything we talked about but didn't think was possible."

"Exactly," Liam confirmed. "I stopped hoping after my dad died, and then again after Kendra ruined our marriage. But now, with you . . ." Liam pulled her close again. "You've always brought me hope, Clara."

Clara closed her eyes, letting the reality of Liam in her life sweep through her. A long-forgotten feeling of contentment, the kind she'd only known before her parents' deaths, settled in her chest.

This is what coming home feels like.

When she opened her eyes again, Clara caught sight of Sally over Liam's shoulder. Clara pulled back. "Sally? You're sure you're okay with this?"

Sally turned in her chair, gripping the back of it tightly.

"Mom?" Liam asked, stepping toward her.

Sally shook her head, a smile growing on her face. "For the first time in a *long* time, I'm excited to live. It may not be for very long—I don't expect more than one miracle. But the time I have left . . . I'll be with you, Liam. I'll be able to watch you and Clara start a life together. What more could I ask for?"

Liam rested his hand on her shoulder. "I'm so glad you're here."

She patted his hand, tears moving down her face. "Look at us—covered in smoke and ash, crying like babies. Fires, motorcycles, time traveling. What a night!"

Clara and Liam laughed. Clara stopped short. "Do you smell that?"

The fresh, crisp scent of snow filled the kitchen. Clara looked at Liam. He picked up his mom, and then they turned at the same time to hurry outside. Ollie eagerly followed behind. A hushed quiet greeted them as they came down the back stairs into the yard.

The quiet that only came with the snow.

"The inhale," Clara whispered. Liam smiled.

A slow, heavy snow started to drift down from the now cloud-filled sky. The pine trees seemed to reach out their branches, eager to pull on their winter coats, as Liam had said. Clara's breath caught in her throat, a flush of joy heating her cheeks. "First snow," she breathed, her fingers coming to her snowflake necklace.

Liam set Sally down, keeping an arm around her for support. He put his other arm around Clara's shoulders. "What do you think?" he asked.

"It's been fifteen years. I haven't seen snow since I left. I hated it."

"And now?"

"It's the most beautiful thing I've ever seen." Releasing her necklace, she extended her hand out to catch the weightless snowflakes, cool for only a tiny moment before melting into her skin.

Liam kissed her temple. "Now, the night really is perfect."

Ollie barked at the sky and went leaping around the yard, as excited as Clara had ever seen her. "Looks like Ollie is a fan, too," Clara said with a laugh.

Sally leaned around Liam and held out her hand to Clara. Clara held on tight. "Thank you for saving my family," Sally said. "I'm so glad Liam found you."

Fresh tears warmed Clara's eyes. "Thank you for making those wishes every year. I think you brought us together."

Liam looked at them both. "My family feels whole again."

"Mine, too," Clara agreed, the tears tracking down her face. The gap in her heart closed, the wound of fifteen years ago finally healed. She looked up at the dove-white sky, dark but also somehow illuminated with the snow.

I'm okay, Mom and Dad.

Grandpa, thank you for everything.

Wishing well—you did a good thing.

The newly-formed family stood together, marveling at the snow and at the night. After a few minutes, Clara said, "You know, there's a beautifully decorated tree in the front room and some hot chocolate in the kitchen. I think it's time to put on some Christmas music, start a fire, and enjoy this first snow—from the warm couch."

Liam laughed. "Let's do it. I feel like celebrating."

"Me, too," Sally said. "Lead the way."

Clara turned, called to Ollie, and headed back to the blue house.

Christmas at the Blue Farmhouse

December 24, 2019

Nat King Cole Christmas songs drifted lightly from the record player. The room simply glowed with the Christmas tree lights and the beeswax candles Clara had lit all around. The fire in the hearth crackled and flickered, adding to the joyous glimmer. Outside, a heavy snow fell, silently tucking them all in for the night.

Clara sat with Grandma Debbie's recipe box on her lap. She lifted each recipe out with a smile, studying Debbie's graceful handwriting. Her favorite part was the corrections and cross-outs. The improvements over years of testing and tweaking. Clara had chosen to try Debbie's roast chicken, mashed potatoes with gravy, and sauteed zucchini for Christmas dinner tomorrow night. But she still needed a dessert.

Liam lounged on the couch beside her, book in hand, feet on the coffee table. Ollie took up the third cushion, her head in Liam's lap. His hair was a mess from absentmindedly running his hand through it. Clara glanced over, grinning when she saw a whole section of it standing nearly straight up.

"What?" Liam asked, not looking up from his page.

"Nothing." She lifted out another recipe.

He peeked over the edge of his book to give her that sexy half-smile. "Is my hair sticking up?"

"Nope," she teased. "Looks great."

He patted at his head, making it worse, and Clara gave a little snort-laugh.

Sally, from the leather chairs—she in one, her feet propped up in the other—laughed. She turned her nearly empty wine glass in her hand. "He's done that since he was a toddler. Half the pictures I had of him, his hair was sticking up or out. Looked like he'd just been electrocuted."

Liam scoffed. "And that's why I wear a hat." He dropped his book and used both his hands to comb back his hair.

Clara's smile fell. "I'm sorry you lost all those pictures in the fire. I would have liked to see them."

Sally nodded. "I know. It's so strange that it's all gone. All I have left is my old owl lighter." She lifted it from the pocket of her cardigan. "Good thing those jammies had a pocket."

Liam nodded. "I wish I had Dad's boots and guitar. It's weird not seeing them every day."

Clara smiled to herself, thinking of the gift she'd gotten Liam.

"But I don't really miss it all as much as I thought I would," Sally added. "Being here feels so good."

"You look better, Mom."

"I feel better. The new meds, though not a cure, sure do help. And the boot cast is an improvement over that plaster thing."

"We can buy new stuff," Liam said. "Speaking of which . . ." He scooted to the edge of the couch and looked toward the tree. "I think there are some presents under that Christmas tree."

Clara pursed her lips, faking surprise. "We decided no gifts."

Liam grinned, his eyes sparkling. "No one ever means that."

Clara furrowed her brow at him as she set the recipe box

aside. He nodded to the tree. Clara stood and went over. "I don't see anything."

"Look back near the trunk. I kind of hid them."

Clara bent down and looked under the tree. Resting near the trunk on the crimson tree skirt were two small boxes wrapped in pine-green paper and tied with gold ribbon. She reached back and pulled them out.

Liam's smile grew. "That one is yours, and that's Mom's," he said pointing to each one. Clara handed Sally hers and then sat back on the couch.

"Open them!" Liam said, his smile so big and excited.

Clara carefully pulled on the ribbon, enjoying the honeyed whisper of its release. She found herself smiling, a little giddy to see what he'd gotten her. She ripped through the paper to find a black jewelry box. Her breath caught. Slowly, she opened it. Inside, laying on creamy silk, was a new necklace. She looked up at Liam, a hand at her throat on her old necklace.

"It's an exact copy of yours," he explained, "only made with real white gold instead of cheap who-knows-what metal. And diamonds on the snowflake. You can't keep wearing that old tarnished thing."

"It's beautiful!" she breathed. "I just . . ."

"Put it on. You can keep the old one in the box, unless you want to trash it."

"Not on your life!" she laughed. Clara reached up to undo her old necklace while Liam lifted out the new one. She turned so he could drop it over her face and fasten it. The metal was cool against her skin, heavier than her old one. Liam's hands lingered at her neck. She looked down at the new necklace, sparkling like sunlight on snow in the glow of the room.

Tears filled her eyes. "It's perfect. Thank you." She leaned back to kiss him. His eyes were also a bit misty.

"Yes, it is," he whispered back.

"It's really gorgeous," Sally said. "Nice work, Liam."

"Thank you. Now, you open yours, Mom."

She smiled and hurried to unwrap the box. She also had a black jewelry box, but inside was a new lighter. She laughed at the sight of it. "The owl is back!"

Liam laughed, too. "Yep. This is also much nicer than the original. And it's engraved."

Sally flipped it over. "'Not for smoking. Love you, Liam.'"

They all laughed. "It's really pretty. Thank you!" Sally said. "I'll try not to rub this one away." She flicked it open. "How did you have the money to get these?"

"My account is still open at the bank. Earned some nice interest."

Sally laughed. "Of course! I'll have to check mine, too."

"So . . . I got you guys something, too," Clara said lifting to her feet again.

"See! No one ever means no gifts," Liam said with a grin.

"I know! Hold on." She hurried upstairs to her old room. She and Liam were sharing the master now. They'd cleaned out and stored Lincoln's things. Sally took the third room upstairs, which used to be Clara's parents' room. In the back of her old closet, Clara had stashed the gift so Liam wouldn't find it. She tugged it out, plus Sally's, and lifted them into her arms.

Back in the living room, she set the gift onto the coffee table. Liam leaned forward. "Clara . . ."

"You can't be without a guitar," Clara said. "I hit a few music shops until I found the right one. Open it."

Liam popped open the clasps and lifted the lid. He brought his hand to his mouth. "It's just like Dad's," he mumbled.

"Yep. As close as I could get, anyway. It may not be the exact same model."

Liam ran his fingers over the strings. "It's perfect." He lifted to his feet and pulled Clara into a hug. "Thank you. You're amazing."

Clara gave him a quick kiss, so happy. She pulled back to hand Sally her gift, while Liam sat to tune the guitar. "Here, Sally, thought you'd like this."

"Thank you, Clara. You're so sweet." She ripped open the wrapping. "Oh! Wow. These are gorgeous," Sally said as she carefully lifted the red silk pajamas. "Is this a hint that my old flannels should be retired?"

Clara laughed. "No! Just thought you deserved something pretty."

Sally rubbed the liquid material between her fingers. "I've never had something so nice. Thanks, honey."

"My pleasure." Clara turned to Liam, who looked so content hunched over his guitar. "Will you play my song?"

"I'd love to." Liam scooted to the edge of the couch. Clara sat beside him, tucking her legs underneath. Ollie came from behind Liam to snuggle against Clara. She stroked the dog's head as Liam started the song.

Liam sang it beautifully, his deep voice soft around the words, his fingers quick on the strings. He finished with a slow strum. Clara leaned over Ollie to give him a kiss. "Love you," she whispered.

"Love you, too."

A knock came at the front door. Clara jumped up. "That's them!"

She swung open the door, and Kiki immediately started to scream. "Clara! You look amazing!" Kiki flung her arms around Clara's neck. She was bundled in an obnoxious, faux fur-lined parka and big boots. Her black hair was piled on top of her head in a messy bun, and her makeup was colorful but tastefully done. Hank, wide and square, panted at her feet.

"This place is freezing," Kiki said as she pulled back from the hug. "And the snow is *insane*. This is why we live in Miami. I made Carlo drive so slow. That's why we're late. Look at this house!"

Clara looked past Kiki to her husband Carlo, a short, powerfully built man with lots of tattoos. His head was shaved smooth, his goatee dark and sharply trimmed. He was a quiet, serene person. Sort of the opposite of his wife. "Hey, Carlo."

"Hey, Clara. Thanks for having us. This place is beautiful."

"Thank you!" She stepped back. "Come in, come in. Meet Liam and his mom, Sally." Ollie trotted over to see Hank. The two dogs sniffed happily at each other. "And Ollie, of course."

"Look! They love each other," Kiki cooed. "Look at this house. It's Christmas perfection. Oh! Hey, Liam!" Kiki smothered him in a hug and then stepped back to examine him. "Yep. You're as rockstar-hot as Clara said. You even play guitar! It sounded amazing as we came up the porch."

Liam blushed and laughed. "Thanks, Kiki. Good to meet you. Carlo, come on in." The men shook hands.

"This is going to be such a fun Christmas," Clara said. "Winnie is coming over, too."

"The old lady?" Kiki said.

Clara laughed. "Yes. You're going to love her."

"Can't wait! What is that amazing smell?"

"I made ginger snaps. My grandma's recipe."

Kiki shrugged off her coat. She wore an off-the-shoulder black sweatshirt with rhinestones around the collar. "You baked? I must have one right now, or I won't believe it's true. Also, I have to tell you all about the two clients I already found you. They can't wait to send you their bikes."

"Really? You're the best, Kiki! Thank you."

"I got you, girl."

"Clive agreed to send me the BMW. Let me finish the job here."

"Perfect! It's going to be fantastic! I'm so happy for you." She grinned and then hooked her arm through Clara's. "Now, where are those cookies?"

Clara laughed. "Kitchen. Come on." They started that way, and Clara called over her shoulder, "You guys better come, too, or we'll eat them all without you." Clara met Liam's gaze; they shared a smile.

He's here.

We're all here.

And it's Christmas.

Clara's whole body filled with joyous warmth.

Winnie had them all laughing until their sides hurt. They sat in the living room, the night growing old. The cookies were gone, the hot chocolate refilled several times. Another wine bottle had been opened. Liam held Clara's hand, enjoying every moment of her delight. His mom also seemed to be enjoying herself more than she had in years.

It's the perfect Christmas.

How did I get so lucky?

Winnie held up her hands to get the group's attention. "Did you know that there's a tradition in Iceland to give books on Christmas Eve and then stay up all night reading?"

Liam nodded. "I read that somewhere. Very cool."

Winnie grinned, her sequined Christmas tree sweater catching the firelight. "Well, I brought each of you a book. Should we try it and adopt a new tradition for ourselves?"

Kiki clapped her hands. "Yes, please. How fabulous!"

Winnie got up and went outside to her truck. She came back with a small box. She set it on the coffee table and started lifting out wrapped books. "Kiki and Carlo, I asked Clara about you both to get an idea of what you might like. After talking with you the last couple hours, I think I picked right."

"I hear your recommendations are the best," Kiki said, smiling at Winnie and then Clara.

"The best!" Clara confirmed.

Everyone accepted their wrapped books with an eager thank you and tore off the paper. Liam leaned over to see Clara's. She laughed. "*The Time Traveler's Wife*. Winnie *is* a book witch. What's yours?"

Liam tilted it to show her. "*A Wrinkle in Time*. I never got around to reading it.*"

Clara laughed again loudly, bringing a hand to her mouth. She lifted her head and turned to Winnie. "Very nice, Winnie. Thank you!"

Winnie winked to acknowledge their shared secret. "You're welcome."

Kiki let out a loud whoop. "Winnie! You're amazing. This is perfect." She turned the book around to show the group. It was *The Art of Racing in the Rain* by Garth Stein. "I've been meaning to read this for years. Thank you! I love books with dogs in them."

Winnie nodded. Carlo had *The Tattoo History Source Book,* which he was already skimming. Sally had *The Man Who Listens to Horses,* which she hugged to her chest. Winnie had brought herself a fresh copy of *The Thorn Birds*. "I read it every Christmas," she explained. "It's divine. Everyone a satisfied customer?"

Everyone nodded, throwing out more thank yous.

"Christmas Eve read-a-thon," Sally said, adjusting her blanket. "This is amazing."

"I also brought chocolates," Winnie said, lifting a bowl from the box. "Everyone enjoy."

Liam settled next to Clara, their bodies touching along the seams. She leaned close to whisper in his ear, "I can't believe this is real."

Liam smiled. "Me, either. Merry Christmas, Clara."

"Merry Christmas, Liam."

They snuggled closer and opened their books.

Outside, the snow fell silently, and Christmas Eve turned to Christmas Day.

ACKNOWLEDGMENTS

My family has a tradition of going out into the mountains every year to hunt for the perfect Christmas tree. To us, that usually means one that is too fat for my parents' living room. But we don't care. Hiking through the deep snow, sun on our faces, we talk and laugh. We breathe in the smell of pine and drink hot chocolate next to the fire. I adore this tradition. That love of trees, snow, and Christmas is woven into this story. Thank you, Mom and Dad, for keeping that alive.

As always, thank you, Matt, for your support while I write my books (and do too many other things). You're a serious rockstar husband.

Thanks, Heather Moore and the Mirror Press team for stellar editing, beautiful covers, and great support.

Teri Harman is the author of *The Moonlight Trilogy*, a witch fantasy series, the magic realism romance, *A Thousand Sleepless Nights,* the magical historical romance, *The Paradox of Love*, and a couple of romance novellas. Her fiction won first place in the "Romance Through the Ages Contest" in 2016 and Kirkus Reviews called her work "unusual and absorbing."

For many years, she's written about books for ksl.com, reviewed books for *The Deseret News,* and contributed book segments to Utah's number one lifestyle show, *Studio 5 with Brooke Walker.* She has taught classes and workshops for writers all over Utah. She works full-time as the National Account Manager for Legends Boxing. Teri lives with her family in Utah, in a blue farmhouse.

Visit her at: www.teriharman.com

Made in United States
North Haven, CT
17 November 2021

11210438R10140